NUMBER 81

NUMBER 81
Are the secrets of the past ever forgotten?

Christine Bhasin

Copyright © 2023 by Christine Bhasin.

All rights reserved. No part of this book may be reproduced or used in any manner without written permission of the copyright owner except for the use of quotations in a book review.

First paperback edition 2024

Book design by Publishing Push.

ISBN 979-88849325-0-0 (paperback)

Disclaimer

Although inspired by my family history in Shrewsbury, Shropshire, this book is a work of fiction with a dash of truth about my great-grandparents' lives. Names have been changed, and some characters are the products of the author's imagination.

Dedication

For my husband Nikhil
and my two wonderful daughters,
Eleanor and Emily.
I love you more than words can say.

For my sister Jean and her friend Jan
for accompanying me along
the shuts and lanes
of Shrewsbury.

My friends, you know who you are.
Thank you for your prayers and
encouragement since my stroke.

PART 1

CHAPTER 1

October 1898
Kingsland Road, Shrewsbury, Shropshire

William had left the Tate family home twelve months earlier with bruised ribs and a black eye. The reason he'd returned was out of respect for his mother. He didn't want some busybody in town revelling in being the first to tell Esther, "I hear your William's getting wed to some Irish girl from down Hills Lane."

He paced the polished wooden floor in the parlour, trying to control his breathing. As the grandfather clock chimed midday, he paused, and his hope that his father would be happy for him dwindled with each swing of its golden pendulum.

On hearing the news, his mother's face had at least lit up in a way he'd not seen in years. Esther Tate's eyes welled as she cradled her son's face in both hands as if his happiness was something she'd long forgotten.

She left the room, dabbing her eyes with a small white handkerchief, only to return a minute later carrying a small red box.

"These were my mother's rings. It'd mean a lot to me if Theresa wore them," she said, passing the box to him and pulling out six shillings from her apron pocket with her other hand. "This is for the priest, but you will pop into Saint George's and let our vicar know, won't you, dear?"

He nodded and slipped the rings and coins into his pocket before they hugged each other again as if neither wanted to be the first to break away.

"Thank you, Mother."

A silver-framed photograph given pride of place on the mantelpiece caught his eye. It pictured George Tate with William's two older brothers beneath a painted sign: G. Tate & Sons Brickmakers. While his father stood proudly with his chest out and shoulders back, Charles and Frederick seemed uncomfortable, either intimidated by the camera or the man pinning each one to a chair.

The crimson climbing rose that danced around the front door tapped the window and interrupted his thoughts. He ran a finger around his collar, annoyed with himself for taking the trouble of wearing the Sunday best suit his mother had given him for his twenty-first birthday. Since working at the foundry, his shoulders had bulked up and his chest broadened, making the tweed jacket uncomfortably tight. As he loosened his tie, he spotted his father marching up the garden path.

Oh bugger.

George Tate, a grey-haired, stocky man, was a good six inches taller than William who took more after his mother. On entering the parlour, William noticed his father glance at him before heading straight for the cut-glass decanter. After undoing the buttons of his waistcoat, George poured himself a large whiskey and checked his silver pocket watch. "Food on the table, Esther?" he called gruffly.

William followed him to the dining room and waited for his father to sit at the table. This was not out of respect but more that he had deduced over the years that throwing a punch from a sitting position was more challenging.

William cleared his throat. "I'm getting married."

"Say that again, boy." George wiped gravy from his bushy grey moustache with the back of his hand. "You're doing what?"

"I'm marrying Theresa Doyle at the end of the month, and you're both welcome to attend."

William noticed his mother step from side to side to block his father's view of him. "Shall I cut you another piece of bread, George?"

George's face reddened as he slammed his knife and fork down and swiped her arm away from the table.

"You fool. I suppose you've got her in the family way."

William stiffened at the remark.

"I'm sure... sure that's not... not the case," Esther said, slicing more bread even though the plate was full.

"Be quiet, woman, and get back to your chores!"

"Father. Her parents have given permission."

"Oh, I bet they have, William. They can see the pound and shilling signs in front of their bloody eyes. These Irish Catholics are all the same." George bashed his fists on the table. "Irish navvies are only interested in drinking down the Gullet Inn and brawling in the street."

Keeping his eyes lowered, George raised himself slowly from his chair, but William knew his father's *moves too well. He doesn't make eye contact. You think you've got away with it, but then a hand or fist flies at you from nowhere. Or maybe you take more punches to protect your mother, who'd also dared not to comply.*

As George rose to his full height, his whiskey glass toppled, and its golden liquid seeped into the pristine white tablecloth. He flicked a finger at Esther who dabbed at it frantically with a cloth.

"It's disappointing enough that you don't want to work at the brickyard like generations of Tates before you," George hissed, his eyes lifting and burning into William.

"I don't want to spend my life sitting behind a desk, and I like to work with my hands."

George brushed his glass off the table with such force it shattered against the panelled wooden wall. "Bricks and mortar are what people need these days, you idiot!"

We need machines and tools too.

"And those Doyles are nothing more than a bunch of layabouts who take jobs from honest Englishmen. Like the rest of them, her father's swilling back his wages."

"You've never even met him."

"Go, William, go," urged Esther.

"I'm fine, Mother." He lifted his slumped shoulders. *Don't let him see he still scares the hell out of you.*

George kicked back his chair, and it slid across the floor. He stepped forwards and curled an arm around his wife's tiny waist. "Yes, little boy, listen to your mother," he mimicked in a high-pitched voice.

William wished he could speak up, but the cowering look on his mother's face said, "Please don't."

George pushed Esther out of the way and towered over William. "And they're bloody Catholics. I wouldn't be surprised if our friends and neighbours never speak to us again. Why can't you court decent women like your brothers do? You've nothing between those ears of yours."

As the verbal assault continued, William focused on a vein pulsing in his father's neck. George spat as the insults flew, and from the corner of his eye, William noticed his mother retrieve her handkerchief from her apron pocket and wipe her eyes.

"You're half-soaked, just like your mother and your simple sister."

"Yes, praise the Lord Lucy Margaret has escaped." William's thoughts had slipped from his lips, and he stepped back.

"What did you say?" George poked William in the chest with his forefinger. "I didn't go to her wedding, and you won't see me in that ruddy Catholic church either."

Then he pushed repeatedly, using both hands flat on William's chest, the second shove more forceful than the first, and William stumbled backwards.

"Please, George, don't," Esther begged as her face drained of colour and she tugged at his arm, but George pushed her away effortlessly.

"I'm going, I'm going," William said, holding up both hands in surrender and turning towards the front door.

"Yes, best you do. Clear off, and don't step foot in this house again. You've made your bed. Now lie in it."

Once outside, William exhaled and took one last look up at the house. He knew his father would never welcome Theresa or their unborn child.

Hopefully, the rings in his pocket would fit, meaning his precious mother would at least play a part in the marriage ceremony. The thought of his mother never meeting Theresa, or her first grandchild, was unthinkable, but he felt sure they could bump into her on market day. That might be the only way.

He pulled a rose from the display around the front door before heading towards town. *The Doyles are my family now.*

William paused halfway through Frankwell as he spotted Granny Tench walking ahead with a gang of unruly children trotting behind her. He quickened his pace as the boys chanted, "Watch out, watch out, Granny Tench is about. She's only four foot eleven and will never go to heaven because she's stealing coal, so watch out!"

William yelled at them. "Clear off, you little buggers. Leave the poor woman in peace."

William knew Granny Tench well as her son lived in Hills Lane. Most people called her Tiny, and she did have a reputation for stealing coal from other people's bunkers. But William had learnt to take any gossip from Hills Lane with a pinch of salt.

His parents' house to town was only a fifteen-minute walk, but felt a world away now, and he doubted his father had ever ventured down the dingy, narrow passages and shuts that zig-zagged across the middle of town. Many opened to unseen courtyards devoid of light, and families lived in wretched houses and endured unspeakable squalor and lack of privacy. They shared a single tap and blocks of lavvies, from which mucky water flowed into gullies. A permanent putrid smell hung in the air outside and a frowsty one inside the homes.

The horseshoe bend of the River Severn enclosed the town, and Hills Lane was only a stone's throw from the river. It was a mishmash of buildings, but better than some as it didn't sit wholly hidden behind a bustling main street. At one end, Rowley's House and Mansion, a dilapidated timber-framed building, had stood since the 1500s. But now the building was linked to and circled by crumbling homes and businesses, including the Old Ship Inn. William paused and kicked a ball back to the two snotty-faced boys playing in the Ship's cobbled yard.

He walked past the three-storey red brick buildings on the left-hand side, each occupied by several families. In reality, tenement slums. They leant forwards, allowing only a sliver of sun to hit the cobbles below.

He nodded at the group of men huddled outside a lodging house.

"Any work going at the foundry, William?" called Jim Ryan.

"Not sure, Jim. I'll ask. Yes, I'll ask around for you," William replied, trying to sound upbeat, but knowing work was scarce and labourers' pay was poor.

William smiled as the Doyle house came into sight. Theresa sprung off the step and ran towards him, clutching her ankle-length skirt. He loved how she could never walk but always skipped or ran with her dark curls cascading behind her. He couldn't resist sweeping her into his arms as she reached him, and he presented her with the rose. "You look beautiful, Theresa."

She turned full circle to show off her blouse with its intricate Irish crochet lace collar.

"A gift from a cousin in Tipperary," she said. "They've sent something for you too." She linked her hands in his before saying, "So, how'd it go with your ma and da?"

"Well... I'm sure they'll come around."

"I must meet them before the wedding though!"

"Yes, yes, of course." Not wanting to say more, he gazed into her eyes and brushed away a strand of her hair. "This is for you."

He took the small box out of his pocket. She bit her lip as she opened it and on seeing the gold band and gemstone ring inside, she squealed and threw her arms around his neck.

"They belonged to my grandmother, Sophia, and Mother would love you to have them."

"Oh, I must go and thank her."

"Maybe another day," he said, removing the engagement ring from the box and slipping it onto her finger. "And we don't want to be late for our party."

They kissed before strolling down the lane, swinging their interlinked hands.

Outside number 48, Mrs Mahoney was brushing her front step. She did it many times a day, and William wondered why she bothered as Old Sam would clatter along with his horse and cart selling coal most days and leave a cloud of drifting black dust. Perhaps the well-swept step was her pride and joy. Rather, she liked to keep an eye on what was happening in the lane.

As they approached, she leant on her broom and said, "Oh, 'ere they come, the bride and groom. You've been fortunate with the weather this afternoon." She gazed up at the bright autumn sky. "The sun shines on the righteous."

"'Ope, we'll be getting an invitation to the wedding," called Alice Tench from the other side of the lane. She was busy helping her husband, Thomas, unload his cart. Everyone knew him as Peddler, and William and Theresa crossed the cobbles to see what he'd bagged that day.

"We're looking for crockery and a few blankets if you come across any," Theresa said.

He flung a bag of rags at his wife. "Catch hold of this, Alice, and put it in the backyard. Yes, Theresa, I'll see what I can do."

"I saw your mother in Frankwell, Peddler, getting pestered by some good-for-nothings," said William.

"Oh, dunna worry about Tiny. She's as tough as old boots and sharper than anyone I know."

Lizzie, Theresa's older sister, beckoned them from the step of number 84. "You two been round the Wrekin? Stop your blethering. The party's started."

As they entered the house, loud cheers, broad smiles, and barrels of ale greeted them. Mr Doyle, a balding man in his mid-fifties, slapped William on the back and placed a tankard of frothy ale into his hand. Theresa raised her left hand, and the women in the room swarmed to admire the gemstone ring.

William knew there'd been a kitty collected for their engagement party as there often was when there was something to celebrate. Nobody seemed to mind tipping a few coins in a hat, knowing a family celebration of their own would come around. Charlie Hughes, the landlord of the Gullet Inn, was more than generous at selling a barrel at a reduced price.

"Cheers, Mr Doyle."

"Call me John. You're one of the family now, William."

Mary Doyle, two years younger than her husband, still looked young for her age. Her dark wavy hair, inherited by all her children, framed her open and lively face. As she approached, John slipped his arm around her waist.

"And this 'ere is the love of me life. I love 'er as much today as I did the day we wed."

"Silly owd sod," she replied, wriggling away from him.

There was another tap on the door.

Mary weaved through the crowded, airless room, chirping, "Lovely news. 'Elp yourself to a drink, dunna be shy."

William took off his jacket and tie, feeling hot and overdressed. The men in the room wore simple collarless shirts and trousers held up with either braces or a tight belt. The Doyle women dressed smarter than most, thanks to Lizzie's needlework skills. A skill that seemed to run in the family.

As Mary greeted more cousins and neighbours, some spilt into the lane, and a human chain formed, and with much cheering and laughter, ale reached those unable to squeeze into the house.

William swept four-year-old Bridget in his arms and jigged up and down with the music as the dancing began.

"Again, again," said Bridget as the first tune ended. "Got summat for me, mon?" she asked as usual.

He knew he'd made a rod for his own back by slipping her coins.

Six-year-old James Doyle, in contrast, rarely spoke and always looked pale. As they heard another Irish jig, William put little Bridget down and smiled as she placed her hands on her hips and tried to hop and kick her little legs. James disappeared into the crowd.

Peddler and Mr Mahoney played the spoons while others clapped along. A loud cheer filled the lane on hearing the rich sound of an accordion.

"Can I go out and play? All this fuss for a silly ole wedding," screeched the Doyle's eldest son, Patrick, over the laughter and singing.

"Clear off then," replied his father, clipping him playfully around his ear.

William ruffled Patrick's hair as the rough-and-tumble boy escaped with his battered football tucked under his arm.

Theresa was across the room, and they held each other's gaze for a moment before a toothless old uncle pulled her outside to dance. She beckoned William to come too, or maybe to rescue her, but he laughed and raised his tankard towards her.

Unlike his parents' house, the Doyle house had no framed pictures, decorative silverware, or patterned china on display. It was homely, even with flaking paintwork, rickety wooden furniture, and well-used pots and pans. There were gifts wrapped in brown paper sitting beside the fireplace, some from neighbours and others sent from family in Ireland. They'd be handmade or second-hand items, and he didn't care. The warmth he felt on seeing them and the ever-present camaraderie made him glad to be part of their community.

Looking almost identical to Theresa, Lizzie approached William. "So, you'll be my brother-in-law." She smiled and checked his tankard to see if it needed topping up.

William couldn't fathom why some bloke hadn't carried her off. At twenty-five, she had dedicated herself to helping John and Mary care for her siblings. He felt sure someone would come along for her and be a lucky man to marry into the Doyle family.

Theresa joined them both, panting from dancing. "I don't know where Uncle Shay gets his energy from." She linked her arm through William's. "I wanted to ask you, Lizzie, if you would make my wedding dress?"

"Oh, for sure. Let's go down to the market and see what material Mrs Turner has on her stall. White, of course!"

Theresa blushed and looked up at William.

"And you must both come and visit me. I'm renting a small room at 81 Whitehall Street. It's a small lodging house, just a bit further on than the Abbey Church. Mrs Hurren, who owns it, says I can share her parlour if I help her with the cleaning and cooking. It's a lovely house with a fireplace in the parlour and the dining room, and a cylinder for hot water. Can you believe that?"

William smiled at Lizzie's enthusiasm.

"It'll free up more space here for the littl'uns, now I'm moving out too," said Theresa as Uncle Shay linked his hand in hers again and pulled her back towards the dancing.

CHAPTER 2

February 1899. Four months after the wedding
Hills Lane

As he entered the Old Gullet Inn, William remembered to duck his head to avoid cracking it on the low wooden beam. The dimly lit inn with its roaring fire was a welcome refuge from the bitter wind outside. It was only a few doors up from the Ship Inn, but most of the men from town preferred the Old Gullet because the landlord was jollier than the woman who ran the Ship.

Men popped in on their way home from work most evenings. Fridays were always livelier when their wives waited outside and tried to tease the men's pay packets out of their pockets before they entered. William's fatter pay packet had helped set up a home with Theresa in a small place on Bridge Street soon after their wedding.

He was now a foreman at the foundry, overseeing the manufacture of economisers for steam engine boilers. The iron industry was changing, and even though it meant long hours and unbearable heat and dust, it thrilled him to be part of moulding iron to build bridges and engines too.

The landlord, Charlie Hughes, nodded as William approached the wooden bar and pulled out a stool. Old Sam, with his familiar coal-blackened face, and Bert Harris sat at the other end of the bar. Those two could make a bottle of ale last all night.

"Adoo, mon," said Charlie, tilting his head towards Sam and Bert as if thinking the same thing as William. "Your usual, William?"

"Yes, a brown ale."

William's father-in-law, John, called over to him. "I'll 'ave another, William."

John sat around a wooden table with four others. A folded playing card stabilised one of the table legs, and Peddler sat at the head, licking his pencil and scribbling on a slip of paper. William strained his neck to see what they were betting on or whether the old devil was taking orders for knock-off wood, rags, or scrap metal.

"How's that fine woman of yours, William?" asked Mr Mahoney, coming up to the bar. "I saw her callin' in on her ma this evenin'. She's a good'un."

"She is. And blooming!" replied William.

"Yes, I've 'eard the good news. And so soon after the wedding!" A grin spread across Mr Mahoney's face, and he winked at William before knocking back his drink.

"Can I get you another, Tom?" William asked.

"No, I best be going, William."

"You need to get that leash of yours lengthened, Tom," somebody called.

William headed towards his father-in-law. The table had cleared, and Peddler's hush-hush business concluded for the evening.

"Thank you, William." John took a large gulp of the frothy ale before lighting up his pipe. His smoke joined the other silvery wisps dancing below the yellowing ceiling.

"How're the littl'uns doing?"

John placed his hand to his ear. "Speak up, William. I canna hear."

A group of Irish labourers from the railway station had fallen through the door. Their raucous laughter added to the cacophony of men cursing, grumbling about their womenfolk, or singing saucy ditties.

"I asked after the littl'uns," William repeated, raising his voice.

"They're growin' up too damn quickly! But at least we've had more room since Theresa and Lizzie moved on. Me and Mary have some privacy at long last!" He chuckled before taking another sip of his ale. "Bit worried about our James though. The lad dunna look well. He's skin and bone."

William stroked his chin. *I wonder if John's heard there's scarlet fever in the town?* "What was Peddler selling this evening?" he asked, hoping to change the subject.

"This and that. You're better off not knowin'. Theresa wouldna forgive her da if you got caught with some of Peddler's knock-off stuff."

"Ha, you're not wrong there, John."

"Are you stoppin' for another, mon?"

"No, I best get myself home," William replied, swigging back his ale and standing.

"Ah, sit down, lad. Canna let the womenfolk stop us from 'avin' a drink or two."

As he was about to sit down, William spotted Theresa in the doorway. Her recently healthy, flushed complexion was like porcelain, and her bright brown eyes were etched with panic. She bobbed up and down with one hand protectively over her belly and the other held to her mouth.

That's odd. Something's wrong. Please don't let it be the baby.

"John, Theresa's at the door for some reason." William elbowed his way towards her, ignoring one labourer who cursed because his ale spilt as William pushed past.

"Fetch Da... He needs... He needs to come home. Now!" she said breathlessly.

He didn't reply but fought a path back to John who bolted out of his seat on seeing William beckoning wildly.

Once outside, William spotted that both front windows at the Doyle house were open. Neighbours huddled in small groups along the lane. As they got closer, heads lowered and hushed tones became silent. People parted to give them access to the front door, and all, barring Mrs Mahoney, averted their eyes. She crossed herself. "It's tragic. Such a sweet young girl."

John gasped for breath, and the colour drained from his face as they entered the front room. Mary Doyle was kneeling on the floor, rocking.

"She went too near. She just went too near." Her eyes lifted to meet her husband's. "She was dancing... She was dancing."

John said nothing but grasped the back of a chair to steady himself as his knees buckled. William stepped forwards to support him.

Something small lay under a charred mat in front of the fireplace. A tiny, blackened hand reached out from beneath as if imploring for help, and a reddened, blistered foot protruded. William's eyes fixed on the chubby little toes, and he scanned the room. Was she under the table? Under a chair? Had she popped out to the lavvie? It couldn't be their darling little Bridget lying there.

The silence that filled the room broke as Doctor Willis said, "Please let me examine your hands, Mrs Doyle."

Mary looked down at the mat. "I tried to put the fire out with my hands and tore at her flannelette nightdress... But it seemed to just melt into her. When her hair caught, I rolled her in the mat."

"Please, Mary. Let the doctor see your hands," said John, stepping forwards.

The doctor beckoned him, and they each put a hand under Mary's elbows and hoisted her from the floor.

"Yes, Ma, please... please," Theresa begged before burying her head into William's chest.

Once standing, Mary held out her hands in a childlike fashion and yelped as she turned them over. She stared wide-eyed, and her lips quivered as a searing pain appeared to rip through her. Easing herself onto a chair, she shook uncontrollably and let out a gut-wrenching cry. The sound resonated in the smoky, rancid-smelling room and into the lane.

"A spark from the fire, Da. That's all it was, and then it 'appened so fast," said Patrick. He cowered in the corner, his arms entwined with his younger brother James, whose eyes were squeezed shut. "I fetched the doctor as quickly as I could run, Da."

"I know you did, son. I know you did." John glanced away from Mary to meet Patrick's glazed expression.

William swallowed a sob and looked up at the ceiling. He clenched his fists and wanted to be angry with someone. Anyone.

John knelt beside the body briefly before slowly lifting a corner of the mat. He bowed his head and mumbled a few words before crossing himself. William helped him back to his feet and watched as Patrick and James stepped out from their safe corner and clung to their father's legs.

"I came as fast as I—" Lizzie's hand flew to her mouth, and she froze in the doorway.

William turned to her and relived the horrific scene again through her eyes. The crying crescendoed, and Lizzie's wails of disbelief caused the neighbours outside to fall silent and stop what they were doing.

"Mary needs to get to the infirmary," said Doctor Willis.

"I'll take her," Lizzie offered, gaining her composure or merely wanting to escape from the room. "You two stay with Da and the boys."

William and Theresa nodded.

Doctor Willis picked up his bag. "You set off straight away, Lizzie, and I'll follow you in a few minutes."

As Lizzie placed a coat around Mary's shoulders and they left, the doctor turned to John. "I'm so sorry for your loss... The undertaker is coming, and I must inform the coroner."

John nodded slowly and sat in his chair. Patrick and James climbed on his lap, seemingly no longer too big for a cuddle. Theresa and William saw the doctor out, but he hesitated and turned.

"This will hit dear John and Mary hard... What with losing the other two littl'uns two years ago. Ann and Mary, was it?"

Theresa nodded. "Yes, both with scarlet fever."

William watched as the doctor battled against the wind and scurried into the darkness.

Mr Mahoney and a few other neighbours stood opposite the house; their heads lowered in prayer. Some held rosary beads, and others small Bibles.

William stepped out onto the cobbles to let the biting wind whip him. "What bloody good that'll do, I don't know. You're on your knees every sodding Sunday, praying and asking for forgiveness. There is no God!"

"William, please don't," Theresa shouted from the doorstep.

"Well, I'm angry, and what good can they do? Waste of time—" He stopped, seeing tears streaming down her face.

"It was an accident, William."

"Yes, but it's God that lets awful things happen. And as the doctor said, Ma and Da have suffered more than their fair share."

CHAPTER 3

**Ten years later
Shrewsbury Cemetery**

Ada and Ethel skipped and hopped around.

"Be careful where you tread," Theresa shouted, but her voice floated away in the breeze.

She eased herself down and tugged at the grass covering the gravestone. The letters of their son's name, John Rupert Tate, were jammed onto the small, rounded, upright stone. It sat next to the flat sandstone memorials that bore the names of her parents, John and Mary, and her siblings, Mary, Ann, Bridget, and James. She found it a great comfort that her son lay close to her family, and a usual calmness descended as she knelt amongst them all.

"Oh, it seems such a long time since we were all together."

She brushed away the needles that had fallen from the overhanging yew tree and wished the dark reddish trunk and branches of waxy leaves didn't cast such a large shadow over the spot where they all rested. The wildflowers she'd brought along added a little colour to the sunless setting. She traced the letters on her parents' grave with her forefinger. It'd been no surprise them dying within a fortnight of each other, and she'd even taken comfort from the fact her ma and da weren't apart for long. Bridget's passing and James' three weeks later to scarlet fever had been too much, and Mary died from a heart attack. John gave up without her.

"Patrick's found work on the railway. And he's courting a girl named Marie. You'd all love her," said Theresa.

Ethel had returned unnoticed to the shady spot. "Who you talking to, Ma?"

"Leave Ma be, Eth," Ada yelled, "Let's run around the yew tree again."

"Try not to get your pinafore too dirty," Theresa called after Ethel.

Ada had been trying to teach her how to skip, but at only three, Ethel struggled. She'd lift her knees, step forwards, but then trip over.

Ada was born five months after the wedding, and Theresa's mother had raised an eyebrow at her daughter, but said nothing. Ada had dealt with losing her baby brother and grandparents and endured her father's dark moods. Now she had an older head on her shoulders than most ten-year-olds.

Theresa watched her girls play, with their unruly hair streaming behind them as they ran. "They look so much like you, Ma."

She ran a protective hand over her swollen belly, hoping for a boy this time. Would a boy lift William's ever-present air of despondency? He'd blamed himself for not calling old Doctor Willis earlier to examine John Rupert. But the convulsions from teething and diarrhoea had been too extreme for his little body. It was nobody's fault, just one of those things.

The Doyles had endured more than most families in Hills Lane, but scarlet fever, bronchitis, and TB had taken a toll on mothers, fathers, and infants. Each passing had gnawed at William, making him withdrawn and cynical. Little Bridget's tragic death haunted him and constantly came up in his conversations. He'd gained no solace when she'd said John Rupert would be playing ball with Bridget and James.

Or that they were all at peace in the arms of her parents and his mother.

William had refused yet again to visit the graves. She coaxed as usual, but an excuse was always on his lips. Their son would have been six now, but William had rarely visited his grave. Her attempts at trying to lift his sombre mood had failed again and again. She felt like giving up and hated to admit it, but she was glad to be out of the house sometimes.

Theresa looked at the two rings on her left hand and fought her tears. "I feel I'm losing him, Ma, bit by bit." A tear trickled down her face, but she swept it away, not wanting Ethel to see because she always asked so many questions.

Ada's head appeared from behind a much bigger headstone and distracted her. "Eth fell over and grazed her knee, but I've given it a rub. Do you need a hand to get up, Ma?"

"Give me another five minutes, Ada." Theresa pinned back a strand of her hair that had escaped from the silver pin her mother-in-law had given her.

Esther Tate had passed away too, and lay beneath an ornate headstone at Saint George's Church in town. Before her death, Theresa had purposely bumped into

Esther on market day as often as possible so the poor woman could see her grandchildren. Theresa had resisted commenting on the bruises on her face or neck. Esther's face brightened on seeing Ada and her new grandson, and she was always reluctant to say goodbye.

Theresa placed her hand lightly on her son's stone again. "Thankfully, your sweet grandma was spared knowing you have passed too."

Theresa had never formally met her father-in-law but once saw him crossing to the other side of Pride Hill as she'd approached. There was plenty of gossip in the town about George Tate and how he treated his wife and children, but William seldom spoke of it, and it was all in the past.

"I miss my little brother," said Ada, reappearing and dropping to her knees beside her mother.

Ethel followed, falling forwards on her hands as she landed. "What we doin' 'ere?"

"We're seeing our broth—" began Ada.

"We're visiting this lovely garden, Ethel," Theresa interrupted.

Ada helped her mother back to her feet. "Will the baby be here soon, Ma?" she asked.

Theresa brushed the grass from her skirt. "Not long now, love."

"Hope Da will be happy then," said Ada as they all headed out of the cemetery hand in hand.

She'll be cross with me when she gets home. It was early afternoon, and William had yet to wash or shave. *What's the point? John Rupert won't know I didn't visit his grave.*

Plopping down at the kitchen table, he slipped his braces from his shoulders. Theresa wanted him to talk to old Doctor Willis, but he didn't intend to. He'd shouted after Theresa as she'd left the house. "We can't change the past by talking about it. And besides, Doctor Willis can hardly see to the end of his nose these days."

I go to work. I come home. I hand over my pay packet, unlike some I know. What more does Theresa want from me?

He glared at the cupboard where he'd hidden the note, hand delivered by a worker from the brickyard three days ago. He'd not seen head nor hair of his brothers since their mother's funeral, and even then, they'd only given polite nods in his general direction.

"Why on earth would I want to visit that vicious sod now just because he's on his deathbed?" he muttered before lighting a cigarette. *Have they all forgotten how our father treated us? Treated our poor mother?*

His thoughts dispersed as Ada and Ethel breezed into the kitchen, followed by their mother.

"I fell over, Da," said Ethel, and she lifted her grey pinafore to show him her grazed knee. "Kiss it better, Da."

"Shoo. I'm sure your ma will see to it."

Ethel's chin dipped to her chest, and she shut her eyes.

"Take Ethel out to play for a while please, Ada," said Theresa.

Ada stuck her tongue out at her father as she ushered her sister outside.

Theresa watched them leave. "Ethel only wanted a little cuddle from you. Is that too much to ask?"

"So, how are all the dead people today?" He ignored her question and repeatedly tapped each side of his Woodbine cigarette packet on the table. He knew his habit of doing that annoyed her.

Theresa had instilled so much hope in him from the first day they'd met, but it'd drained since losing darling Bridget. At work, he could function even after a few hours of fitful sleep. But he'd built a wall around himself at home.

"It helps me to go there. I haven't stopped loving my family because they're—"

"They're dead and buried," he said, a little louder than he intended.

She bit her lip, her eyes moist with tears, and for a moment, he remembered how those eyes used to bring him happiness. They were a lively mix of brown, hazel, and honey. Warm, rich, and irresistible. If it hadn't been for her, where would he be now? Working at the brickmakers? Drinking too much? Up Roushill looking for a woman to spend the night with? Still trying to escape his bullish father?

He watched as she slid onto the chair beside him, removed the silver pin from her hair, and put it on the table. "I'll treasure this and pass it to Ada on her wedding day. I think Esther would've liked that."

William stared at her, his body softening at the mention of his mother.

Theresa reached for his hand and placed it on her belly, on their unborn child. "We have so much to look forward to," she said, covering his hand with hers. "Why don't you take Ada and Ethel to see your father?"

He snatched his hand away. "You don't miss a bloody thing, do you?"

"Well, you didn't hide it very well, William. Please don't be angry with me. You're always angry. Forgiveness might bring you some peace."

"Ha, peace?" He threw his hands in the air. "You and your Catholic faith have the answer to flaming everything."

"Come to church with me, William. Father O'Connor would love to see you; he might talk to you about how you're feeling." She reached for his hand again, touching her late da's signet ring that William wore on his left hand.

He pulled away again. "Will your God forgive my father when he arrives at the gates of heaven? I hope the bastard rots in hell."

"Hush, William, you don't want the girls to hear you."

"Should I forgive God for taking our only son John Rupert, James, and little... little Bridget?" He mouthed "little Bridget" again.

"She's at peace and with—"

"At peace? She barely had a life, and my sodding father lives well into his old age." William pushed back his chair and began pacing the floor. "Be in no doubt. I'll never forgive him."

"Forgive us our trespasses as we forgive those who trespass—"

"Don't start bloody quoting that shit at me, Theresa."

"But your daughters, William. Can you not find joy in their faces? And in the new baby?"

He slumped back onto his chair, placed his head in his hands, and tried to ignore the sweat trickling down his back and his racing heart. William fought his tears because that was something he only gave into when he was alone.

Ada appeared at the door, and he lifted his eyes on feeling her arm resting along his shoulders. "It's okay. Don't get upset, Da."

"You're a good girl and have your mother's beautiful hair and eyes."

Ethel returned to the kitchen. "Am I a good girl too?" she asked, her eyes still downcast but her fingers searching for his.

"Sorry, love. Of course, you are. Now, let us see that poorly knee of yours."

CHAPTER 4

1912
Shrewsbury Market Hall

Emillie's mother, Martha Rogers, lifted her head after examining the vegetables displayed at a nearby stall. She could feel the colour rushing to her cheeks.

"Emillie Rogers has been caught at it again," said Mrs Smith over the noise of market traders selling their produce.

"No," replied Mrs Evans, stepping closer to her friend to hear more. "Not again!"

"Flo Edwards from the milliners in town caught her husband round the back of the shop with Emillie." Folding her arms across her generous bosom, Mrs Smith continued, "Yes, a right brazen mare she is."

"Oh my word! So, what did Flo do?" asked Mrs Evans.

"Emillie got her marching orders, and she gave 'er old man a right flea in his ear, I can tell you."

"What can I get you this fine morning, Mrs Rogers?" asked the greengrocer.

Mrs Smith swung round. "Oh, Martha. I didn't see you there. How's the family?"

She ignored the question and passed her basket to the stall keeper for him to pop in the few potatoes and carrots she wanted to buy.

"Take no notice of those old gossips, Mrs Rogers," he said.

Mrs Smith turned to her friend, raised her eyebrows, but said no more. Martha nodded at the stall keeper with appreciation and fumbled in her coat pocket for the coins to pay him. As she weaved her way out of the crowded market hall, she ignored the cries from her usual butcher about the excellent rabbit on sale that day.

Once outside, she caught her breath, hoping not to see anyone she knew. Shrewsbury's market hall stretched from Mardol Head to Shoplatch and had been built in the Italianate style using white, black, and blue bricks. It was always a hive of activity, and farmers were still waiting outside to unload their carts laden with meat and dairy produce. Martha stared at the town's coat of arms displayed above the market entrance, with its three leopards' faces and the words *"Floreat Salopia"*.

Yes, it looks like Shrewsbury is flourishing. But I won't be showing my face here for a while.

After crossing Market Street, she paused again to stare at the clock tower. It was almost eleven o'clock, and she couldn't help but wonder if Emillie was already home. Minutes later, she stormed up Coffee House Passage towards number 10, ready to give her daughter a piece of her mind.

Emillie sat on a wooden bench, staring into a small, tarnished mirror. "'Ello, Mum."

"Why aren't you at work, Emillie?"

"Mrs Edwards gave me the day off," she replied, not meeting her mother's accusing stare.

Martha dropped her basket on the table with a thud. "Don't flamin' well lie to me."

Emillie fiddled with her mousy brown hair, curling it around her forefinger. "I'll find summat else."

Martha sighed. "If you preened less... like you're summat you're not."

"I'm gunna find another job. Dunna get your knickers in a twist."

"Not with your bloody reputation around town, you won't!"

"Whadya mean by that?"

"Don't give me that innocent look, Emillie. You and the butcher in Mardol carryin' on, and now Mr Edwards from the milliners."

"Summat and nothin'. Flo Edwards didna take to me from day one."

Martha threw her hands in the air. "You were damn well canoodling with her husband!"

A smirk slid across her daughter's face. "Well, canna blame him, being married to that miserable old cow."

"How d'you expect me to put food on the table without your money? Shoulda wed Edwin from next door when you 'ad the chance."

"Ugh, I wouldn't touch him with a barge pole. He's nothin' but a fat, sweaty oaf." She puffed out her cheeks to mimic him.

"Grow up, Emillie."

"And besides, I inna gonna end up in an 'ole like this and 'avin' a life like yours, Mum."

Martha stepped forwards, grabbed Emillie by the arm, and yanked her to her feet. James Rogers appeared through the door as she raised her hand to strike.

"Martha!"

She held her husband's gaze for a moment before stepping back.

He sat on the small wooden stool by the front door, tutting to himself as he unlaced and kicked off his heavy work boots. "I could 'ear you two bickerin' from a mile away."

"She's only gone and 'ad the sack again," Martha said, wringing her hands.

James shook his head at Emillie. "How many more times?" She shrugged at him. "You've upset your poor mother again."

Martha banged the kettle on the stove. "And that ol' gossip Mrs Smith told all and sundry in the market today... revelling in it she was. Bleedin' revellin' in it."

"My dear, try not to fret so much."

"Don't... don't know how I'll show my face again."

James sighed and watched as Emillie re-tied the ribbon on her bonnet. "You should have married Edwin. You're knocking thirty. What man will take you on now?"

"I beg your pardon!" She glared at her father.

"We can't live on fresh air," Martha said as she poured boiling water onto the used tea leaves in the pot.

"Dunna wanna stay in this boring old town anyway. I'll board a ship and sail away and... Life would be so much bet—"

Martha turned. "Stupid girl! You'd need a husband with a good trade and some money behind him to emigrate."

"But look at this place!"

Martha fought back her tears again as she looked at the room. Like other shuts in Shrewsbury, the passage was narrow, allowing only a streak of sunlight to fall between the homes. Everyone lived in semi-darkness, whatever time of day or season it was.

"But I've done my best for you."

"I want more than this!" Emillie picked up her mirror and bonnet and stomped up the wooden stairs to her bedroom.

"James, 'ow on earth will we cope without her money?" Martha asked, pouring him a cup of tea.

"We'll manage, love. We'll manage. I'll see if there's any overtime going on this weekend."

"It's that madam upstairs who needs to—"

"Wait a minute," he said. "The foreman at work is looking for help with his children because his wife is very ill."

"Deary me. Anyone we know?"

"Surname of Tate. I think 'is wife came from down Hills Lane, but they live along Marine Terrace now. Tell

Emillie to go round there first thing," he said, placing a comforting hand over his wife's.

———◆———

The following morning, Emillie slammed the door behind her as she left and flounced up Coffee House Passage.

"Need to get to Marine Terrace early," her mother yelled. "Loads of womenfolk will be after earning an extra bob or two from Mr Tate."

Emillie's attempts to sweet talk her father, as usual, had failed. "I'll earn more money in a shop than skivvying," she'd told him. But James Rogers wasn't having any of it.

She'd dragged herself out of bed, regretting getting the sack from the milliners. She wouldn't miss Mr Edwards' fumbling and sloppy kisses, but she'd miss the coins he used to slip her on top of her wages. The cloth bag under her bed now held a reasonable sum. *The sooner I escape from this godforsaken town, the better.*

Marine Terrace was a good fifteen-minute walk from Coffee House Passage, but it took her longer because she dawdled down Wyle Cop. She paused outside the watchmakers, tobacconists, drapers, and clothiers, hoping if she were late, Mr Tate would have given the job to someone else, with a bit of luck.

She held her breath as she knocked on the door of number 8, hoping there was no one at home or the job had gone. The house was three storeys and overlooked the river. She couldn't help wondering if the house had ever flooded when the river was swollen. *I couldn't be doing with having to clean that mess up.*

A girl of about twelve answered the door. *I 'ope all the children are this age. Canna be doin' with washing nappies.*

"Hello, do you want my da?"

"Yes," she replied, forcing a thin smile.

"Come in. I'll fetch him for you."

Despite several washes, her white lace blouse still had a musty smell and Emillie ran her fingers around the collar, convinced it was bringing her out in a rash. She admired herself in the mirror of the polished carved oak hall stand before removing and placing down her straw bonnet. *Hopefully, it's just a little cleaning.*

"Da's in here," called the girl.

Mr Tate was looking out of the window into the yard outside. He wore a sleeveless white vest and charcoal grey trousers and didn't turn round as she entered. Emillie spotted two children playing on the floor. *Oh bugger, two more brats.*

"'ello, Mr Tate. My father said you're lookin' for someone to 'elp in the 'ouse?"

"And your father is?" he asked, facing her.

"James Rogers. We live along Coffee House Passage."

He looked blankly at her. Her father had said Mr Tate was in his thirties, but the man staring at her with red-rimmed eyes and greying hair appeared much older.

"So, this is Ada, Ethel, and Dorothy," he said, pointing to each one.

"I'm twelve, Ethel's five and Dorothy's two," chirped Ada, glaring at Emillie and placing an arm across her father's shoulder as he sat.

"What 'elp do you need, Mr Tate?" She sensed three pairs of wide eyes glued to her every word and movement.

"The missus has been ill for some time. I must work, and the house... well, it's getting on top of me as you can see."

She saw plates, pots, and pans littering the kitchen and a pile of clothes scattered on the floor.

"But Aunt Lizzie can help us some more, Da," said Ada, "And I polished the hall stand this morning."

Emillie shuffled her feet. *I'll be off then if you dunna need me.*

"Lizzie needs to work."

She noticed tears welling in Ada's eyes at his dismissive tone.

"And besides, now Ma's not going to..." He paused, seeing Ada's face streaked with tears. "Cleaning and cooking... And you can come every weekday?"

"Yes, I ca—"

He didn't seem to hear her but continued. "Yes, lots of cleaning, washing, and plenty of fresh air needed in the missus' room especially."

"Yes, Ma just needs some fresh air," Ada added, wiping her face.

"Sorry, what did you say your name was?"

"I'm Emillie. Emillie Rogers."

He nodded, but she sensed he wouldn't remember her name by the morning.

"Well, start tomorrow. I can give you ten bob a week and more if we tick along nicely."

She smiled. *I'll tell Mum it's five bob.*

"Be here by 6 a.m. though," he called as she returned to the hallway and rechecked her appearance in the hall stand mirror. As she replaced her bonnet, she was aware of Ada already holding open the front door.

A week later

Emillie sat at the kitchen table, peeling potatoes and watching Ethel and Dorothy playing with two wooden spinning tops. Little Dorothy, as her father always called her, sucked on the metal tip more than trying to spin it.

Keeping the house clean had been easier than she had thought, and she enjoyed the afternoons when she had time to sit down. The family seldom used the parlour, but she guessed William slept there every night. Each morning, she folded his blanket and moved around a few ornaments to make it seem like she'd dusted.

The kitchen was airy, with plenty of shelves for pans, and the free-standing sink and reliable stove made cooking meals easier than she'd ever known. Her mother momentarily came to mind, pumping water from a communal tap and struggling to cook food over a fire.

Ada, returning from school and heading straight upstairs to check on her mother, distracted Emillie. She'd felt like clipping the young girl round the ear on more than one occasion in the past week but had reminded herself how much she needed the job. Ada usually whined that her mother's pillow wasn't plumped enough or that dinner wasn't as tasty as Ma's. Emillie would nod, force a smile, but bite her lip.

A little later, she heard Ada running down the stairs to meet her father. Emillie had cottoned on that Ada kept a watch for him coming home to moan about the housekeeping as soon as her poor father came through the door.

He sat on a kitchen chair, removed his flat cap, undid a few shirt buttons, and sighed loudly. Despite being a skilled foreman at the foundry, Emillie noticed he looked just as exhausted each night as her father, and he was a labourer. His daughters huddled around him, and Ethel giggled, pointing at her father's dusty, sweaty face.

"Give me some room," he barked as he struggled to remove his boots.

Ada pulled her sisters back, but rested a hand on her father's chair.

"How's Theresa today?" he asked, turning to Emillie.

"She's getting better," said Ada, sticking out her chin.

He ignored her because her hopeful response was the same every evening.

"I washed her hands and face and made sure she was comfortable," Emillie said, lowering her gaze. *But what's the point? The woman's dying.*

William nodded. "I'll get myself washed. Food smells good."

"I've cooked a stew with the rabbit you brought home yesterday."

He nodded again, and she noticed the hopelessness in his downcast eyes that increased each evening, something she noticed even his daughters' smiles and laughter couldn't ease. His wife was on her deathbed, and he'd not run up the stairs for the past few days as soon as he was home to see her.

Ada slipped her hand into his. "Shall we go up and see Ma?"

"I'll eat first, Ada, and why don't you join us, Emillie?"

She could sense Ada's eyes burning into her as she sat.

"That's Ma's chair," Ada hissed under her breath as Emillie ladled stew into everyone's bowl.

William finished his meal, ignoring his eldest daughter's silence and Ethel and Dorothy's chatter about spinning tops. Ada pushed the brown meat around her bowl, prodded the suet dumplings, and every so often stared at Emillie. *I know the dumplings aren't as good as your ma's.*

"Can you get your sisters ready for bed, Ada?"

"Another cup of tea, Mr Tate?" Emillie asked, topping up the kettle.

Ada glared one last time before leaving the room with her sisters.

William remained sat at the table with a blank expression on his face.

She placed a cup of tea in front of him. "I dusted the parlour today and did all the washing."

He stared straight ahead.

"You have a lovely photograph in there. Is it your mother and father? I'd love to 'ave my picture taken one day." She cupped her face and smiled as if posing for a camera.

"Not bloody likely!"

Emillie froze, not knowing what she'd said wrong.

"Sorry, I didn't mean to... It's Theresa's mum and dad, John and Mary Doyle," he said, gesturing for Emillie to join him at the table. "John was more of a father to me than my own."

"Got any brothers and sisters, Mr Tate?" she asked as she joined him.

He sipped his tea and said, "Please call me William."

"That's very kind of you, Mr Tate. I mean, William."

"I haven't seen my two brothers in years, not since my mother's funeral. We didn't speak even then. I slipped out the back of the church when it was over."

Seeing a faraway look on his face, she clasped her hands around her cup, unsure what to say next.

"Mother's at rest now, away from that brute."

"Your father a bad'un?"

"He died twelve months ago. I couldn't bring myself to attend his funeral, even though Theresa nagged me. She said I'd regret it. But I don't. And then the bastard cut me out of his will anyway. He left G. Tate & Sons Brickmakers to my brothers Charles and Frederick. Me and my sister Lucy Margaret got nowt."

"Oh yes, I'd 'eard of George Tate." She refilled his teacup and quietly recalled all the gossip in town about George Tate. *He was a sod to his workers and was cruel to his wife and children.*

William took a sip of his tea before continuing. "But a few years back, Lucy Margaret emigrated to Canada along with her husband."

"'Ow exciting!"

"She wanted to escape Father if truth be told. Like me, she married someone he disapproved of. But Fred Brittle was a decent, hardworking chap, and I liked him."

"I'd love to sail to Canada and have a fresh start," she said, looking dreamily out the window. "Where'd she settle?"

"A town called Woodstock in Ontario."

She'd not heard of it but nodded in appreciation. "How lovely, setting sail from Liverpool and off into the sunset."

"Ha, don't you believe it! They said the voyage was like hell on Earth. Liverpool was a nightmare because they had to wait a week in some awful lodging house until the ship docked. They slept with one eye open and kept a tight grip on their belongings."

"Oh, but wouldn't it be worth it? New country and new people."

A small smile slipped onto his face at her enthusiasm, and she held his gaze.

"What does the doctor say about Theresa?" she asked, looking away.

"Just a matter of time. I've lost her... lost her already. She's been in bed these past two months."

She moved her hand closer to his, and he didn't move. "But you 'ave your daughters."

"Yes," he replied, biting his lip. "I can see Theresa in all of them. The dark wavy hair and those eyes. And Ada... she has Theresa's strength and fire." He grimaced as if the words were searing through him. He lowered his head again. "How on earth will I cope? When they're a constant reminder. Girls need their mothers, don't you think?"

She stood and placed her arm along his heaving shoulders. She'd never seen a man cry before.

"I-I feel so... so trapped," he stuttered. Tears streamed down his face, but he brushed away her arm before pushing back his chair.

I know what it's like to feel trapped.

Minutes later, as she reached for her coat from the stand in the hallway, she saw him disappear into the bedroom where his wife lay.

CHAPTER 5

Early next morning, a cold, wet cloth swept over Theresa's face, and she shivered.

"Who are you?" she mouthed, looking up at the unfamiliar face. "You're not Lizzie."

"I'm Emillie, Mrs Tate. Here to look after you."

Theresa tried to sit up, but her usual morning cough began. Emillie reached for the china bowl from the side table and held it at arm's length. Theresa felt like the sputum was coming up from her boots, not just her chest. Her shivers turned into a sweat, and she reached towards the wet cloth Emillie had left on the side table. *You silly woman, that'll take the polish off my table.*

Theresa coughed again, and the blood that appeared slid slowly down the bowl, contrasting vividly with its white and blue floral design. Emillie placed the cloth on Theresa's forehead as she lay back on her pillow. Water ran down Theresa's face, making her shiver. *The fool didn't wring the cloth out.* Emillie stepped back, recoiling in disgust at seeing the sputum and blood in the bowl.

Theresa focused on Emillie who'd moved nearer to the mirrored dressing table. Emillie picked up Theresa's ornate silver hairbrush, a gift from William on their first wedding anniversary. She pulled a pin from her hair and shook her head to loosen her mousy-coloured hair. Theresa coughed as Emillie lifted the brush. *Cheeky madam! I need to get up.* Theresa couldn't remember the last time she was up and about. She felt the tightness in her chest that had been there for months and would never ease. When the doctor called, he always whispered to William; she wished he'd talk straight to her. Theresa coughed again. Emillie spun around and placed the hairbrush back.

I'm nobody's fool, missy.

Theresa had seen consumption before. She knew she was wasting away and had seen folk from down Hills Lane coughing, sneezing, and spitting. *That's probably where I picked it up.*

Before leaving the room, Emillie flung open the bedroom window, and the morning air flowed over Theresa as she closed her eyes and sighed.

Hearing noises, Ada slipped out of bed and tip-toed onto the landing. She didn't know what time it was, but Ethel was still sound asleep at the other end of the bed, and Dorothy seemed happy lying in her cot, gurgling and trying to catch her feet. She wore a thin nightdress and wished she'd pulled on her woollen socks. *If I put the kettle on for Da's tea, it might make him smile.*

The sun was just up, so it surprised her that the kitchen door was ajar, and a chink of light cut across the hall floor. She paused outside the door and saw her father and Emillie talking at the kitchen table. *Why's she here on a Saturday morning? Aunt Lizzie will be coming to help.*

"But I couldn't leave the girls."

"Life's so much better in Canada, Will. And gettin' a job wouldna be a problem for you."

"It's all talk, Emillie."

Ada stepped closer. *Is Da going to Canada?*

She watched as her father rose from his seat and paced the floor. That was something she'd noticed he did a lot since her ma took ill. He paused, and she moved back into the darkness and held her breath.

Ada had seen a welcome change in her father when Dorothy was born; his spirits had lifted. He'd always ask how she was getting on at school and often came home with coloured ribbons for her hair or a wooden toy for Ethel. Without fail, he'd bounce little Dorothy on his knee before having tea. But most of all, she'd loved how he tried to kiss her mother while she was busy at the sink or making the beds. Theresa would shoo him away, saying she didn't have time. Then he'd pull a sheepish, hurt face and pretend to cry to make them all laugh, and her mother would relent and fall into his arms. But since Ma took ill...

"You wanna have a better way of life, don't you?" Ada heard Emillie say.

As she inched forwards, she saw her father sit again, and Emillie covered his hand with hers.

"I'm not sure. Theresa might—"

"Will, you 'eard what the doctor said yesterday. She's got the consumption, and you canna survive that... It's only a matter of—"

"I know!" he said, rubbing the back of his neck.

Ada shivered and wrapped both arms around herself. *Please, God, don't let Ma die.* Half of her wanted to creep back to her warm, cosy blankets, but the other half wanted to hear more of the conversation, so she stayed put.

"Your sister's out in Woodstock already, so you'd 'ave a place to stay as soon as you got there. Canna you see why so many people are leaving England?"

"I'm not sure I'd want to. Not certain I could."

Emillie pushed back her chair, scraping it on the floor, and flounced to the kitchen sink. "Think about it. It'd be a better life, for sure. Full of opportunities."

Ada turned back to the stairs. *I'll be glad when that witch leaves, but if she goes, Ma will have...* She wiped her eyes as she headed upstairs and slipped between the sheets, not wishing to disturb her younger sisters or her dying mother in the next bedroom.

———•———

Later that morning, Lizzie Doyle arrived at Marine Terrace. Her two younger nieces greeted her with wide smiles, and Dorothy wrapped her chubby toddler arms around one of Lizzie's legs. Ethel slipped her hand into Lizzie's and began pulling her towards the parlour.

"Hello, my dears, let me through the door, let me through."

Ada looked pale, and Lizzie reasoned that was down to the fact that she, unlike her sisters, was more aware of the grave situation.

"How's your precious ma today, Ada?" she asked, releasing herself from Ethel and Dorothy's clutches.

"Not so good." A single tear meandered down Ada's cheek.

Lizzie moved forwards with outstretched arms and hugged her eldest niece. "I'll pop up and see your ma, first job. You put the kettle on, and then we'll have a nice cup of tea and a good chat."

Lizzie watched Ada gather her two younger sisters and guide them towards the parlour. She saw her brother-in-law sitting at the table, his head in his hands. She bit her lip as she noticed Emillie flitting about the kitchen. *Why is that interfering madam here at the weekend?*

Upstairs, Lizzie sat in the rocking chair beside Theresa's bed and cradled her sister's limp hand in her warm one. She hoped Father O'Connor would call in again today. Last Saturday, she'd knelt and prayed alongside him as he'd anointed Theresa's forehead with holy oil. She sensed it wouldn't be long until she placed rosary beads in her sister's hands.

Ada's face appeared at the bedroom door. "Tea's brewing, Aunt Lizzie."

"Thank you, my dear. I'll be down in a minute."

"Can I ask you something, Aunty?"

Lizzie stood, kissed Theresa's forehead, and followed her niece out of the bedroom. "What is it, dear?"

"Is Da going to leave us?"

"Why on earth would you think that?"

"I overheard him and Emillie talking this morning."

"Ada, nothing good ever came out of eavesdropping, and besides, Emillie's always gossiping."

Ada stepped forwards and buried herself in Lizzie's arms, sobbing. "Emillie was telling Da how good life is in Canada. And... and Aunt Lucy Margaret lives there already, you know."

Lizzie fished a handkerchief from her skirt pocket and pressed it into Ada's hand.

"And she put her hand on Da's!"

Did she indeed? "Probably trying to comfort him, Ada." *Surely nothing more?* "With your Ma being so ill, she's here to help. That's all, Ada. You know I'd be here every day if I could."

"But I can help Da. I can get a job and earn some money. And—"

"Sssh. Sssh now, Ada, don't get yourself all upset. I'm sure you've misunderstood. Let's have that cup of tea."

Lizzie knew all about Emillie Rogers. People had raised their eyebrows on hearing that she was helping William nurse his dying wife.

"Wouldna trust 'er as far as I could throw her," people would say. "She got the sack from the milliners, and Flo Edwards keeps 'er husband on a tight leash now."

As she followed Ada downstairs, Lizzie saw William in the hallway, putting on his coat.

"I need some fresh air," he growled, not looking up at them.

"I can come with you, Da," Ada offered.

"No, look after your sisters," he replied, keeping his eyes downcast as if to avoid his daughter's hurt expression or Lizzie's questioning one.

Lizzie stood open-mouthed in the hallway, tempted to shout after him as he left and to give him a piece of her mind. *Pull yourself together, William. They need you.*

Ada's eyes glistened with tears again. "See, Aunty. He doesn't want us!"

Lizzie reached out to her, hoping to reassure her, but Ada brushed her arms away and fled upstairs. She watched her go and sighed before popping her head around the parlour door to check on her other two nieces. They sat side by side in an armchair, oblivious to their father's departure or Ada's sobbing.

Dorothy's head of dark hair rested on her sister's shoulders, and her eyelids fluttered and fought to stay open. Lizzie glanced up at the ceiling, picturing her sister lying in bed upstairs.

"Be a good girl, Ethel. I'll be next door in the kitchen."

Ethel grinned before returning to walking her peg doll along the arm of the chair. Lizzie smiled, closed the parlour door, and headed to the kitchen. She paused outside, pushed her shoulders back, and fiddled with the lace cuffs on her blouse.

Lizzie didn't speak as she entered but watched Emillie at the sink for a few seconds as she wrang out a shirt of William's. Emillie hummed a tune as she worked and sipped tea from one of Theresa's best china cups. *She's made herself right at home here, that's for sure.*

"There's no need for you to be here on a Saturday. I'm sure your mother and father must miss you," Lizzie began.

Emillie glanced over her shoulder. "I'll just finish—"

"No. You don't need to be here."

Emillie squeezed the last drop of water from the shirt before turning.

"Is William paying you for today?"

"Of course. He thought you were too busy to—"

Lizzie felt the colour rush to her cheeks. "I'm never too busy for my family."

Emillie dried her hands slowly on a small cloth and held Lizzie's gaze. "If you've got summat to say, spit it out."

"I reckon you know what I'm about to say."

Emillie turned away and washed the china cup.

"Don't turn your back on me, madam. Have you no respect, Emillie?"

Emillie shrugged.

"William isn't coping. And we don't want you putting ideas in his head."

"Still dunna know what you're on about." Emillie shrugged again and gazed out of the window.

Lizzie moved closer and placed a hand on Emillie's shoulder to get her attention.

"Dunna touch me!"

"Ada overheard you talking about immigrating to Canada, and if you're wanting Will—"

"Got nowt to do with you or any bugger else if I wanna go to Canada."

"It flaming well does if you're persuading William to go too. Have you no shame?"

Emillie crossed the kitchen and returned the cup to the cupboard but didn't reply.

"Don't play the innocent. You know what I'm talking about. Cat got your tongue suddenly?"

"I'll stay for as long as he wants me to."

"That'd be grand if everyone thought your intentions were godly and not—"

"Who's everyone?" interrupted Emillie, placing her hands on her hips and facing Lizzie.

"Your reputation precedes you, my dear," Lizzie hissed.

"That ain't my fault." Emillie pulled out a kitchen chair and slid onto it.

"You deserve what people say about you. You're a right—"

"If he tells me to leave, then I will," Emillie said with a sickly smile. "If you're too bloody busy runnin' your fancy lodgin' 'ouse up Whitehall Street, that inna my fault."

"Listen here, madam, it's not my lodging house. I work for Mrs—"

"Whatever you say, Miss Doyle, whatever you say." A smirk crept across her face. "If you canna care for your dyin' sister and her children, that inna my fault."

"If you think for one minute, I will let you take advantage of a grieving man..."

William suddenly appeared in the room.

"Oh, I didna 'ear you come back. Shall I make some tea?" asked Emillie, throwing a triumphant smile at Lizzie as he nodded.

"William, Emillie isn't needed here. I can always come at the weekends," Lizzie said.

He slumped into a chair. "Sorry, I forgot what day it was."

"Ada's upstairs, and she's distraught. She has some mad idea you're going to go to Canada."

Emillie huffed and clanged the kettle onto the stove.

"Go up and talk to her, William." Lizzie ignored the noise Emillie was making.

He nodded, and his eyes lifted, and met hers. "Yes, I'll go in a minute." He placed his clasped hands down on the table.

Lizzie sat beside him and put her hand over his. "Ada needs you. They all do."

"He'll go in a minute! *I'll* make us some tea first." Another smug smile slid across Emillie's face, and Lizzie couldn't help but notice the emphasis on the "I'll".

William lifted his soulless eyes. "It won't be long now, will it, Lizzie?" he asked with a pleading look on his face.

"It's in God's hands."

Ada burst into the kitchen and threw her arms around him.

Lizzie swallowed a sob. "You should leave," she said, waving her hand dismissively at Emillie. "I'll stay here till Monday morning. So, leave right now, please."

Emillie looked hopefully at William, but his head was down, and the sounds of his despair filled the room.

CHAPTER 6

The following morning, William jolted awake and escaped the dreams that had plagued him through the night. Part of him wanted to return to sleep, no matter how restless, so he would have more time to prepare for what the day might bring.

He concentrated on the thin strip of morning light that fell across the foot of Theresa's bed, his eyes not wanting to move up to her face. He gripped the arms of the wooden rocking chair as the room came into focus.

Seeing Lizzie appear in the bedroom carrying a hot drink, he stood and stretched his back.

She placed the cup in his hand. "Plenty of sugar in there for you."

He nodded in appreciation, took a sip, and returned to watching the moving slither of daylight.

They'd both taken turns over the weekend to sit with Theresa, aware that the end was near. As Lizzie switched on the lamp, the room took on an orange glow, and he watched as she knelt beside the bed in prayer. Her words swam over him, and he fought the urge to challenge her about her Catholic faith, as he'd increasingly wanted to challenge Theresa as each untimely loss chipped away at his belief.

Lizzie lifted herself from the floor and crossed herself. "We should let the girls come in to say goodbye. It's time. I'll get them dressed while you have a moment alone."

His eyes followed her as she left before being drawn back to Theresa. Her thick wavy hair was lank, and her face was almost translucent. He struggled to recall the last time he'd played with her hair, stroked her rosy cheeks, or seen her bright, playful eyes.

He leant forward and kissed her forehead before tenderly adjusting her head on the white embroidered pillowcase. *It seems like only yesterday that Mrs Mahoney gave us this pillowcase as a wedding present.*

As the door opened, he turned to see Lizzie ushering Ada, Ethel, and Dorothy into the dim room. All looked bleary-eyed and confused. Ethel held her peg doll and Dorothy a small pink blanket. They made a chain of little hands and lowered heads.

William kissed the gemstone ring and wedding band on his wife's finger, then placed her hand beneath the sheets. Lizzie gestured for Ada to sit beside the bed and Ethel and Dorothy to sit on the small floral armchair in the corner. The pink chair was the only brightness in the room, and Lizzie helped Dorothy climb onto its plump cushion. He glanced across at them as they huddled together, their little legs intertwined. Dorothy fiddled with her blanket, rolling the corner between her thumb and forefinger, and Ethel stroked the scraps of material her mother had used to dress her peg doll.

Ada picked up their wedding photograph from the dressing table. "You looked so beautiful, Ma, on your wedding day. And the flowers on your hat were so pretty."

William nodded. "Yes, you did, my darling. The flowers were white and pink. We were so happy that day." Thirteen years of marriage, three daughters and one precious son who passed away before he could walk.

Was it a comfort that Theresa would soon be with John Rupert? No, he wanted his wife to stay. To fling open the curtains and let the daylight bathe her. To relive their laughter. To hold on to their love. To run down Hills Lane together, just one more time. Theresa always ran or skipped.

He couldn't remember when tiredness and her dreadful cough first began. She'd often rally for a few weeks but then only for a day or two. Her night fevers and bloody sputum had led them to this tearful room. Theresa's breathing was almost silent, her concave chest barely rising. TB had consumed her lungs, larynx, and intestines. Switches were flicked off one by one. Was that her last breath?

Ada straightened the quilted maroon eiderdown before kneeling on the rag rug she'd made with her mother's help. "Love you, Ma," she whispered. "It's my birthday next week. I'll be thirteen."

William put his hand to his mouth and noticed Lizzie turn away.

As Theresa passed, his sob cut through the silence and the strip of daylight he'd been watching finally reached the head of the bed. They all watched as Lizzie placed rosary beads in her sister's hands and knelt to pray. Ada knelt too, and Ethel, looking unsure, approached with her eyes downcast. Little Dorothy slid off the armchair, and as her feet hit the floor, she stumbled and let out a little giggle.

William beckoned his daughters over and gathered them to his chest. He stroked their dark wavy hair. Theresa's hair. *How will we manage without you, my love?*

A week later

Others knelt to pray, but William stayed upright and motionless in the front pew. He stared at the stained glass window above the altar, gaining no comfort from the priest's words of hope and that Theresa was at peace now. What was the point? Theresa's faith hadn't saved her, and what future would her children have without her guidance? He felt unprepared as a father and incapable as a man.

It was a huge turnout, and relatives and neighbours occupied every church pew. Even Granny Tench was there, and William couldn't help wondering how she was still going at ninety-seven, and Theresa was gone at thirty-two. He'd tried not to make eye contact with anyone. As Irish voices reverberated around the church, he'd felt like screaming out for them all to be quiet. Their singing made it real. Their tears made it real. The wooden coffin within arm's reach of him made it real and he didn't want it to be.

Ada sniffled throughout the service, but Ethel and Dorothy were silent, with their eyes fixed straight ahead. Lizzie, Patrick, and his wife Marie sat on the other side of the girls, reaching out with a hand to reassure Ada or nodding at the younger two to acknowledge their silence.

Later, as William stared down at the mound of freshly dug soil, he noticed the wildflowers scattered on top were already fighting for light because of the overhanging yew tree. Theresa's body rested beside their son, her parents, and her younger siblings.

He stayed behind after the other mourners drifted away from the graveside. He'd noticed the concern on Lizzie's face as he lingered, but he had no intention of spending hours engaged in hushed small talk or eating dry curled-up sandwiches. Although grateful to Lizzie and old Mrs Mahoney for laying on a spread, he had bit his tongue earlier when they'd said, "Let's make Theresa proud and give her a good send-off."

The autumn breeze whipped copper leaves from the beech tree in the graveyard. Tearing his eyes from the grave, he lifted his head and breathed deeply. He focused on one leaf as it lost touch with its branch. It floated one last time to the left, then the right, like a ship without a sail, and landed at his feet. Like himself, he felt the leaves were saying goodbye. Goodbye to the summer months, eager to be with others in the feast of colour running along the ground.

He wanted to run too and shake off the burden of being a widower.

"Goodbye, my love," he said and turned away.

CHAPTER 7

1912. Two weeks later

William took his time walking home from work, knowing Emillie had become used to him being late. At first, she'd complained about having to put Ethel and Dorothy to bed and arguing with Ada, who insisted on waiting for her da to come home. The moaning stopped once he started slipping Emillie a few extra coins at the end of the week.

Calling in at the Boars Head for a drink had become his routine because nobody knew him there. He wasn't the man who'd recently buried his wife and left alone to bring up three daughters. Nobody asked questions or gave him sympathetic looks, which suited him after a hard day's graft.

He no longer ate with the other workers at the foundry or participated in their games of pitch-and-toss. *I'm bound to lose my money the way my luck is at the moment.*

After sitting in the far corner of the bar for half an hour, he retrieved the airmail letter that had sat in his inside jacket pocket for four days. He studied the Canadian postage stamp and turned the unopened letter over several times in his hands. Emillie had urged him repeatedly to open it, but it scared him. From his sister's last letter, he'd known that her husband, Fred, had been ill, and he wasn't sure he wanted to hear any more bad news. He tore at it after taking a large swig of his brown ale.

Lucy Margaret offered her condolences and apologised that they didn't make it to Theresa's funeral. But Fred's health was improving, and he hoped to return to work soon at the foundry in Woodstock. William smiled, knowing Fred was on the mend and how she'd signed off with how much she missed him and her three nieces. She also spoke about the growing English community in Woodstock and how they weren't looking forward to the harsh winter.

He glanced up at the clock and swigged back his drink. Emillie never appeared in a hurry to return home to Coffee House Passage, and he knew she'd ask about the letter. She'd taken great delight the day before in telling him she almost had enough money in her hidden cloth bag to escape England. Her enthusiasm was exhausting, but it distracted him from his constant sadness and loss of direction.

As he entered the house later, he saw Ada sitting on the stairs. Her face was tear-stained. "You're late again, Da."

"Sorry, pet."

Ada rushed forwards and buried herself in his chest.

"She wouldna go to bed till you were 'ome. She'll be tired for school tomorrow," Emillie called from the kitchen.

Ada scowled. "No, I won't!"

"Best get to bed now, Ada. I'll come and tuck you up in a bit," he said, taking off his jacket.

She gave her father one last hug before heading upstairs.

"The girls been all right today, Emillie?" he asked.

"Ethel and Dorothy 'ave been as good as gold. But Ada's been givin' me some lip."

He ignored the remark but nodded in appreciation as she placed a chicken stew on the table.

She sat beside him. "You opened that letter yet, Will?"

He finished chewing his food before replying. "I did, Emillie, and thankfully, it wasn't bad news."

"Did Lucy Margaret say any more about Canada?"

He couldn't help smiling at her eagerness. "Yes, they seem well settled. Fred is a lot better, thank goodness," he said before taking another mouthful.

"I bet you'd love to see them."

William put his knife and fork down. "Yes, I miss Lucy Margaret." He smiled again as the usual dreamy expression spread across Emillie's face. "What do your parents think about your plans to emigrate?" he asked.

"I haven't told them. I'm not a child. I've been saving for a couple of years and—"

"I know, I know, you've told me a hundred times. You almost have enough money."

"No bugger will miss me. And 'ave you ever been down Coffee House Passage?" She wrinkled her nose in disgust.

"I'm sure it's not that bad. There are worse places in town." The slums in Hills Lane and Barker Street came into his mind.

"It all needs knockin' down. And I dunna want to end up like my mother! She said I should 'ave married Edwin from next door."

"You didn't care for him?" William asked, taking a last mouthful of chicken.

"No, Edwin is the size of a house!" She held her hands out to the side to make her point.

William chuckled.

She smiled at him before continuing. "Is it wrong to want a new life? This town is full of ol' gossips, and I've 'ad enough of 'em."

"Not sure I like the idea of spending weeks in the steerage of a crowded ship though. I'd be seasick," said William.

"You'd get used to it." She swayed and made wave-like movements with her hands.

"Emillie, you have heard what happened to the Titanic?"

"It'll never 'appen again. It dunna put me off anyway. We'll have each other to lean on." She reached for his hand and held it tightly.

Perhaps it would work if Emillie was by my side.

"Da? You didn't come and say goodnight, and now Ethel is crying," said Ada, appearing in the kitchen.

Emillie pushed back her chair. "You want me to see to them?"

"No, we want Da. Shouldn't you be getting home?"

Emillie raised both hands in surrender.

"Best you get off," William said before following Ada out of the kitchen.

After Emillie had left and he'd settled Ada down, William crawled into his bed. As usual, he reached out in the night with his arm. The other side of the bed was cold and empty. He looked at the bedside clock at 2 a.m., his mind full of ships, the sea, and Emillie's excitement.

Three days later

William cleared his throat and adjusted his tie. He had been dreading this moment and was only outside number 81 because Emillie had insisted they shouldn't delay further. Ada burst into tears when he'd said they were going to Aunt Lizzie's, and she'd demanded to go with him instead of Emillie.

"I like to skip when I cross the English Bridge, just like Ma and I used to do when we visited Aunt Lizzie," she'd said.

"We've no time for that silliness," Emillie had replied.

William knocked on the front door as Emillie linked her arm through his, and they heard the metal bolt back from inside.

Lizzie opened the door, and he took in her dark wavy hair: the same hair, same smile, same eyes as Theresa. Since Theresa's death, a pain had burrowed deep into his chest. It intensified every time Lizzie smiled Theresa's smile, Dorothy climbed on his knee, Ethel showed him her peg doll, or Ada tried to fill her mother's shoes around the house.

"Ah, William, come in, come in. Get yourself out of this chilly wind," said Lizzie.

"We won't stay long," Emillie replied as she unpinned her hat and placed it on the hall stand.

William waited as she glanced in the mirror and adjusted the back of her hair. His eyes were drawn to the nape of her neck. Emillie always wore lavender perfume, and he had wondered where she got it.

He leant against the door and fought the urge to step closer to her. *Pull yourself together.* He'd finally caved in the night before and fallen into Emillie's arms.

"I can't do it," he'd said.

"Well, let me help you," Emillie had replied, "It'll be easier if we stick together."

"Tell me what to do," he'd whimpered as she nuzzled his neck.

The closeness of a woman stirred something in him, and he was ashamed to admit it. *I need someone, and Emillie could help me.*

He followed Lizzie through to her kitchen, and she pulled out just one chair and offered it to him. He grimaced before pulling out another one for Emillie to sit on.

"How are those beautiful girls of yours, William?" asked Lizzie.

Before he could answer, Emillie sat beside him and placed her hand over his. He sighed and reached for the cigarette packet in his pocket. *Yes, I'll let Emillie do the talking.*

"Would you take care of the girls for a while?" Emillie asked.

Lizzie cleared her throat as she filled the kettle and put it on the stove. "Why would you want me to do that?"

William lit a cigarette and Emillie glared at him before tilting her head towards Lizzie as if to say, "Go on, go on, tell her."

"You know Lucy Margaret, Will's sister, lives—"

Lizzie turned and interrupted. "Can't you speak for yourself, William?"

"We're thinking... thinking of going to Canada," he stuttered. "A better life and... we'll send for the girls once we're settled."

"When *we're* settled?"

Lizzie turned her back to them again and reached for her china cups. He watched as she placed her familiar red cake tin on the table, poured boiling water into the teapot, and covered it with a knitted tea cosy that Theresa had made as a Christmas gift.

He bit his lip as a recurring pain welled up inside.

"We've got our tickets already. We leave at the end of the month!" said Emillie.

Lizzie swung around. "What? So soon? And with the winter coming?"

"The girls are delighted at the thought of staying with you for a few weeks," he said, fiddling with his cigarette packet. He wished he could explain that every inch of their house, every street in the town, and every time anyone mentioned her name was like his heart ripping in two.

"Well, it'll be longer than a few weeks, Will."

"For God's sake, shut up, Emillie." Lizzie slammed the kettle back on the stove.

"I'll leave you some money for their keep," he offered. "And, of course, I'll send more each week."

"They'll be fine. Lizzie earns plenty runnin' this place and doin' her dressmaking."

Lizzie stood with her hands on her hips and her face reddening. "So, William, you've come round here to tell me you're going off with this hussy when my lovely sister, God bless her soul, is barely cold in her grave."

She dropped the teapot on the table, causing the tea to ebb out of the spout onto her tablecloth. Reaching for a cloth, she cursed under her breath.

"She's been planning this all along. Surely to God you can see that? And you'll not be the first to fall for her conniving. Where'd you think she gets all her cheap perfume from? Other fools like you!"

Emillie stood.

"Sit down. You're going nowhere till we've sorted this out. You're her ticket out of here, William. All she had to do was flutter her eyelashes at a grief-stricken man and Bob's your uncle, Fanny's your aunt. She reeled you in like all the other fools in town."

"You never know, p'raps, we'll marry once we get to Canada," Emillie said with a smirk.

"Shut up! Let the man speak for Christ's sake."

William rubbed the back of his neck and looked from one woman to the other. His sister-in-law was red in the face, and Emillie jutted her chin out in defiance.

"William, you still have family here. Patrick, Marie, and I will help you, and once Dorothy's at school, it'll be easier."

He heard her words but didn't reply.

"Why not talk to a doctor? See if he can give you something to help you cope?"

"Silly old doctors dunna know anything," Emillie said, throwing her arms in the air.

"Be quiet, Emillie," Lizzie said through gritted teeth.

"It's hard to explain," he said in a whisper. "I want to do the best for them."

"By traipsing them across the Atlantic when their dear ma has only recently passed away?" Lizzie sat beside him.

"My sister Lucy Margaret can help me with them out there because..." William stopped speaking as he lost his train of thought, and Lizzie reached out to him.

"She's got no children of her own," said Emillie, finishing his sentence. "And he'd earn more money out there."

"That'd suit you fine, missy, wouldn't it?"

"Will you take care of them or not, Lizzie?" he asked.

"Of course, I will." Tears streamed down Lizzie's face, and she dabbed her eyes with a handkerchief. "They're all I have left of my beloved sister."

"We'll send—I mean, I'll send for them once—"

Lizzie rolled her eyes. "I should think so! Lost their lovely ma, and now their father's crossing the sea, with this right—"

"Come on, Will, let's leave," said Emillie, standing again.

"Please, please, William, don't do this."

Lizzie's imploring words rang in his ears as they left number 81.

CHAPTER 8

Lizzie smiled as her brother Patrick tapped the kitchen window before appearing through the back door. He was wearing his grey British Rail uniform and a flat cap.

"Ow bist, Lizzie?" he asked.

"Trying to keep busy," she replied. "Can you believe it? They're catching the train to Liverpool this evening."

"I'm working this evening, and if I see him on the platform, I'll give him an ear full."

Lizzie cut a slice of cake for Patrick and placed the teapot on the table. "What's the point? His mind's made up, or rather, it's been made up for him."

Patrick sat at the table, removed his cap, and ran his fingers through his dark wavy hair. "Can't help wondering what Ma and Da woulda made of it. They welcomed William to our family with open arms," he said, taking a bite of cake.

Lizzie nodded.

"William lost his wife, but we've suffered too. There's only me and thee left now, Lizzie," said Patrick, shaking his head slowly.

"We're made of sterner stuff, and William never had the upbringing we did." Lizzie fought her tears. *I need to be strong.*

Patrick reached across the kitchen table and put his hand over hers. "There's been a lot of gossip about Emillie and William in the town," he said. "I've heard it in the Gullet Inn, and Marie's heard it going round the market hall."

"What are they saying?" asked Lizzie.

"What a fool William must be. Do you know the butcher from down Mardol...? His missus stands outside his shop on a Friday, making sure he's not meeting Emillie. Flo Edwards, who runs the milliners, takes all her husband's pay packet off him as soon as he gets it. She reckons he earns more now than he ever did in the past."

Lizzie threw her hands in the air. "Yes, because he ain't giving any to Emillie now!"

She had barely slept since hearing about William and Emillie's decision to leave Shrewsbury. He was ill. She was sure of it. She'd asked their family doctor to call on him, but he'd been refused entry. Who by, she didn't know, but could make a damn good guess. Lizzie had also sought advice from Father O'Connor, but that had been no comfort either. She'd had the impression he had little sympathy for William. All he said was, "William has never been a God-fearing man."

"I'll do an hour in your garden at the weekend if I can have more fruit cake," Patrick said with a smile. "It's time to put the garden to bed for the winter."

At least Patrick never changes. He can always get stuck in and eat like a horse. "I expect William will bring the girls around this afternoon."

"You gonna be all right? You look exhausted, Lizzie. You know, Marie and I will help as much as possible," he said, taking his last slurp of tea.

"But you'll have littl'uns of your own one day."

That afternoon, as Lizzie watched her three nieces head upstairs, her chest ached with sadness. Each girl carried a small cloth bag, and it surprised her how little luggage they had. *I expect she packed for them and threw stuff out without asking.*

Ada took the stairs two at a time, and Ethel followed with her head down so no one could see her tear-stained face. To little Dorothy, every step was a mountain.

"Put your bags in the bedroom at the back," Lizzie called, giving Dorothy a heave to the top of the stairs.

She only had one room left to rent out now, but with plenty of dressmaking on the go, she'd take in washing if push came to shove. Mrs Hurren, the owner of number 81, had offered to lower the rent until William sent for his daughters, but Lizzie was not one for taking charity. She wasn't convinced her nieces' stay would even be short-term. Would he expect them to make the journey alone? Return to collect them? Did Emillie even want them?

"Will Da be on the big ship now, Aunty?" asked Ethel, sinking into the bed's soft mattress.

"Who cares?" snapped Ada. "P'raps they'll go down like the Titan—"

"Ada!" Lizzie shouted before holding her forefinger to her lips and shaking her head.

"I can't wait to go on a ship. I've never, ever seen the sea," said Ethel.

"He won't come back for—"

Lizzie shot Ada a look. A look that said, "You could be right, but this isn't the time to shoot down your younger sister's hopes."

Ada pulled a small, framed photograph out from her bag.

"You could put that beside the bed," Lizzie suggested.

But Ada removed the picture from its frame, folded it in two, and was about to rip her father's face away from her mother's.

"No!" Lizzie shrieked.

"But I don't want to see his face ever again," Ada replied.

"Why not?" Ethel's eyes flicked from Ada to Lizzie.

"Here, you have it," Ada said, passing William and Theresa's wedding photograph to Ethel. "I'm sorry, but I've broken the frame."

"Well, I'm going to keep it under my pillow until Da comes back for us," replied Ethel.

"So, that's all settled then," said Lizzie. "It's a nice big comfy bed. You can all top and tail," she added, hoping to move on and distract little Dorothy from Ada's outburst.

"Can't I have the box room?" complained Ada.

"Afraid not, pet. It's rented out to Mr Wilman now." Ada went to speak again, but Lizzie cut her off. "It's kind of Mrs Hurren to let you have this room."

Ada bit her lip and said nothing more.

"Unpack your bags now. There's one drawer each." Lizzie pointed to the chest of drawers. "And please help your sisters, Ada."

"You know she sold all our furniture... Ma's dressing table and her silver brush set. I wanted that to remember Ma," said Ada with her hands on her hips. "Emillie put everything outside the front door and sold it all to passers-by. Two bob for this and half a crown for that!"

Lizzie sighed as she returned downstairs, struggling to believe Emillie could be so heartless.

William had spent no more than five minutes at the front door to say goodbye. It was for the best, and she didn't have any fight left to argue with him anymore. Emillie hadn't bothered to come with him as she was in town buying important stuff they needed for the journey.

"You'll never have any money with her about," Lizzie had said as she hugged him for the last time.

Later, as she made bread and jam for the girls' tea, she paused to look out over the fading pink hydrangeas at the end of the back garden. Everything in the flower beds was well past its best and the fragrant flowers on her wisteria were long gone. It was as if Lizzie's sadness had spread out into the garden. It had been her pride and joy for years. Mrs Hurren had kindly agreed to reduce the rent if Lizzie kept it tidy. *I'll have less time now, so I'll take up Patrick's offer to help.* Thoughts of the winter filled her mind and added to her dark mood.

She thought of Theresa and imagined how bereft she'd be knowing William had left his daughters.

"I'll look after them, Theresa," Lizzie said, looking up and crossing herself.

She felt guilty for not heeding Ada's words and acting on her suspicions about Emillie sooner. Lizzie didn't listen to gossip about people, but she wished she'd paid attention to what folk had said about Emillie Rogers. She'd played on William's grief, but Emillie also knew he had an excellent trade to land a job as soon as they arrived in Canada.

Lizzie shook her head to dispel her thoughts, knowing she would have to get on with things and do her best for her nieces.

CHAPTER 9

December 1915
43 Finkle Street, Woodstock, Ontario

Three years in Canada, and my God, it's been an eternity of nagging.

William had never hit a woman; he'd never hit anyone. But as he sat at the kitchen table, taking the last mouthfuls of his dinner, he tried to abate the rage building inside.

Because it was classed as a reserved occupation during the war, work at the foundry was intense; fewer hands than were needed. All William wanted when he came home in the evening was some peace and quiet.

He watched as Emillie stood at the sink, washing a pot before clattering it down onto the draining board. "No room for our new dinner service in these cupboards," she said, reaching for a cup and banging the cupboard shut.

"Do we have a new dinner service?" William asked.

She ignored his question. "It would be nice if we could 'ave a separate dining room. We could entertain friends for a meal or have a drinks party," she said.

He lit a cigarette before playing with his box of matches, rotating it and tapping each edge on the table. He knew that annoyed her, but her enthusiasm to get on in life drained him. There was a war on, and she only cared about having more space and more things. "I want, I want" were the only words that came out of her mouth. She gave him nothing in return. No appreciation, thanks, or understanding.

She'd cajoled him from the moment they left Liverpool, saying it wasn't decent to travel together unless they were husband and wife, so she wrote Mrs Emillie Tate on the ship's passenger list. She'd assumed his sister would give them free board and lodgings once they reached Woodstock without even asking. And he'd gone along with it, gone along with everything she said. But the penny had finally dropped. The rent for their apartment was far more than he'd ever wanted to pay, so from day one, he'd taken on more and more overtime. It suited him now though. If he was busy, he didn't have time to think.

The only clear evidence of his toiling was a wardrobe full of coats and dresses and an ornate mantel clock that she'd sworn wasn't expensive. He often came home with just a plate of cold meat left out for him and no note to say where she was or when she'd return.

He wondered how they still hadn't saved enough money for the girls' passage to Canada. *I've been a damn fool.* There was no final straw; her nagging was the same as it regularly had been. But the wave of anger that had simmered for some time now had, for some reason, reached the surface.

As they'd neared the ship, Emillie had breezed along the landing stage at Liverpool, smiling, waving, and swinging her small suitcase. She'd talked to any fellow passenger willing to listen.

"My husband's an engineer. Big wage. We'll buy a nice house... blah blah. Canada will be so much better than England."

Now, he wondered what her audience would have thought if they'd known that they weren't married at that point. Or that his wife had been barely cold in her grave.

Some people seemed apprehensive about the voyage and stopped to take a good hard look at the ship,

Lake Manitoba, before they boarded. There was talk of terrible Atlantic winter storms, and the English weren't always welcome in Canada. Poverty and unemployment had brought most of the passengers to Liverpool that day. William had glanced over his shoulder at the crowds waving and cheering goodbye. There was no one to wave them off though.

He had a decent, well-paid job in Shrewsbury and family there. So, what made him get on the ship? That was a question he'd often asked himself.

For him, the voyage was a mixture of seasickness and uncertainty that led to many sleepless nights and vivid dreams of Theresa. He'd spent days watching but not joining in the joviality and camaraderie up on deck as others danced and sang to pass the time. Nothing quelled their or Emillie's excitement about the "New World".

She'd given no sympathy to his inability to keep food down or his crying out "Theresa" in the middle of the night. Emillie told him to shut up or said, "What will people think of us?"

Now the words "Marry in haste, repent at your leisure" and Lizzie's parting words came into his mind: "You'll never have any money with her about."

"You listening to me, Will? Will!"

Her voice grated on him. "Yes, yes, I'm listening. Did you post the letter as I asked you to? And put the money order inside for Lizzie and the postal notes for the girls?" he asked.

She swung round to face him. "Of course, I did! Though why you bother when there's a war on, I don't know."

"Christmas is coming, and we can't expect Lizzie to—"

"So, doing even more overtime would 'elp them too." A look of satisfaction spread across her face.

"Hundreds of men are returning to England to defend their country of birth. Dying for their country, and all you're bothered about is me earning a few more dollars."

"You're doin' your bit."

But am I? "We're better off than a lot of folk in the world."

"But we could get a bigger place, William."

"For Christ's sake, Emillie. If I worked every hour God sent, it wouldn't satisfy you."

"Annie and Jim have moved to a lovely new house on Dundas Street," she whined.

"Why don't you get off your backside and find a job?"

With her hands on her hips, she glared at him. A look he'd seen many times, a look that said, "You're a disappointment." The same look his father gave when he'd refused to join the family business and when he'd married Theresa.

"You'd always let Theresa 'ave whatever she wanted. Love her more than me, did you?" Her high-pitched, saccharine, yet mocking question made his fists clench.

His heart quickened. Had he become the type of man who raised his fists to his wife? Had he become his father? He stubbed out his cigarette, got up, and flung his dinner plate into the sink.

She glared at him. "I keep 'ouse for you but get nothin' in return. Was the lovely Theresa so perfect? At least we'll never have to see 'er blasted offspring again!"

"What? What the hell did you say?"

He swung at her. The back of his right hand sliced the side of her face, and his signet ring caught under her eye. She stumbled backwards, and only the wooden kitchen table saved her from landing on the floor.

"You bitch! Theresa was an angel, and I loved her far more." He paused. "I still love her," he mouthed.

William shook his head before turning away and covering his mouth. Emillie cradled the side of her face but didn't look up at him.

He hooked his heavy winter coat off the back of the kitchen chair and slipped it on as he headed for the door. He turned his collar up as he stepped outside into the bitter December wind and tucked his head down to avoid catching anyone's eye as he walked up Finkle Street. He was sure everyone knew he'd just hit his wife.

William paused at the corner, unfastened his coat, and loosened the top button of his shirt. It didn't help; he was sweating, and a heavy weight pressed on his chest. He couldn't understand why he felt so hot and why there was an unfamiliar pain radiating across his shoulders.

He tried to justify himself as he strode on, but there was no excuse. *What sort of man am I? I hit my wife, I left my children, and I'm not fighting for my country.*

Nausea enveloped him, and he paused again at the corner of Dundas and Graham Street and lit a cigarette, hoping to calm himself. He closed his eyes as he inhaled, only to picture Englishmen bedded down in the muddy trenches or scrambling over the top and running towards the enemy.

What am I doing? Nothing. I'm not even protecting my children.

"You all right there, mate?" called someone from the other side of the street.

"Heartburn. I'll be on my way in a minute," he replied, rubbing his fist up and down his chest.

Thoughts of Ada, Ethel, and little Dorothy filled his mind. He'd continued to send letters and money orders to them, even though he hadn't heard from Lizzie for over a year. The war affected the postal service, but he'd hoped they all arrived eventually. Hearing that working at the foundry was a reserved occupation and not part of the Canadian Expeditionary Force would comfort them.

Walking down Hunter Street, he wondered if Emillie had ever loved him. Was he caught up in her plans to escape? Or was it his weaknesses that had brought him to this point? His trait of turning away to avoid what life threw at him and relying on others so much? How could he have run away now?

He stubbed out his cigarette before descending the steps into the public library. They weren't steep, but he needed to hold the handrail. The building was his escape from Emillie, a sanctuary where he could lose himself and forget the present and the past. He'd met his good friend Charles Bevan there, and their mutual interest in anything mechanical meant they'd poured over every engineering book on the shelves.

It was almost empty inside, and Charles waved from their usual table as he saw William enter. The door had barely closed behind him when a shadowy veil descended over his eyes, and he clutched his chest. A sharp dagger-like pain cut down his arm, and he crumpled to the floor.

The blackness that surrounded him momentarily cleared. He was standing on the landing stage at Liverpool. He dislodged his arm from Emillie's and turned back. He saw Ethel and little Dorothy running towards him with outstretched arms, and he scooped them both up. Hugging them tightly, he nestled his face into their dark wavy hair.

"Hello, my dears," he said.

"Da. Da. We can't breathe," they chorused.

"We're ever so good at spinning our tops now, Da," said Ethel as he put them down.

The Liverpool morning mist parted, and he looked out to sea. He saw their mother and watched Theresa remove her bonnet, allowing her dark wavy hair to cascade onto her shoulders. John Rupert was sitting on her hip, holding his bottle and waving his chubby fingers.

William's heart overflowed with love, and he waved enthusiastically at them. Someone appeared from behind Ethel. It was Ada. She didn't smile or wave but pulled on her sisters' arms instead. They all faded as they turned away, but he saw Ada's hand wave dismissively at him. Theresa and John Rupert disappeared into the morning mist that blanketed the sea.

He stepped forwards and saw Charles rush towards him, but the blackness returned—a brutish, almost palpable blackness.

———•———

Emillie banged on the kitchen window, thinking William would glance back as he left their apartment. She'd wanted him to see her bloodied face.

"Go to hell," she shouted as he scurried up Finkle Street.

He'd never struck her before, and she struggled to comprehend why he'd done it now. They didn't argue about much. He would moan and seem disinterested but always accepted everything she said or did. Life with him had been much easier than she'd thought, and the war had helped her cause too.

What was the point of sending money orders to Lizzie when the mail service was so poor? And surely it wasn't safe for his daughters to join them during a war. She had no intention of being a stepmother to them. No, she was far too young and having far too much fun.

They'd wed a month after arriving in Woodstock; his sister Lucy Margaret and her husband Fred were the witnesses. After the ceremony, they shared a delicious meal at the Oxford Hotel in town. Emillie wished her parents and the old gossips from Shrewsbury could have seen her there, wearing her fancy white lace dress.

She retrieved a handkerchief and a compact mirror from her handbag and examined her face. Her cheek burnt, and she dabbed the cut under her eye.

"Wait till I tell your sister about this. She wanna think you're so bloody perfect then, will she? Nor that Miss high and mighty Lizzie Doyle."

The signet ring that had caused the cut once belonged to William's father-in-law, John Doyle. Emillie had persuaded William to move it to his right hand after their wedding. She had plans to mislay or sell it if he ever took it off. Deep in thought, he often sat, turning it round and round and that annoyed her.

"It's like Theresa's still in our flamin' lives," Emillie said between gritted teeth. "I never wanna set eyes on her brats again, that's for sure. Ada especially. She always 'ad summat to say 'bout everythin'."

Emillie turned her face from side to side as she looked in the mirror, relieved that she'd not arranged to meet any of her friends that week. Especially not Jack, who owned the tailor's shop along Main Street. The onset of war had curtailed her regular trips into town, but some people had organised small gatherings at their homes. However, she'd made excuses not to host one herself, fearing William would appear and ask about Jack or embarrass her by talking about his daughters.

She retrieved William's latest letter from her handbag and, without hesitation, tore it open and pulled out the money orders. Screwing up his letter, she threw it to the far corner of the room. *Lizzie won't be needing this one either. I'll just write my name on the payee line.*

It was tempting to camouflage the redness on her cheek with powder, but wanting Lucy Margaret to see the marks, Emillie grabbed her coat and cursed under her breath as she headed for the door.

A smartly dressed gentleman met her on the path outside. He tipped his hat towards her. "Are you, by any chance, Mrs Tate?" He shuffled his feet and looked down at the ground before continuing. "I'm... I'm Charles Bevan, a good friend of your husband's."

"Well, pick your friends more carefully," she growled, lifting her face to show him.

He cleared his throat. "Mrs Tate, I'm—"

"If you're sellin' summat, I'm not bloody interested," she said, brushing past him. "I've got business to deal with."

"Mrs Tate, I'm afraid I have some terrible news about your husband."

She stood in front of him, her face inches from his. "More's the pity 'e is my flamin' 'usband. Can you see what he's done to my face? He's a good-for-nothin—"

"Unfortunately, he suffered a heart attack," Charles interrupted. "We often meet at the library, as I'm sure you know."

Emillie didn't know.

"Yes, it happened as he came through the door."

"Oh, for God's sake. So, now I'll 'ave to get to the hospital, lookin' like this." She raised her face again to show Charles. "What'll people think of me?"

"No, no, Mrs Tate. I'm afraid William passed away. It was quick. He didn't suff..." Charles stopped mid-sentence as Emillie put a hand to her mouth.

She stared at him as if processing the words and then mouthed, "But he was 'ere an hour—"

"I believe he had a younger sister, Mrs Tate. She lives on Dundas Street, I believe. Would you like me to take you there? You shouldn't be on your own at a time like this."

She held his gaze and then, without replying, turned and headed back inside, ignoring Charles as he called after her.

Once back in the apartment, she headed straight to the sideboard and slammed down their framed wedding photograph. "How dare he. How bloody dare he!"

She scanned the room as thoughts raced through her mind about what she should do first. *I must tell his sister. Then, tell the boss at the foundry and the bank manager. I suppose I should write and let Lizzie know.*

William was buried in Woodstock Cemetery on a cold but sunny afternoon five days later. Emillie told herself repeatedly that she'd loved him, but her tears had not flowed easily. Apart from recognising Charles Bevan, she had no idea who most of the mourners were.

"Will you return to Shrewsbury now?" he asked as they stood beside the small spread Lucy Margaret had put on for everyone at her house. "I believe your parents are both still alive. And you'll surely want to take comfort from William's children."

Emillie coughed and held her handkerchief to her mouth. "It's still such a shock. I'm... I'm not sure what I shall do," she stuttered on seeing the sympathy in his eyes.

"Please let me know if there is anything I can do to help you. Lucy Margaret has kindly given me an address for your sister-in-law, Miss Elizabeth Doyle. And I intend to pay my condolences to her."

Do what you like. She nodded and turned away, choosing to stand with the small circle of friends she'd invited back after the funeral.

"That stupid chap thinks I might want to head back to England now," she whispered to Jack. "Why on earth would I want to go back there?"

He winked at her.

William's sister had offered Emillie a home with them, but she'd refused. She had no intention of wearing black for months on end or having her goody-goody sister-in-law know all her business. Lucy Margaret had already asked if he'd made a will. Much to Emillie's relief, he hadn't because she intended to take the lot as his widow.

William had always trusted her to look after their money. In fact, he'd trusted her with everything. She had a nice little nest egg, and Jack had offered to "see her right".

The day after Theresa's funeral, William had cried in Emillie's arms for her to take the responsibilities and organisation off his shoulders. *I only did what he asked of me.* Yes, she'd played on his grief and used him to escape her miserable life, but hadn't men used her in the past?

The thought of going back to Coffee House Passage made her shudder. If she let her parents know, they would surely ask her to come home. She'd not bothered to write to them since arriving in Canada, so why bother now?

A week later, Emillie picked up the last of William's pay from the foundry and nodded gratefully as the boss said he'd put a little extra in for her. She also took an envelope with a mourning card inside to the post office addressed to: Miss Elizabeth Doyle, 81 Whitehall Street, Shrewsbury, England.

CHAPTER 10

February 1916
81 Whitehall Street

Lizzie spread her newspaper on the kitchen table to look at the headlines. There was rarely a good one, and today's was no exception. A German Zeppelin heading for Merseyside had dropped its bombs on Tipton, Wednesbury, and Walsall, ninety miles off target. Sixty-seven died, one hundred and eleven people were injured, and fourteen houses were destroyed.

Bowing her head, she crossed herself. "The Father, the Son, the Holy Spirit. Amen."

Lower down the front page was a picture of a Red Cross train pulling into Shrewsbury station carrying a hundred and forty-two wounded soldiers. The Shrewsbury Volunteer Medical Corps had worked alongside the Red Cross and St John's Ambulance to transport the men, many of whom were on stretchers, to the Royal Salop Infirmary.

She longed to see the headline "Shrewsbury men return home" and thought about her brother, Patrick, in France. "Please, Lord, keep him safe."

Ada, Ethel, and Dorothy were at least keeping her busy and giving her a routine to get through each day. Crossing herself again, she sighed, folded the paper, and put it beside the fireplace. The clatter of the letterbox distracted her from melancholy thoughts.

Like every woman, Lizzie constantly dreaded a certain letter or telegram from overseas. But as she stooped to retrieve the creased envelope and recognised the handwriting, all she could think was, *Why is that bloody hussy writing to me?* She crossed herself again in a faint hope God would forgive her wicked thoughts and the utter loathing she held for Emillie Rogers, the sender.

She could barely make out the postmark: maybe 27 December 1915. *You'd have thought the ship must have called in every port, and the mailman had stopped at every pub along his journey.* There had been no news from William for almost two years, and her three nieces no longer asked after their father.

Lizzie had a small purse where she kept coins paid to her for doing washing and dressmaking. She still let out the third bedroom to a travelling salesman, and his money helped to pay her rent to Mrs Hurren. Money was tight, but Ada had just found a job which would help to keep the wolf from the door. She'd stopped hoping a money order from her brother-in-law might fall through the letterbox.

And now this, from that bloody good-for-nothing woman. She crossed herself again before returning to the kitchen, relieved the girls hadn't heard the letterbox.

Once she'd sat at the table, she tore open the envelope and pulled out a postcard. There was a picture of William wearing a dapper brown tweed suit and a nifty hat on one side, and on the other, she read:

> I GUESS YOU KNOW WHO THIS IS WITHOUT MY TELLING YOU. PASSED AWAY ON DECEMBER 12, 1915.

She raised her hand to her mouth and fumbled to find her handkerchief as her eyes welled with tears. *No, no, surely not?*

At that moment, the three girls breezed into the kitchen, laughing and chattering. She slipped the envelope and card inside her apron pocket, sat straight, and wiped a tear from her cheek.

"You all right, Aunty?" asked Ada.

"My arthritis is playing up," she replied, lowering her head and rubbing her knee.

"Can I make you some tea?"

"Yes please, pet." *I need time to think before I give you all the awful news.* "By the way, Ada, did you try on the new dress while you were upstairs?" she asked, trying to push William's death out of her mind.

Ada placed a kiss on the top of her aunty's head. "It's smashing and fits me a treat. I shall be the smartest girl working at the army pay office," she said, dancing around the kitchen table.

"All the Doyle women were handy with a needle and thread. Your dear mother was the same," Lizzie said, crossing herself for the fourth time that morning.

"Can we do more knitting this evening?" asked Ethel. "I want to help the soldiers."

She'd kept the girls and herself busy through the long winter evenings knitting socks. There'd been a notice in *The Shrewsbury Chronicle*: The Shropshires at the front could do with some socks. It had pointed out what a great comfort it was for soldiers to have a dry change coming out of the trenches.

She'd answered many calls for help with the war effort that the Catholic Church had given out and attended several patriotic fundraising concerts at the music hall in town. She'd also packed comfort boxes to send to the front: a chocolate bar, socks, a small Bible, and some cigarettes. She didn't enjoy putting in a packet of Woodbine cigarettes because it reminded her of William and it would perhaps rot the soldiers' teeth, but she knew the Bible would be a great comfort to her brother Patrick.

Lizzie enjoyed involving the girls, sitting in front of the fire, showing them how to undo old outgrown woollen jumpers, and teaching them how to knit. Ada and Ethel needed guidance with the heels, and she had to re-knit in places where they'd gone wrong. Dorothy tried to rewind the old wool into balls but only got tangled up.

Every evening since the war started, she had drawn the curtains, hoping to block out her worries for a few hours. She'd told the girls stories about their grandparents, John and Mary. Their great-grandfather Bartholomew Doyle had been a tenant farmer in Ireland when the potato famine struck, and his son John met Mary Kelly on the ship over to Liverpool. Both had been in search of work and a better life.

"Did Grandma Mary have hair like mine?" Ethel would often ask.

"Yes, that's where we all get our wavy dark hair," Lizzie had replied.

"I'll help with the knitting," said little Dorothy, climbing onto Lizzie's lap and bringing Lizzie back from her thoughts and memories.

"Let me finish my tea and get us something to eat first." She ruffled Dorothy's hair as she jumped down.

How could Emillie think those few words would be enough? Standing at the sink peeling potatoes, she glanced down at the envelope in her apron pocket. *Did he die fighting? Where's he buried?*

"My God, you must have loved mailing that, you cruel trollop."

She crossed herself for the fifth time that morning.

A few days later, Lizzie nestled into her comfy armchair by the window and picked up the cross-stitch sampler she'd started after Theresa died. It had filled many winter evenings after the girls had retired to bed. The sampler bore her late parents' names and her siblings' initials. As a spinster, and with Patrick fighting in France, she'd wanted something to give to her nieces; otherwise, it was almost as if the Doyle family never existed. Passing the thread back and forth was a chance to reflect on life, and she was proud of the memoriam she'd made.

The mourning card had been in her apron pocket all weekend, and she'd thought of nothing else. As she pulled the thread, she cast her mind back to William and Theresa's engagement party and wedding day. Their eyes had been so full of love for each other. She regretted the harsh manner she'd parted ways with William but still hadn't forgiven him and wasn't sure she ever would. Even with her strong faith, she struggled to understand his motivation for leaving his daughters.

Was it all Emillie's fault? Was his grief so intense he lost his mind? Theresa helped him escape from his violent father. Was he so weak he couldn't carry on once she'd passed?

Lizzie sighed and put down her needlework as the parlour door opened, and three smiling faces appeared, one above the other, around the door. "Come in, come in," she beckoned.

The girls bustled into the parlour, Ada settling on the other armchair and Ethel and Dorothy sprawling on the wooden floor.

"I have..." She paused and looked at each girl in turn. *Ada thinks she's all grown up now, Ethel's still full of questions, and Dorothy's still innocent and unknowing.*

Lizzie took a deep breath and started again. "I have something to tell you."

Ada twiddled her hair and appeared disinterested, but her younger sisters stared up with wide eyes.

"Don't tell me they've cancelled the church bazaar," said Ada.

"No, I've had a letter from Emillie."

Ada's eyes widened. "What the dev—"

"Let me speak, Ada, please."

Ethel and Dorothy came closer and sat cross-legged in front of her.

"I'm afraid your da has passed away."

Her younger nieces stared at each other. She beckoned them both, and Dorothy climbed up onto her lap.

"Your da is in heaven now."

"So, is he an angel now?" asked Ethel.

"I doubt it," snapped Ada.

"Ada, be quiet," said Lizzie, and she watched as Ada lifted her legs onto the armchair and hugged her knees to her chest.

"I feel sad," said Ethel, lowering her head onto Lizzie's shoulder.

She drew both of them to her and planted a kiss on the top of their heads. "He'll be with your ma in heaven."

"Will we ever see them again?" asked Ethel.

Lizzie fought her tears. "Yes, one day. We can say a special prayer and light a candle for them both in church on Sunday if you'd like."

"What's 'eaven?" asked Dorothy.

"It's where angels live, silly," said Ethel, poking her younger sister in the arm.

Ada brushed a tear from her cheek. "Emillie won't come and live here with us now, will she?"

"So, Da's not coming home, not ever?" whimpered Ethel, climbing onto Lizzie's other knee.

"How did it go at the army pay office today, Ada?" Lizzie asked, trying to distract the two younger girls. She stared at Ada, hoping for a reply to ease Ethel's sobbing.

"Who is Em... Emillie?" asked Dorothy.

She ignored Dorothy's question but shook her head at Ada. "I know how you feel about Emillie. But your da was a good man, who perhaps wasn't very well and now may he rest in peace."

"Well, he wasn't a good father!" replied Ada, standing up. "He never came back for us. He promised me he would. He promised."

"So, how's the army pay office, Ada?" Lizzie asked again as Ethel and Dorothy nuzzled closer.

Ada sniffled. "Yes, it's wonderful." She blew her nose before saying, "And you'll never, never guess how much my pay is."

"Half a crown?" guessed Lizzie before mouthing "thank you" at Ada for distracting her sisters.

Ada brushed away another tear. "No, a pound a week, and I'll learn shorthand, typing, and bookkeeping." She smiled and held her hands towards her sisters, who jumped off Lizzie's knee.

"A pound a week, a pound a week. Can you believe it?" she repeated, doing a little jig to make them laugh.

Lizzie exhaled, relieved that she'd done the job. But she knew more questions would come in the days, weeks, and even months to come, and there was no need to share the postcard with them.

"Aunty, can we measure ourselves again? I'm sure I've grown," Ethel said, standing to attention to prove her point.

"All right, you find the pencil and line up in the hall. And no cheating, Ethel, by standing on the stairs," Lizzie replied with a smile, and as they left the room, she called out, "And remember, we still have plenty to do for the church bazaar on Saturday."

As Ada moved to follow her sisters, Lizzie whispered, "We'll have another chat later, pet, when they're both in bed."

"No need. I'll never forgive Da," said Ada.

CHAPTER 11

March 1916

As Lizzie headed for the door, she noticed Ada stuffing something in the wide sash of her costume. "Everything all right, Ada? Have you got everything you need?"

"Yes, Aunty, I was just checking I had a handkerchief."

As they entered the church hall, Lizzie smiled at the vivid colours and the smell of freshly baked cakes and biscuits. There were Union Jacks hung proudly on the walls, and the colourful costumes of the stall holders were imaginative. Mrs Egan sat at the piano, and her husband Billy sat in a wheelchair wearing his army uniform with one trouser leg pinned up to his waist. Lizzie spotted his shiny medals spread across his chest. *Poor soul, I'm sure he'd rather have his leg than them.*

It had been a good idea to give the event an Oriental theme, and the entire community had embraced it.

Everything on sale was homemade or simple household bric-a-brac. The organisers hoped that with the help of the costumes, a piano, cups of tea, and cake, they could all escape their worries of war for a few hours and enjoy themselves.

Mrs O'Malley behind the Egyptian stall had risen to the occasion and wore a pharaoh's headdress made of gold paper and dressed in a white bedsheet, which she'd secured with a golden curtain sash.

"You look like Cleopatra brought back to life, Mrs O'Malley," Lizzie said with a smile, making the poor woman blush.

Mrs O'Brien stood behind the Korean stall wearing a white blouse with large bell sleeves.

"You're looking wonderful too, Mrs O'Brien. I'll be back later to buy some of your delicious cake," Lizzie said as she walked on.

The two ladies at the Moorish stall had used red scarves to cover half their faces.

"Mrs Mahoney? Is that you behind there?" she called, laughing.

The bazaar was held to raise funds for the war effort and repairs to the church's west wing because the stonework was crumbling. Lizzie and her nieces joined in with the loud "hear, hears" as Sir Francis Smyth declared the event open, saying he hoped everyone present had come with full hearts and large purses.

Lizzie smiled as she watched Ethel and Dorothy skipping around the hall. Unlike Ada, they seemed to have forgotten the news of their father's death, at least for now. Lizzie had made Ada's Japanese costume out of an old red curtain, and the colour contrasted beautifully with her dark hair. Ada looked sheepish and fiddled with the wide sash around her waist.

As Lizzie approached, Ada asked, "How do I look, Aunty?"

"You look grand, dear, and I'm sure your stall will make lots of money. I'll start you off by buying this shiny red cake tin."

Ada giggled. "But Aunt Lizzie, you're buying back the tin you donated!"

"It's all for a good cause, dear. I plan on buying some of Mrs O'Brien's cake to put in it, and we can have some for our tea. And besides, I love my cake tin!"

"Are the mayor and mayoress coming today?" asked Ada, passing the tin over and dropping the coins into a small cardboard box.

"Yes, and the chap from *The Chronicle* too, so you better stand up straight if he takes a picture," Lizzie said, glad to see a smile on Ada's face.

Lizzie moved to the next stall, and John O'Reilly caught her eye as he approached Ada.

"Sorry to hear 'bout your da, Ada," he said, glancing over the items on her stall.

"Oh... oh, thank you, John, that's kind of you."

It surprised Lizzie to overhear his words of sympathy. *Those O'Reillys usually don't have anything kind to say to anyone. Biggest gossips in town.*

"Shame your ma died a few years back, and your da cleared off with 'is fancy woman 'cause he didna want you or your snotty little sisters," John added with a sneer.

Lizzie held her breath as Ada bit her lip, but she could see Ada's cheeks redden and her eyes fill with tears.

"I'll be having a word with your father, John," Lizzie said, looking stern and shooing him away. *Oh, the little bugger.* Lizzie glared at him and raised her fist.

She was relieved to see Ethel and Dorothy running towards their sister and hoped Ada could hold back her tears until they got home.

"Isn't this wonderful? And Aunty has bought some cake for our tea," said Ethel. "What's in your sash, Ada? Is it a letter?"

"It's nothing, Ethel. Forget about it." Ada put her hand deeper inside her sash and distracted her sister, saying, "So, tell me more about our cake, Ethel."

The afternoon was a great success, and once home, Lizzie couldn't wait to put the kettle on the stove and try the Ceylon tea Sir Francis had donated to the event. He'd also donated some spices, but she didn't like the smell or know what to do with them.

She watched as Ada shot up the stairs as soon as they were home, mumbling something about her costume being itchy. *I'll clip that little ragamuffin, John O'Reilly, round the ear if he upsets my Ada again.*

That evening, Lizzie finished sewing her cross-stitch sampler and held it up to admire her needlework. She traced each name, initial, and the clover leaf or flower beside each one with her forefinger. *The Doyles and Hills Lane will always be remembered if I have anything to do with it.*

She pulled out some blue ribbon from her sewing bag and some tissue paper from the sideboard. After rolling up and tying the sampler securely with the ribbon, she placed it in her old cake tin. She added the small and sadly creased wedding photograph of William and Theresa that Ethel had soon forgotten about keeping under her pillow. Finally, she placed the mourning card. She looked forward to seeing their church bazaar event reported in *The Shrewsbury Chronicle* and planned to cut the article out and add it to the other items in her tin.

Ada closed the bureau silently and swung round to face Lizzie.

What's she up to?

"You all right, pet? Are you looking for something?" Lizzie asked. "You're looking a little pale."

"No, I'm fine."

Ada joined her sisters at the table and kept her head down as she played with buttons from Lizzie's sewing box.

"Where you off to, Aunty?" asked Ethel, watching Lizzie button up her long winter coat.

"I have a few errands to run this morning, but I won't be long, dearies."

"I'm getting good at tiggerlywinks," said Dorothy as a button rattled into a small tin.

Ethel peered inside Lizzie's basket. "What's in here?" she asked, picking up a small package wrapped in brown paper.

"Now, Ethel, your nose will get you into trouble one day." Lizzie laughed and tapped her on the nose before returning the package to the basket.

"You mean, tiddlywinks, Dorothy," Ada groaned.

Tempted to ask Ada whether she'd got out of the wrong side of the bed, Lizzie bit her tongue instead.

"Can't I come with you, Aunty?"

The fresh air might do Ada good, but... "Not today, Ada. Keep an eye on your sisters, please."

Ada nodded and said no more.

Lizzie shivered as she stepped outside, and looking up at the dove grey sky, she retrieved her woollen gloves from her coat pocket. It was mid-morning but still bitter, and a hoar frost glistened on the wallflowers she'd planted last autumn. She'd prayed they'd survive the long winter and bring some early March colour; a beam of hope that the war might end soon.

She hurried to the bottom of Whitehall Street but paused outside the Abbey Church to look up at its sandstone west tower. *Please help me to be strong, Lord.*

Halfway over the English Bridge, she stopped again to look at the swollen River Severn rushing down from the Welsh Cambrian Mountains. There was talk of flooding, and as she watched the water, she concluded that the talk might be right.

Making her way up Wyle Cop, she stopped to catch her breath, still unsure whether calling on Martha and James Rogers was a good idea. She only knew them by sight, but if there was the slightest chance they had more information about William's death, she owed it to his daughters to find out.

The wind whistled down Coffee House Passage, and Lizzie lowered her head as she entered from the town square's end. Number 10 was about halfway along, and she knocked on the door.

"Hello, Mrs Rogers?"

Martha Rogers opened the door and, for a moment, looked blankly at Lizzie. "Oh, Miss Doyle. Please, please come in," she said, beckoning.

After clearing a chair of old newspapers for Lizzie to sit down, Martha reached for the kettle.

Lizzie had never spoken to Martha, so she was surprised she had known her name. "I'm sorry to call on you uninvited."

She paused as she placed her basket down on the table. There was a rasping, coughing noise coming from upstairs.

"My James 'as taken to his bed," Martha explained. "It seems to take him longer each time to get over his bronchitis."

"Sorry to hear that."

Lizzie watched Martha place two cups and a teapot on the table before sitting down.

"Have you had a letter from your Emillie recently?" Lizzie asked.

Tears sprung to Martha's eyes. "Miss Doyle, we've heard nowt from her since she left. Nothin' for three years. And now her poor father—"

Lizzie moved her chair closer and placed her hand over Martha's. "Not a single word from her?"

It beggars belief.

They both heard the rasping cough again, and Lizzie paused and glanced up at the ceiling, concerned. Martha poured the weak tea from the pot, and they both sat silently for a few minutes.

"She always was a wicked girl. Never one to worry 'bout anyone but 'erself," Martha said, clasping her teacup.

Lizzie pulled out the mourning card and placed it in front of Martha. "I received this a week ago."

Martha turned the card over several times and gasped. "Was that it? That's all she wrote?"

"Yes, that was it."

"How did he die? Where's he buried? Where's Emillie?"

She shook her head and shrugged at each of Martha's questions. "For the first year or so, he wrote regularly and sent money for his daughters—"

"Those poor, poor little girls," Martha interrupted, shaking her head from side to side. "You know I'd 'elp if I could."

"My dear Martha, I wouldn't expect you to. None of this is your fault."

"Did... did he... die fighting?" stuttered Martha, staring straight ahead.

"I only know what's written on the mourning card." Lizzie stared out of the small window and wrung a handkerchief in her hands. *We're so lucky to live at number 81.* For a moment, she remembered the house on Hills

Lane. It seemed like a palace compared with Coffee House Passage, which was practically devoid of light.

"Do you have an address for Emillie? Do you think she'll come home?" Martha asked, turning to face Lizzie.

She reached inside her pocket and passed Martha a folded piece of paper. "Here. I'm planning to write to this address. It's the only one I've ever had. Think I owe it to the girls, especially Ada, to find out what happened and where William's buried."

Again, the coughing from upstairs disturbed them both.

"'E's never been the same since Emillie left. 'E could only ever see good in 'er. Like most fathers, I suppose," Martha said, taking the paper. "Let's 'ope Emillie is still at this address."

"Emillie's not one for letting the grass grow under her feet." Lizzie's thoughts had slipped out, and for a second, she thought she might have offended Martha. But Martha seemed lost in her thoughts about her daughter and stared into her teacup.

"Perhaps James would like some of this for his tea?" said Lizzie, unwrapping the brown paper package from her basket and revealing a chunk of cake.

"That's so kind of you, Miss Doyle. There was so much gossip about William and Emillie when they first left town. I didn't have the strength to show my face in the market, and I saw people whispering behind their hands when I passed by. She'd been carrying on with a couple of others before William."

"She was a bad'un, that's for sure, Martha. But they're married now... William mentioned it in the first letter I received from him," said Lizzie.

Martha's eyes widened. "She's wed? And didn't even see fit to tell us?"

Lizzie placed her arm around Martha's shoulders as she sobbed.

"Her father will be heartbroken not to have walked her down the... the aisle."

"Everything all right, Martha?" called a croaky voice from the stairs.

Martha wiped away her tears. "Yes, James, I'll bring you some tea in a minute."

Lizzie heard James shuffle along back to his bed. "I best get home to the girls now."

"If I hear from her, I'll let you know, Miss Doyle."

As Lizzie left and walked towards the market square, she couldn't help feeling that poor Martha and James would never see their daughter again. It also hit her that she had sole responsibility for her nieces now until they were of age. Lizzie looked up. *With God's help, we'll manage. And please, may William rest in peace.*

PART II

CHAPTER 12

2016
A flat opposite 81 Whitehall Street, Shrewsbury

Howard Vaughan groaned as he woke, realising he'd fallen asleep on the sofa. His neck was stiff, his head pounding, and his mouth felt like sandpaper. He sat up and ran his fingers through his lank hair. *Shit. Did I have a drink last night?* His eyes scoured the floor for an abandoned bottle or glass. Discarded clothes and unwashed dinner plates littered the living room, but he couldn't see any booze.

On entering the kitchen, he wrinkled his nose at the smell. Cleaning up was another chore he couldn't be bothered to do. His habit of eating straight out of tins and then discarding them on the worktops for the flies to enjoy didn't help. Unpacked boxes filled the floor, creating more surfaces to dump used crockery and take-out boxes.

He rubbed his stiff neck as he checked the kitchen cupboard and sighed on seeing his secret bottle with its golden contents still untouched, but his daily internal battle began.

The fight with his familiar friend seemed relentless, but he lit a cigarette instead and inhaled. Licking his lips, he tried to tear his eyes away from the liquid. He could taste the burn on his tongue, and his eyes flicked between the whiskey bottle and the glasses beside it.

The temptation, and another chance to turn down the reality and volume of his life, was powerful. It was all too much, and he reached out. Only the daily newspaper clattering through his letterbox distracted him from the brink. *I need to check the odds on my gee-gees.* He returned the bottle and tried to reason with the voices in his head. *But I still get bloody headaches and the shakes even when I don't have a drink.*

"Well, Bill, it was like this: I only had a small snifter because I thought I had a cold coming and thought a drink might help." *Bill will never buy that.*

The phone call with Beth, his thirteen-year-old daughter, hadn't gone well the day before, and he knew Bill, his probation officer, would ask him about it. She'd hung up on him. *I'm on top of the drink. Why won't she believe me?* He clenched his fist.

"Spect, it's that bitch of a mother who's been putting doubts in her head. Bad-mouthing me as usual."

Grumbling to himself, he flipped the kettle on and made a strong black coffee. But drinking it didn't help, and after taking the last mouthful, his temptation resumed. He returned to the cupboard and let his fingers linger on the bottle before gripping it and pulling it out. His eyes moved to the sink, but he couldn't pour his old friend away and returned it to its hiding place.

Trying to control his breathing and think of other things, he went to the living room, looked out the window, and spotted Betty standing outside number 81. He'd ignored Bill's advice not to do odd jobs for people and concentrate on rehabilitation and finding paid employment. Like most professional help he'd received, he ignored it and had already arranged to clean Betty's windows today. *No need to break my back over it though. The silly old bat won't see whether I've done them.*

Betty Harris had lived at number 81, the pretty Georgian townhouse opposite, for over sixty years. The day Howard moved into his flat three months earlier, he noticed an ambulance outside her house. He'd watched as two paramedics helped a petite grey-haired lady inside. The sight had made him question why a pensioner needed a three-bedroom place like that when she'd be better off in a care home. He'd popped a note through her door later that day, offering to do odd jobs, and he was now a regular visitor.

After a quick, cold shower and a long overdue change of clothes, Howard picked his keys up from a shelf and glanced at the photograph of his three daughters. *I'll be able to see them at weekends as soon as I have a bigger place to live.* His three daughters had lovely chestnut-coloured hair, just like his mother when she was young. He leant in closer to the photograph. "Please keep your wavy brown hair and never go blonde like your jumped-up mother."

I hope Jenny can still remember me; she's only five. Bill had told him to keep looking at the picture to remind himself of his end goal. It was the only personal item in the flat. Howard wasn't one for knick-knacks; this place was just somewhere to rest his head for the time being. There was no point in making it too comfortable because, one way or another, he didn't plan on living there for long.

"Morning, Betty," he called as he crossed the street towards her. "What are you doing standing outside without your stick? You know what the doctor said after your last fall."

"Doctors are silly old buggers who talk rubbish," Betty chuckled as she turned, and he followed her into the house. "Fancy a cup of tea, Howard?"

"I'll make a start on your windows first. Give me half an hour."

"Right you are."

Howard retrieved a bucket and squeegee from under the sink. "You're looking pale, Betty. Are you feeling okay today?" he asked, filling the bucket with water and adding soap.

"My breathing isn't too good, but I'm not doing too bad for eighty-five, am I?"

"True. That's very true, and you know I'm always here to help you. This is a big house for you to manage on your own." He looked around the kitchen and out of the window at the garden.

Betty tucked her grey curls behind her ears and sat straighter in her chair. "Bert and I used to dance around this kitchen." She swayed both arms to a tune only she could hear. "He was so wonderfully light on his feet. The waltz and the quickstep were our favourites. The other girls envied me on a Saturday night at the music hall in town. My Bert was a handsome chap." She clutched both hands to her chest and smiled.

"Yes, he was. You've shown me pictures of him in his army uniform." *You've shown me loads of bloody times.*

Howard had endured several afternoons sitting alongside Betty, looking at old photographs and asking questions. He'd established that she had no family, and she'd said she planned to leave everything to a dog rescue charity.

Betty gazed upwards. "We married soon after the war, and he looked so smart on our wedding day with his colourful medals spreading across his chest."

Yeah, yeah, blah, blah. I've heard it all before.

"And you were married when you inherited this house?" He'd asked her these questions many times. *I'll damn well find her will if it's the last thing I do.*

"That's right. It was a lodging house when Bert's father bought it. His father had a decent job, working in an office. Good with figures, you see. And when his father died, he left the house to us."

"So, you never had children, Betty?" he asked and sighed as she didn't answer. *Oh Lord, she's back in the 1940s, as usual.*

Betty coughed before saying, "No, we weren't blessed with children. The house was rented back then by a lovely Irish lady. A Miss... Miss... Oh, what was her name?" Betty stroked her chin as she tried to remember. "The name is on the tip of my tongue. She didn't own it but took in lodgers and brought up three girls here. Her nieces, I believe."

Who cares? "Right, I'll get on then, Betty." He sighed. "I said I'll be getting on." *Turn up your flaming hearing aid, for God's sake.*

"You're so kind to me, Howard. How will I ever repay you?"

By destroying your will and making a new one, leaving this house to me. "No, I'm happy to help Betty. It keeps me busy because you know how much I'm struggling to find a new home big enough to have my three daughters stay." *And you never know, they might want to live with me permanently one day.*

Betty nodded slowly but didn't comment on his situation. "Now the lady had lovely dark hair... even in old age. She must have dyed it with something. Not sure what happened to her. She was frail at the time."

He lifted the bucket from the sink, ignoring her reminiscing.

"I wish I could remember her name. Miss... Miss..."

He left the kitchen whilst Betty was still rambling. As he washed the dining room window, he gazed inside at the wooden bureau. He'd been through it three times already because it seemed the most logical place to store official paperwork, but he'd found nothing.

On his return, he emptied his bucket and reached for the Windolene. "I'll do the inside of the dining room window, and then shall we have a cuppa?"

"Oh yes, and I've got some nice fruit cake somewhere," she replied as she left the room. "You're so kind to me, Howard. I don't know what I'd do without you."

Howard sat at the bureau and pulled various envelopes onto the fold-down desk. He ran his fingers across everything in each wooden compartment but saw nothing he hadn't seen before. There were plenty of electric and gas bills but no solicitor's letters or anything official.

"I'll recognise your kindness in my will," she'd said several times over the last month. "I've not got much, but I've no one to leave it to."

"But you have this house..." he'd started to say but stopped himself.

He slammed the bureau shut as Betty appeared in the room with teacups and wedges of fruit cake.

"Everything okay?" she asked.

"Yes. Yes, I might give your bureau a polish."

"That'd be kind of you. It belonged to the lady who lived here before. I think Bert's father gave her a few bob for it. Gosh, I wish I could remember her name." Betty made herself comfortable in her armchair facing the garden and rubbed her chest at the sound of her raspy breathing.

"Do you need to call on your solicitor to amend—"

"All taken care of, Howard. All taken care of. The garden was so colourful and well-stocked when we moved in, and my Bert always loved his gardening until he—"

Here she goes again.

"The Irish lady I've told you about had kept it beautiful. Wisteria hung from a metal archway. The flowers were like bunches of grapes, and the smell was divine. Bert's father was an excellent gardener too. There used to be a path on the left-hand side, and the metal archway stood at one end. It's rusting away in the cellar alongside a lovely wooden sideboard. They both belonged to... the Irish lady that used to live... Gosh, I wish I could remember her name."

Move on, Betty, for Christ's sake. Who cares?

"Bert planting this fir tree so close to the house was a mistake though." She pointed at the long, bowed branches.

"Well, I've tidied the garden up for you," Howard said, relieved her eyesight was poor and the lofty fir tree blocked most of her view.

A wry smile appeared on her lips, and just for a moment, he thought he spotted a twinkle in her eye. She nodded and, staring past him, said, "I know, I know, don't worry."

Howard looked over his shoulder. *She's losing it. On another planet most days, for sure. God, I need a fag.*

CHAPTER 13

William

It's a quiet and steady existence here at number 81. A gentle rhythm of the sun rising and setting and the moon waxing and waning. The weather seems less harsh here than I remember, but I expect the River Severn still floods the town regularly. In Canada, the snow gift-wrapped the trees and swallowed up the streets, and the summers lasted forever. Ada, Ethel, and little Dorothy would have loved it if they'd come over to join me.

I pat myself down, hoping to look smarter because my brown tweed suit is baggy. My hat is in my pocket, and it's lost its shape. I wore this to have my picture taken when I first arrived in Canada. My cigarette packet is still in the top pocket and is a comfort. I'm smoking far too much, but what's the point of stopping now?

I'm often lucid and see people in the house. I stand by the fireplace, and it's lovely to hear Betty talk about the garden. I remember how beautiful Lizzie kept it. A neighbour often visits and talks to Betty. I'm wary of him and often stand just behind him when he's talking. I sense he's got problems, but don't we all?

I often recall the past and hear voices when I'm here. You see, sometimes I'm in the light and lift my face, hoping to feel warmth. Then I'm in the blackest darkness. It's seamless and impenetrable.

My confusion ebbs and flows like the ache that runs down my arm or radiates across my chest. But I accept that's how it is. I'm unsure how or why I'm in Lizzie's house, how long I've been here, or whether I'm always here. But I suppose I'm waiting. Yes, that's it. And I've been waiting a long time.

I prefer to stay in the dining room and look through the window into the garden. This room is quieter, and my aches ease a little. I don't enjoy going upstairs because I hear girls' voices following me, climbing the stairs with me.

Today I must go upstairs because I'm very fond of Betty and enjoy our time together. She often calls me Bert, but I don't mind, and she's not herself right now. Two ladies are here, dressed in spotless blue uniforms and talking sweetly to her as they change the bed linen and wash her hands and face.

"We're just making you more comfortable, Betty," they whisper.

I doubt she can hear them. Her eyes are closed, and she has an almost translucent look. It's not a look of resistance or fight but a look of acceptance. The sad scene is familiar to me. The curtains are closed to the morning sun, the bedside lamp has an orange glow, and the ladies speak in low tones.

"Her breathing is hushed today," says the older lady as she combs Betty's hair.

"Has she any family we should call?" asks the other.

"No. It's written in the file to contact Hargrove Solicitors." She lifts Betty's head and plumps the pillows. "A neighbour... a Mr Vaughan has been caring for her and the house for some time."

"Not sure he's doing a great job. We should have called social services. Have you seen downstairs?" replies the young one.

My awareness heightens as someone enters the house, and I move to the top of the stairs. It's Howard, the neighbour, and he's let himself in. I watch as he climbs the stairs two at a time and pauses on the landing to stub out his cigarette on the window ledge. His manners appal me, and he walks straight into the bedroom as bold as brass. Doesn't even knock!

"Hello, ladies. How is she today?" he asks, standing with his hands on his hips, surveying the scene.

"Sssh, show some respect," I say.

"She's not good, I'm afraid, Mr Vaughan," says the younger lady.

The other lady is writing in her notebook and says, "It won't be long. Sometimes people hang on, waiting for someone special to arrive to say goodbye."

Howard stands straighter. "She has no family, and I've done my best to care for her. Doing odd jobs in the house and keeping the garden tidy."

I notice the older lady raise her eyebrows at her colleague.

"What? It's a jungle out there, and the fir tree is almost in the house!" I shout. "And don't get me started on downstairs. My Theresa would have whipped a duster round there in the blink of an eye and mopped the kitchen floor."

I steady myself, hearing whispers. It often happens when thoughts of Theresa fill my head.

"That's neighbourly of you, Mr Vaughan. It's a lovely house," replies the younger lady as she takes off her apron.

I watch the ladies pack their bags as they say, "We'll be back this afternoon, Mr Vaughan."

He touches the younger lady's arm. "Please, call me Howard."

She's a pretty lady, and I sense her discomfort as they all leave the room.

Howard lingers in the hallway and watches them drive off. Is he going to sit with Betty until the ladies come back?

No. He heads into the dining room and begins rifling through the wooden bureau in the corner. He throws papers onto the floor and then flicks through the books on Betty's shelf. He storms into the parlour and flings the cushions from the sofa. He's sweating and swearing under his breath. I stand beside him, and he swings around and stares straight at me.

"Excuse me, Howard, what the devil are you doing?"

He takes no notice of me.

Howard leans on the fireplace. "Shit. Betty said she'd changed her will. She wouldn't lie to me. It'll all work out, Howie. Don't panic."

I'm baffled. "What the hell are you searching for? Betty said she'd changed her will? You crafty bugger, what are you up to?"

Howard leaves and slams the front door behind him. I watch from the window as he storms across the road.

I sit on Betty's bed. It seems intimate, but being close to her and comforting her feels like the right thing to do. The wedding photograph on her bedside table catches my eye. Betty and Bert look so happy and in love, like Theresa and I did on our wedding day.

Betty hasn't used her walking stick for a while, and it's propped against the wardrobe that stores clothes that need airing. A commode is alongside the bed, and boxes of tablets are stacked on her dressing table. Her false teeth sit in a glass beside the small thing she always puts in her ear.

"Hello."

I hear the deep voice clearly and study Betty's face. Her expression has changed, and there's a smile on her lips.

A man stands by the bed, wearing a khaki brown uniform. His shoulders are pinned back, and five polished medals with bright ribbons are spread across his chest. My eyes flick to the photograph on the bedside table.

I lower my gaze. I never wore a uniform or fought for my country. What sort of man does that make me compared to the man standing here?

He removes the jauntily placed beret from his head and holds his hand towards me. I stand up, and my hand reaches for his. The handshake is strangely firm, warm, and somehow comforting.

"Pleased to make your acquaintance," he says. "I'm Albert Harris, but most people call me Bert. I'm Betty's husband."

"I'm William Tate." I struggle to lift my eyes to meet his, and instead, I stare past him as someone approaches. It's a small blurry outline; a female silhouette.

"Please..." I say. I straighten my shirt collar. Could it be my Theresa?

A woman taps Bert on the shoulder, and he sweeps her in his arms. I see the smiling face. It's Betty!

And yet she's still lying in bed, with her head positioned awkwardly, and her eyes... well, they're open, but staring as if she's seeing something or someone for the first time. It isn't an expression of fear but one of tenderness.

"Oh, my darling, you're here at last," says Bert.

They face each other, and her left hand meets his right. She moves in closer to place her other hand on his shoulder, and he circles his hand around her waist.

I look down at the floor, feeling I'm prying on an intimate moment they're sharing. They stare into each other's eyes and sway in time to music only they can hear. They are comfortable and familiar with each other, and their fluid movements mirror each other perfectly.

I can sense their love. A love I remember.

"Theresa?" I try to see beyond them as they dance, but nothing. No one.

Bert lets go of one of her hands and, lifting the other, Betty circles and twirls under his arm several times.

"Betty, William's been watching over you for a long while," he says, letting go of her hand and pointing at me.

She holds out her hands. Not the age-spotted ones still tucked in the bed, but fleshy pink hands. I study her unlined face, bright eyes, and glossy hair pinned back with a fancy silver pin. It reminds me of the pin my mother gave to Theresa.

"Ah, was it you?" Betty asks.

I'm not sure what she means.

"I often felt like someone was there right beside me."

I nod.

"Thank you, William. You got the measure of that Howard bloke," says Bert.

"But what's he searching for?" I ask.

"My will! And if he'd found all the airmail letters from our nephew, Peter, who lives in Canada, he would know we had family to leave the house to."

I scratch my head. "But why would Howard...?"

"He was up to no good, that's for sure," adds Bert.

"He must have thought I was born yesterday." Betty chuckles. "But he never did find the secret compartment in Miss Doyle's old bureau!"

Bert smiles. "No flies on my Betty. She deposited her will with a solicitor many years ago."

"I should have burnt Peter's letters. If Howard had found out I was lying—"

Bert finishes her sentence. "He'd have known we had a relative to leave the house to."

"Oh, I see."

"I told Howard I'd changed my will because we had no family. I think he thought he'd get the house."

"The rogue thinks he's getting the lot," says Bert.

"Was it wrong of me, Bert, to tell lies?"

He searches for her hand and kisses it. "No, my love. You can't pull the wool over my Betty's eyes. Howard didn't step up to the plate and turned to drink instead. Never turn your back on the ones you love."

Bert's eyes meet mine as he finishes speaking. He raises his eyebrows, and I glance over my shoulder, unsure if he's talking to me or someone else.

As they turn and walk away hand in hand, I call out, "Can I come with you?"

But they don't look back and don't answer my question.

I'm here again, and number 81 could do with cleaning. A pile of letters and leaflets sits on the mat in the hallway, and there's a musty smell. I hear noises, a creaking floorboard, a window not entirely shut, and memories circle in my head. The house is stagnant, in limbo, and missing a family's warmth and laughter.

I feel sorry for the wooden bureau, the only piece of furniture left behind. Left behind just like me. Staring at it reminds me of Betty sitting there, reading the airmail letters from her nephew Peter.

Did my letters reach Lizzie? On hearing the letterbox rattle, did she run to the doormat to retrieve them and share my news with Ada, Ethel, and Dorothy? Did they write back? I'm unsure because the war broke out, and the world turned upside down.

I hear a key in the front door, and a young man wearing a dapper navy suit steps inside and walks into the parlour. I've seen nothing like it! His hair is pulled back into a bun, just like ladies do their hair. He's a good-looking chap, maybe in his twenties. Why would he do such a thing?

"There's a barber's shop in town. I'm sure they'd sort that out for you, mate," I say.

He stands admiring the fireplace and pulls something out from his inside pocket. I move closer. It's oblong, and he lifts it. Woah! It flashes. Blimey, is it a camera?

I follow him into the hallway, where he raises the doodah again and flashes it at the beautiful cornicing, then the floor tiles. He likes the sash windows and the fireplaces, and the flash goes off repeatedly. From the dining room, he stares out over the garden; his shoulders slump, and he sighs. He lifts the doodah to his ear and speaks. What on earth is he doing?

"The garden is a right mess," he says.

"When Lizzie lived here, it was always so tidy," I say. "Wisteria, roses, and delphiniums all brought so much colour."

He walks out to the hallway, and I follow. He peers into the darkness after opening the cellar door and flicking on the light.

"Full of junk, I expect," I tell him.

He doesn't go down the steps. I don't blame him; he wouldn't want to ruin that smart suit, and I suspect there are mice. I haven't dared go down the cellar myself. I can't stand the little blighters.

I'm sorry to see the man head for the front door. He didn't comment on anything I told him about the house. Sadly, it seems no one can hear me. He retrieves something from a car. It's a sign on a wooden pole, and he hammers it into the flower bed at the front.

Sale by Auction 15 Sept 2016
Contact Hargrove Solicitors
01743 364782

Number 81 is up for sale.

I catch sight of Howard marching across the road with his arms flailing.

"Oh Lord, why's he back?"

"Hey, what the hell do you think you're doing?" he shouts.

"I beg your pardon?" replies the young man.

Howard gestures towards the sign.

"Mrs Harris' house is up for auction, as you can see, and if you ring—"

"Well, Hargrove should be bloody well ringing me. Who'd you think you are, coming here with your stupid... stupid man bun?"

The young man looks taken aback. "Sorry, sir, but who are you?"

Howard steps forwards and towers over him. "This house is mine. So, you can clear off and take your ruddy sign with you."

I'm impressed by the younger man's composure because Howard's face is puce, and as he speaks, he spits in the man's face.

Their confrontation brings my father into my mind, but I shake my head to disperse the picture. I don't want to think about that old sod.

"Have you been drinking, sir?" the younger man asks, stepping back and moving closer to his sign.

"Yes, good move," I say. "Wouldn't put it past Howard to kick it over."

I move towards Howard. Yes, I can smell drink on him.

"Sir, Mrs Harris' nephew has instructed us to sell the house."

Again, I'm impressed by the young man's politeness.

Howard steps backwards and falls off the kerb into the road. "She hasn't got a sod-sodding nephew. What the 'ell you on about?"

A car beeps its horn at Howard as he zig-zags across the road and raises a fist at the petite lady behind the wheel.

"Probably best if you go home, sir," the young man calls. "You don't want me to have to call the police." He heads for his car and, under his breath, adds, "You drunken old bugger."

I smile. I like my visitor. "Remember to call at the barber's shop on your way home," I shout as he gets into his car.

CHAPTER 14

Kate Walker pulled up outside number 81, turned off the engine of her new BMW convertible, and smiled. She sat for a minute, stroking its leather steering wheel and walnut dashboard while breathing in its "new car" smell.

She'd kept her emotions in check as she'd driven from Warwick and smiled on seeing views of Shropshire, a county she'd never visited. Days out in historic market towns and exploring the rolling Shropshire Hills were on her to-do list, although that part of her list might have to wait until the spring.

Had she been impulsive buying a property at auction without viewing it? No. The car and the house were the best decisions she'd made in a long time. A very long time. Selling her bed-and-breakfast business and starting again was scary, but she had no doubts about her decision as she looked up at the house. She didn't know a soul in Shrewsbury, but importantly, nobody knew her either. She needed a project, and this house would hopefully fit the bill.

Number 81 sat in the middle of a terrace of five Georgian townhouses that stood proudly in the autumn sun near the end of Whitehall Street. Their sash windows, Welsh slate roofs, and decorative fanlights made them stand out. Crowned with terracotta chimney pots, they were taller than the plainer Victorian terraces in the street.

There'd be plenty of work to do inside, but after pouring over the auctioneer's photographs, she was up for the challenge. It was an aesthetic renovation, and there was no rush; she had all the time in the world for decorating and would employ tradespeople to do big jobs. Kate longed to fill her mind with finding antique furniture and deciding on colour schemes, anything to block out the hurt and grief of the last two months.

I still can't believe I won't see him again.

She retrieved her bottle of Pinot Grigio from the back seat and keys from her leather handbag before stepping onto the pavement. She looked up and down the street as an overwhelming desire to skip or run up the path came over her. Skipping was something she'd not done since childhood, but like her recent retail therapy and house purchase, it felt liberating. On reaching the door, she turned and laughed.

The opposite building was converted into flats, and she'd noticed all the doorbells inside the entrance. A middle-aged man watched her from a second-floor window. He stood with his hands on his hips and looked like he was chuntering to himself. Knowing he must have seen her skipping, she raised her bottle of wine towards him and smiled. *He'll think I'm a right silly devil.* He held her gaze for a moment before turning away. *I don't care what he thinks. If I want to skip up my path, I jolly well will.*

Holding her breath, she slipped the key into the door and stepped over the leaflets and take-out menus that littered the doormat. There were patterned maroon and green Georgian-style floor tiles in the hallway and decorative cornicing. The mustiness, dust, cobwebs, and even the striped lime green wallpaper that greeted her all failed to quell the excitement of her first impression.

Leaving the front door ajar, hoping her removal lorry wasn't too far behind, she placed her handbag and wine bottle at the bottom of the stairs. She ventured further inside, and the cast iron fireplace with its original metal basket in the front room caught her eye. There was more intricate cornicing and another fireplace but with a white marble hearth in the room at the back. Yes, they needed a damn good clean, and no doubt the chimney hadn't been swept in years. *Cosy winter evenings spent in front of an open fire. I can't wait!*

An antique wooden bureau sat in one corner of the back room, and shelves furnished each side of the fireplace. Kate had seen endless property renovating programmes and knew with a sanding machine, the wooden floor would come up grand. She coughed as she drew back the thick, dusty curtains to see the garden.

The French windows barely allowed any daylight in because of a fir tree outside. Its unruly, long branches almost stroked the house. She grimaced, looking out over the garden. It was long and narrow, with no pathway in sight. Some fencing panels had fallen, and there were none at the end. Invasive tendrils of ivy choked the sagging roof of a shed, and brambles and nettles devoured every corner. It was a battleground, and any lawn or flowering shrub that had once been there was now well-defeated.

She checked the kitchen out next and smiled on seeing the splendid red quarry-tiled floor that would also buff up with a bit of elbow grease. The kitchen units and worktops were functional if dated, but she loved the Belfast sink even if it required scrubbing.

Once back in the hallway, she threw her leather jacket over the wooden newel post and sat on the stairs. She was keen to see the three bedrooms upstairs, but light-headedness swept over her and, realising she'd not eaten since early morning, she dipped into her handbag to retrieve the sandwiches she'd bought from the motorway services.

As she took a bite, a loose edge of the blinding green wallpaper caught her attention, and she reached down. She teased it away from the skirting board and pulled upwards, only to reveal the faded remnants of a pink floral paper underneath. She glanced up and saw the same green wallpaper continuing onto the landing. *I'll need a steamer if every room in the house has multiple layers of wallpaper like the hallway.*

She felt better after eating and couldn't resist tearing at the wallpaper again. Beneath the floral pattern, a dark grey painted wall appeared. The wall had cracks running in all directions, and a cloud of grey dust fell to the floor along with the shards of wallpaper. *I hope this wall isn't damp.*

It was an old house, so she had to expect the unexpected, but she had the funds to deal with any problems. She was eager to start and wouldn't worry about what it threw at her.

As she was about to turn away, she spotted something and reached for her reading glasses out of her handbag. In black pencil, Kate saw the names Ada, Ethel, and Dorothy written on the wall, and there was a thick horizontal line beside each name. The date was smudged. Maybe 1916.

"Wow. Hello, girls! Did you live in this house back then? Ah, Dorothy, I see you were the smallest."

She smiled and expected more lines higher up the wall to prove the three girls had grown taller. But not wanting to add to the mess she'd already made on the hall floor, she let it be.

The front door slamming jolted her from her thoughts, and she glanced through to the kitchen, wondering whether someone had come in and created a draft. But the house was silent, and a coldness swept past her, causing her to shiver. *I need to get the heating on.*

With her fingers crossed, she found the boiler and switched it on. It fired up immediately, and she turned the thermostat up. She looked around the back room. *My new dining table and chairs will sit well alongside the bureau.* Kate wasn't sure she liked the white marble hearth, but the fir tree would be the first job that needed tackling.

"I shouldn't leave your front door open, love. You never know who might walk in."

Kate jumped. She hadn't heard the plump removal man arrive.

He scooped up the papers from the doormat and handed her the flyer from the top of the pile. With a cheeky grin, he said, "You'll need this, by the look of things. And a decorator for the hall."

"Yes, tell me about it," Kate replied. The flyer, from Jake Madden, advertised his gardening business.

"I should call him as soon as possible, love. I think clearing the garden will be a hell of a big job, by the looks of it."

"You're not wrong there! The house has been empty for a few months."

"I reckon it's been neglected for longer than that! But houses go downhill rapidly when left to their own devices." He gave her a toothless grin. "We'll start unloading now, Miss Walker, if you can direct us to where you want everything. And the priority is, of course, to find the kettle."

"That's very true." Kate slipped Jake Madden's flyer into her jeans back pocket. *I'll ring him this evening.*

One lorry and two men were enough to transport all her furniture and possessions, but she'd enjoyed shedding the layers and bad memories of her previous life. Her B&B had given her a comfortable living, but selling the furniture with the business hadn't left her with much. She wanted her new home to be different and filled with stuff that didn't remind her of things, or people. Endless trips to the council refuse tip had been therapeutic. And ridding herself of personal items and updating her wardrobe had made her feel re-energised, perhaps even a little younger.

The house became a hive of lifting, positioning, unwrapping, and Kate trying to ignore the removal man's builder's bottom. Her online food delivery arrived, and the removal man plumbed in her washing machine and put her new bed up in the front bedroom. The bedroom smelt old and stale, and the pink carpet had several imprints where furniture had once stood, but it seemed the best choice; the fir tree was the only thing visible from the other two bedrooms at the back.

She opened the bedroom window to let in some air before returning downstairs.

After they'd finished their third cup of tea, Kate was relieved to say goodbye to both men. She thanked them for the last time in the doorway and noticed the same man in the building opposite, in his window again. It was almost dark outside now, but she could see his silhouette. She waved at him to be neighbourly, but he remained motionless. *Blimey, let's pray the other neighbours are more friendly.*

It was time to relax and open her bottle of wine, but the wooden slatted door in the hallway caught her interest as she passed by. She pressed on the latch handle and peered into the thick gloom. After fumbling for a switch, an old fluorescent tube light pinged into life. The cobwebs didn't deter her, and she leant on the whitewashed wall for support as she journeyed down the stone steps. A piercing cold hit her as she reached the bottom, and she shivered, wondering again whether there was a damp problem in the house.

Paint cans and old tools sat on shelves that ran the length of one wall. A 1960s kitchen cabinet that looked like one her grandmother used to have stood against another wall. Her eyes were drawn to the far wall though, and she pushed a large, rusty metal archway out of the way to get closer. A khaki-coloured, heavy-duty dust sheet shrouded something bulky. She removed the wallpaper rolls, pots of stiff paintbrushes, and four crumbling house bricks from the top. Then, covering her mouth with her left hand, she pulled and teased the heavy sheet with her right. Dead flies and a cloud of reddish dust flew into the air, free after years of stillness.

Wow, another piece of antique furniture to bring back to life. It was an impressive oak sideboard with two doors at the front and three drawers, all ornately carved. Unfortunately, all the brass handles were missing bar one. She stooped down, tugged on the remaining handle, and sighed at the emptiness inside. Behind the other door, she found several dusty glass jars. *Oh well, if I ever want to make jam.* She took two out and spotted something else at the back. After reaching inside, she pulled out a tin with flecks of red clinging to its silvery base.

She placed it on top of the sideboard and tried to open it. The dented lid wouldn't budge, sealed by rust and age. She shook the tin. There was something inside, and she scanned the cellar for an implement. Using a screwdriver she found on one of the shelves, she prised the tin open, and the lid clattered onto the concrete floor.

Inside, she saw a small package wrapped in brown tissue paper tied with a faded blue ribbon, a postcard, and a yellowing newspaper cutting lay on top. Kate glanced over her shoulder; a sense that she was prying came over her. *Don't be daft. The house is yours now!*

She wished her reading glasses were on the top of her head to read the newspaper. As she unfolded it, a small black-and-white photograph floated to the floor. There was a heavy crease down the middle, but two smiling faces looked up as she retrieved it: a handsome groom with a fine moustache and a stunning bride with dark wavy hair. *Ah, that's lovely. I hope you had a happier ending than Lionel and me.*

The tube light flickered and, annoyed with herself for letting Lionel pop into her head, she replaced everything in the tin. A scurrying noise from the far corner of the cellar quickened her pace back up the stone steps. And besides, there was still that bottle of Pinot upstairs with her name on it. Most evenings, having a glass of wine had become a habit and an attempt to forget about the future she thought she had with Lionel. *I hope the couple in the photograph lived happily ever after.*

CHAPTER 15

The following morning, Kate reached over to the emptiness on the other side of her bed. She was glad she'd closed the bedroom window before bed because it had been chilly once the heating went off. She'd stayed up until midnight drinking wine and thinking.

My head's pounding.

She opened one eye, aware of a knocking sound, followed by an infuriating beeping. Flipping onto her back, she stared at the unfamiliar white ceiling rose, trying to focus and figure out what the hell the noise was from outside.

Daylight streamed into the bedroom, and she reached for her phone to check the time. *What? I never sleep till nine.* She grabbed her dressing gown from the end of the bed and moved to the window.

Parked behind her new car was a dirty white van and a tall, dark-haired man beside it, waving at her. The catch on the sash window was stiff, and as she struggled to raise it, her dressing gown slipped open.

"Are you having trouble there?" he called, with a wide grin spreading across his face. "I tried just knocking on your front door."

"Can I help you?"

"I'm Jake. Jake Madden. We spoke on the phone last night. You said I could start your garden early this morning."

"Oh. Oh sh—yes, that's right," she replied, pulling the belt of her dressing gown tighter and trying to flatten her bed hair. "Yes, if you go round to the garden, I'll... I'll come down in a minute." She pointed to the path along the back of the terrace.

The condition of Jake's white van made his capabilities an immediate concern to her. It looked barely roadworthy. And someone had scrawled "PLEASE CLEAN ME" in the grime on one side. Kate stepped back but watched as he unloaded a wheelbarrow and various cutters, trimmers, and a large chainsaw. After removing his denim jacket, he slipped his muscular frame into khaki overalls.

He has all the right equipment! She hid behind the curtain as he glanced up at her window again.

Even though her head screamed to be back on a pillow, she washed, dressed, and swept her hair up in a rough top knot, grimacing at how florid her complexion was in the mirror. *Lord, how much wine did I drink last night?* Holding the banister, she went downstairs and wondered why she'd told him to come so soon and so early.

She stepped onto the single paving slab outside the kitchen door and waved at him.

"You weren't kidding, Kate, when you described it as a jungle," he called from behind a clump of nettles.

She bristled at him calling her by her first name and couldn't remember much about her phone call with him.

"Yes, it is. Is it too big a job for you?"

"No, I can cope with this. No problem. Is the kettle on?" he asked with yet another cheeky grin.

"Tea or coffee?"

"Coffee, please. No sugar, I'm sweet enough."

Yeah, yeah, I've heard it all before. But Kate smiled as she returned inside, made two drinks, and popped down some bread to toast. She felt light-headed again and prayed she'd feel better after eating breakfast.

The overgrown garden meant Kate couldn't pass Jake his coffee from the kitchen door. Instead, she left through the front and headed to the path at the side. As she walked, she noticed all the other back gardens on the terrace were tidy and well-planted. *Gosh, the state of mine must annoy the neighbours something rotten.*

She smiled, seeing Jake had already started work and cleared a flattened path through the nettles and weeds to reach the fir tree.

"The first job will be to cut this fir and bring some light into the back of the house."

She nodded in agreement, passed him his coffee, and they gazed up at the offending tree and its long, bowed branches.

"So, you're from Warwick?" he asked as he sipped his coffee. "Lots of tourists there, I suppose, visiting the castle."

She nodded.

"And will you run a B&B from here once you've tidied the place?"

"No, I've retired now."

"You're not that old!"

Even though she was tempted to tell him she was forty-two and financially secure, she kept quiet and decided not to elaborate. "Blimey, did I give you my life story last night?"

"You were very chatty, let's say."

She looked back at the fir tree.

"And it's just you moving in, I gather?"

"Yes, just little old me... in this beautiful old house."

"You told me how you'd given up on men. We're all a load of—" Jake chuckled before taking another sip of his coffee and lifting his dark eyes to meet hers.

She turned away and fiddled with a piece of her hair that had escaped. She could feel her cheeks reddening. "Hope I didn't talk too much and bore you."

She felt her neck colour as his deep, dark brown eyes twinkled with amusement.

"No. Not at all. You were very entertaining, Kate."

"Do you live locally?" She hoped to change the subject and remembered how Lionel often teased her by saying, "Wine always gives you verbal diarrhoea."

"Yes, I've lived in a rented flat just around the corner since I split from my girlfriend. I'll buy a place once our house sale goes through."

"I'm sorry to hear that."

"No, no, don't be. I'm not. And we both agreed about that on the phone last night."

Shit. I still have no recollection of the phone call.

He smirked. "Your memory's not as good as mine."

"Sorry, I was celebrating last night. You know, what with the move and everything. And yes, I had a glass of wine."

He raised his eyebrows.

"Maybe more than one," she admitted with a smile. *I probably drank half the bottle. But I still dreamt of Lionel.*

"You said marriage and relationships are overrated."

Did I tell Jake, an absolute stranger, all about Lionel? And now, is he enjoying teasing me about it?

Jake carried on with an expression of satisfaction on his face. "I'm better off on my own too. My money is mine and I can spend it how I like."

As she turned to leave, she heard him say under his breath, "And marriage and children are such a bloody commitment."

She noted the bitterness in his voice and wasn't sure what to make of Jake Madden, but what he might think of her strangely bothered her. She kicked herself for looking back as she left the garden. They locked eyes briefly before he turned away and fired up his chainsaw.

She was no sooner in the house than there was a knock at the front door. Her stomach rumbled, and her toast was cold. *Ugh, will I ever get my breakfast?*

Surprised to see the nosey neighbour from the building opposite at her door, she gave him a tentative smile. He held a bunch of pink roses wrapped in a sheet of newspaper in one hand, and they looked exactly like the roses from the front garden of number 87.

His face was puce, and his T-shirt looked like it had yesterday's dinner spilt on it. A cigarette hung from his mouth, and he struggled to find and remove it from his lips.

"Are you okay?" he asked, stepping from side to side.

"Of course. Why wouldn't I be?" *Is he hungover too?*

"Well, you haven't drawn back your curtains." He stumbled back and pointed at the front room window. "I told my neighbour, Mrs Trow, that it was odd."

Not that it's anything to do with you, but... "I'm having a busy morning and just haven't—"

He swung an arm towards Jake's van. "And, that wide boy pulled up in his clapped-out van early this morning making a 'ell of a racket. 'ell of a racket."

You're right about the van. But what the devil's a wide boy? She took a step back and placed one hand on the door. "I'm sorry about the noise if it woke y—"

"But, but, your cur... curtains?" he repeated, stepping closer. "And I wouldn't trust that bloke as far as I could throw him. Seen plenty of his sort before!"

"I've not had time to draw the curtains back yet, and Jake is—" *For God's sake, I don't need this.*

"You should be careful who you let into your house," he said, pushing the roses towards her face. "I'm How... Howard Vaughan. Pleased to meet you."

Oh dear, I'm feeling a bit sick. She took the flowers and, for a second, admired them, hoping that would be enough to make him go away.

"Thank you, they're lovely," she said, closing the door slightly. "I best get on now. I've plenty of unpacking to do."

He stepped closer again, and a whiff of alcohol and cigarettes wafted over her, adding to her delicate feeling. *Shit.*

"And your name is?" he asked.

"Kate, Kate Walker."

"And will Mr Walker be joining you?"

"Erm, no, I..."

He didn't wait for her answer but rambled on. "I could have cleared the garden for you. I 'elp most people on this street. I 'elped Mrs Harris, the lady who lived here before. She died in that room just up there." He pointed upwards towards the bedroom and staggered backwards.

Relieved, Kate gripped the door, poised to shut it if he came closer again. *Please go away.*

"Yeah, a sweet old lady. A good... good age." He was halfway down the path but continued talking even after replacing his cigarette in the corner of his mouth. "'ad a nephew, but 'e didn't sod... sodding bother. 'e didn't give a shit about 'er. I was more like a son to her than anyone!"

Howard paused, stared at Kate's car and, turning to her, shrugged before staggering across the road.

What is his problem? She closed the door and held her breath momentarily, praying he wouldn't knock again. *What a vile, rude man.* She examined the roses, debating whether to bin them or go straight to number 87 to apologise.

Jake waved his coffee mug outside the window as she returned to the kitchen and she opened the window to take it.

"Wow, lovely roses. Do you have an admirer?" he asked.

"Hardly. They're from this creepy man who lives in the building opposite. I clocked him yesterday, watching me as I was moving in here. He gives me the heebie-jeebies, to be honest, and stinks of cigarettes and booze."

"Is he a rough-looking bloke who doesn't own a comb or soap?" Jake asked.

"Yes, I think he must stand in his window all day long, just nosing what's happening."

"I saw him earlier while I was unloading my tools. I thought he looked dodgy, so I double-checked that I'd locked my van. My tools are expensive to replace."

"Funny that. He said you looked dodgy too. A wide boy, he called you! Luckily, I don't know what that means."

"I know my van is a bit run-down, but once my ex and I sell the house, I'll get another."

"So, no children?" The question slipped out of nowhere, and she lowered her eyes. "Sorry, sorry, I didn't mean to pry. None of my—"

"No, it's okay. I don't mind, and you gave me all the gossip about yourself and Lionel."

Shit. I did give him all the gory details of my love life.

"She wanted marriage and children," he said flatly.
"And you didn't?

A "The Boys Are Back in Town" ringtone sounded.

"Sorry, I best take this," he mouthed and turned away.

She ate two pieces of toast and marmalade and stared out the window at Jake on his phone. He waved his hand and shook his head as he talked. The smell of her coffee made her feel woozy as she raised her cup to her lips. *Gosh, I must stop drinking wine.*

CHAPTER 16

William

There's a new lady here at number 81. And, oh my! She skipped up the path to the house, just like Theresa used to do when she came to greet me on Hills Lane.

The lady is pretty with light brown hair that's swept up into an untidy bun. Unlike Theresa though, she doesn't use pins to keep it in place, and strands hang at the sides of her face. She's wearing a baggy woollen jumper and faded blue trousers that aren't very ladylike.

I hope she'll stay in the house. Yes, I like her, but she looks pale and sickly.

I'm thrilled to see the dining room almost how Lizzie used to keep it: an elegant table and chairs sitting alongside the bureau. But the parlour is full of cardboard boxes and bags, and a blue sofa still sits in the middle. A long, shiny car with a sleek bonnet is parked outside, but it hasn't much room for luggage or passengers.

She has a comfy-looking armchair and has positioned it just right to gaze out over the back garden. It's lovely that she's brought colour and warmth into the house.

That damned fool Howard called round, bothering my new lady, so I followed him back to his flat to see what he's up to. I won't stand by and have him upset this lady by popping around uninvited.

Once inside, Howard goes straight to a cupboard and takes out a bottle. Whiskey, I suspect.

"I think you've had enough to drink, chummy," I say.

Don't get me wrong. I used to enjoy a drink myself. The ale down the Gullet Inn was head and shoulders above any Canadian beer I tasted... or maybe the company in the Gullet made it so good. I miss my father-in-law John, Mr Mahoney, and even that old devil, Peddler! He's probably down some alleyway right now selling knock-off stuff.

Howard slumps into a chair and lights a cigarette. I smoke too, but he's a chain smoker. Yes, one after another. He reeks of smoke, and his fingers and teeth are stained far worse than mine.

He coughs. It's a familiar wheezing, crackling noise.

"Should be me moving into that house, not some posh tart with a flash car," he says after filling his glass. He takes a mouthful. "Why the hell does she need a three-bedroom house?" He punches the arm of his chair. "Skipping up the flaming path like some silly bloody schoolgirl."

"Language, please!" Oh, Howard, I enjoyed how the new lady skipped up the path.

Unwashed plates and glasses litter the floor, along with silvery containers that pong. Howard picks up a flat cardboard box from under his chair, pulls out a triangular piece of bread, and rams it into his mouth.

And from nowhere, Theresa's delicious rabbit stew comes to mind. I can smell it and it's damn good. Tastier than this congealed thing Howard is struggling to chew.

It amazed me how John Doyle could always get a rabbit for his family. I think Peddler had a hand in it.

Most people in Hills Lane shared what they had. Well, what little they had.

Howard swigs back his whiskey and tops his glass up again.

"Steady on, mate. Is life so bad?"

"I searched bloody everywhere. Everywhere!" he says. His face is red, and he runs a hand through his uncombed hair. He kicks at a plate that's on the floor, and a crust of bread flies into the air.

I laugh.

"You should eat the crust. It'll make your hair curl." The words slip from my mouth, and in my head, I hear, *"But, Da, our hair is already curly!"*

I shake my head and cover my ears, and the giggles fade.

"Every cupboard and every bloomin' drawer." Howard stares up at the ceiling and shakes his fist. "What a conniving old bat you were, Betty. Lies, it was all lies."

Then it comes to me. "Yes, yes, you did. I remember now. You searched the house when my last lady, lovely Betty, fell asleep in the afternoons or as you were cleaning her windows. You were up to no good!"

Howard shrugs. "I went through her mothball-smelling wardrobe, looked under the beds, and emptied every cupboard in the house. Even rooted through her sodding underwear." He throws his hands in the air,

"That wasn't very gentleman-like," I say.

Scratching his belly with one hand, he stubs out his cigarette on a saucer with the other. It's already overflowing with butts. After he finishes his whiskey, his eyes flicker and close.

"Why can't I spend time with my daughters? God, I hate my ex," he mumbles before loud snoring fills the room, and his glass joins the others on the floor.

"I'm not sure they'd want to see you in this state," I whisper, not wanting to wake him. "You need to smarten yourself up, mate."

"Why can't I spend time with my daughters?" Howard's question repeats in my head as I return to number 81.

I'm in the garden, standing in the shadow cast by the overgrown fir tree. Branches are falling left, right, and centre. And the noise! A solid-looking chap is here wielding a machine. It's as if he's cutting through butter! I've seen nothing like it! Oh, I'd love to have a go with it. And if I ever meet my dear friend Charles Bevan again, I must tell him all about it. He'd be fascinated. I wonder if he still works in the foundry in Woodstock and goes to the library.

My new lady comes to the back door and distracts me. She smiles at the man and gives him a thumbs up. "Fancy a cuppa?"

"Don't think he can hear you," I shout.

He takes off his yellow helmet and large glasses. "Yes please, and I'll soon have this sorted for you, Kate."

Ah, my new lady's name is Kate.

I give her a thumbs up too. "Yes, he looks more than capable, Kate. People from the lane would say he's built like a brick shit house."

I wish I had something to cover my ears. Hopefully, the racket won't go on too long. To see the garden how it used to be would be so wonderful. Lizzie had wisteria hanging from a metal archway that ran along the path. Ada, Ethel, and Dorothy loved to jump and try to touch the violet-coloured fragrant flowers. There was a well-stocked flower bed on the right-hand side in the summer and daffodils there in the spring. Oh, and hydrangeas at the end of the garden. Yes, they were pink.

"Yes. Ada, Ethel, and little Dorothy enjoyed playing in my garden."

"Lizzie?" I shake my head, hoping to dispel her voice.

I follow Kate into the house to get away from the revving noise. There's more light in the dining room now, and Kate sits in her armchair. I study her face, reminded of what my mother-in-law used to say when Theresa was expecting. Mary Doyle always knew before we'd told her our news.

"A woman has a certain look, a twinkle in her eye, or a hand placed unconsciously over her belly," she'd say.

I can see that look on Kate's face.

Kate reaches for an object at the side of her chair. It's a tin, like the cake tin Lizzie used to have. Surely it can't be. This one is dented and only has flecks of red paint on it. Lizzie's was very shiny and always took pride of place on the table at teatime.

Placing it on her lap, Kate doesn't tug on the lid but rests her head back and closes her eyes. Damn, I wanted to find out what's inside. But she's tired, so she should nap for a while.

I watch her doze, surprised she can sleep through the noise the man is making outside. But wait... yes, he turns the machine off and heads towards the house.

He taps on the French doors and makes Kate jump and the tin slips from her lap.

"I'm gonna call it a day, Kate." He removes his helmet. "Sorry to wake you."

Her cheeks redden as she stands and opens the door. "Gosh, I can't believe I nodded off. Must have gone out like a light."

He removes an odd thing from his ears and runs both hands through his flattened hair. "I've hired a woodchipper for tomorrow and won't be able to do much else until all these branches are cleared away."

"That's fine, Jake, and good to do our bit for the environment."

So, the man's name is Jake, but I've never heard the word environment.

"Once that's done, we could talk in more detail about how you want the garden," he says.

"Yes, I'll think about it this evening. I found a metal archway in the cellar. It might be nice to incorporate it somehow. It's old though, and probably beyond saving."

"I'll look at it, or we could search for a similar one. I think there's a pathway over on the left-hand side, so we could perhaps position it there."

"Yes, you're quite right, Jake," I say. "The path was on the left of the garden, and Lizzie had a metal archway."

"I found an old sideboard in the cellar too," Kate says. "Not sure how it got down there or how difficult it would be to get it back up."

He laughs. "If it got down there, there must be a way to bring it back up."

I remember Lizzie had a lovely oak sideboard in her dining room. It had shiny brass handles.

"Funny what you remember and what you choose to forget."

I shrug at the voice in my head.

Kate wraps her arms protectively around her waist. "Well, there's no rush to do everything at once. No one to please here but myself."

It seems Kate is alone, and that's sad. I must be mistaken about a baby.

"I can turn my hand to most things if there are other jobs to do," Jake offers.

"Plenty of wallpaper to scrape off. You should see the stripy one in the hallway!"

"Bit eighties, is it?" he asks. "I'd love to help. This is a beautiful place, and if there's anything I can't do, I'll know a man who can."

"I'm concerned the place is damp the way some of the wallpaper has peeled off," she replies.

"I have a mate who could help check that out for you."

"You'll let me have quotes for any work though."

Kate sounds defensive, and there's a moment of silence.

"Of course. Right, I'll be back in the morning. I'll come straight round to the garden. No need to wake you if you have another lie-in."

I can tell he's teasing, but her cheeks flush again.

CHAPTER 17

After Jake left, Kate opened the French doors to let air into the house. She settled down in her armchair and closed her eyes, surprised she still felt tired. Even though she'd not finished all her unpacking, she felt at home at number 81. A warm early autumn sun flooded her dining room because the fir tree was half its former self. Jake had worked hard, and she was pleased with what he'd already achieved in the garden. Perhaps he wasn't the wide boy Howard thought he was.

Since he'd offered, she decided to ask Jake for quotes on other jobs that needed doing. She shook her head to dispel the picture of his dark hair and eyes. He was going through a breakup too, so maybe his offer to help was to keep himself busy and nothing more. She liked him. And that was a good thing, surely? The time wasn't right, but she shouldn't let Lionel cause her to judge every man in a poor light. *Oh, Kate, you silly old fool. Jake is so much younger than you.*

He'd said his ex wanted marriage and children, and Kate could sympathise. Hadn't that been what she'd always dreamt of for herself? A familiar annoyance rose inside her because she'd wasted time with Lionel, and that silly old biological clock was ticking. She was tempted to open another bottle of wine, but her stomach felt delicate, and she'd been surprised that Jake had to tap the window to wake her up earlier.

Stifling a yawn, she retrieved her reading glasses from her handbag and reached for the metal tin she'd found in the cellar the day before. It had seen better days. Though hopefully, it had protected the contents. The small, square wedding photograph lay at the top, its heavy crease down the centre determined to separate the happy couple. Kate studied the long-sleeved lace wedding dress covering the woman up to her neck. *There's no flesh on show, unlike brides these days.*

The groom was a handsome man with a moustache and wore an uncomfortable-looking stiff-collared white shirt, a waistcoat, and a jacket. The bride's wide-brimmed hat was adorned with flowers, and Kate couldn't help wondering what colour they'd been. She flicked over the photograph and sighed, disappointed not to see names or dates written on the back.

Next, she lifted out the small package and pulled on the thin blue ribbon that secured it. Two brittle sheets of tissue paper protected whatever was inside. Kate glanced over her shoulders as the feeling that she was snooping came over her.

"Gosh, that's beautiful!"

A cross-stitch sampler unfolded onto her lap. Green threads that had lost their vibrancy formed the name "Doyle" across the top. Beneath, in a navy thread, were the names John and Mary. Then came seven initials, each with a stitched flower or clover leaf beside it. Using her forefinger, Kate traced each initial: A, M, E, T, P, J, and lastly B. The red rose beside the letter T was intricate, and the thread was more vivid than any others. At the bottom of the sampler and clinging to the frayed edge were the words: "Lizzie, 1916. 84 Hills Lane".

"I wonder if the sewn initial E stands for Elizabeth? Lizzie? And could this be a hundred years old?" She picked up the wedding photograph again. "Are you Lizzie? And is this your beautiful needlework? And how did it get here if you lived at 84 Hills Lane?" *I'm going to try to find out.*

The yellowing newspaper cutting beneath the sampler caught her eye, and she carefully unfolded it. It gave details of a church bazaar held in Shrewsbury in 1916 to raise money for the Catholic Church and the war effort.

"Wow, 1916 again. The same year beside the names in the hall."

She couldn't help smiling as she read the reporter's polite English tone:

> SIR FRANCIS SMYTH, WHO HOPED EVERYONE PRESENT HAD COME WITH FULL HEARTS AND LARGE PURSES, OPENED THE ORIENTAL BAZAAR.

"Oh, I say, Sir Francis Smyth," she said aloud in a la-di-da voice.

At the end of the article, it gave stallholders' names, and she spotted Ada Tate on the Japanese stall. *Wait a minute.* Placing the tin down, she headed to the hallway. Yes, Ada was one of the names written on the wall.

"Aha. The plot thickens!" Kate chuckled. "So, were you the tallest and, I assume, the eldest, Ada? Was Lizzie your mum?"

She returned to her armchair and reread the cutting before folding it up. Times were different then, and there was a world war on. *I'm not sure dressing up as an "Oriental" would be politically correct now.*

Looking back in the tin, she spotted something else. It was a postcard with a grainy brown picture of a man dressed in a tweed suit and a hat. She compared the image to the wedding photo. The same moustache, maybe.

Someone had written on the back of the card:

> I GUESS YOU KNOW WHO THIS IS WITHOUT MY TELLING YOU. PASSED AWAY ON DECEMBER 12, 1915.

"Well, that was short and to the point! Who was he?" She pushed her glasses onto her head, relaxed in her chair, and closed her eyes.

Kate had loved the house from the moment she'd walked inside. Finding the tin hidden since 1916 added another dimension. It added a story, a history. She opened her eyes and stared at the bare wall above the fireplace.

"Lizzie, I will frame your beautiful sampler and give it pride of place in this room. If you lived here in 1916, you'll be here again in 2016. I'm talking to myself, and that's the first sign of madness!"

"Hello, anyone there?" called a gruff voice.

The voice made Kate jump out of her armchair. Her glasses and the tin fell to the floor. The postcard floated towards the French doors.

Howard stood just outside in the garden with a cigarette hanging from his mouth. He wore a smart pink striped shirt, formal trousers, and some hair product slicked down his hair.

Kate stepped forwards. "Can I help you?"

"I wanted to see how that chap was getting on with your garden," he replied, stepping closer.

Nosey bugger. With her arms folded, she stepped towards the door, hoping to block him from entering.

"I could have done all this for you, love." He waved an arm at the garden.

Don't you "love" me.

"I used to do Betty's gardening all the time. Can turn my hand to most things."

How come it's like a jungle now then? "So, have you called round for a reason?"

"Once Betty took seriously ill, there was stuff inside to do too..."

The house wasn't exactly tip-top either.

He strained his neck to look over her and into the dining room. "Anyway, did you find a vase for my flowers?"

She bit her lip, knowing they were in the bin. "Yes. They're in..."

He removed his dangling cigarette and glared at her, waiting for an answer.

"I've put them in the other room, Howard." She turned and reached for her mobile phone from the arm of her chair. "I need to make an important call, so if you could leave now."

He spotted the postcard on the floor, stepped inside, and stooped to retrieve it.

"It's fine. I'll... I'll get it," said Kate, bending and meeting his eyes as they both tried to scoop it up.

She noticed his closed-lipped smile, a look of satisfaction at getting there first.

"Thank you... I best get on now. Lionel will be home soon, and we have more unpacking." It surprised her how easily the name Lionel had rolled off her tongue, but maybe it would do the trick and get rid of Howard.

No, he ignored what she'd said and examined the picture on the card while inhaling his cigarette. "So, who's this then?"

"I think somebody who may have lived here years ago." She held out her hand to take the card from him. The smell of sickly aftershave and smoke wafted over her as she gestured towards the door.

"I thought you said there wasn't a Mr..." He paused.

"He's my boyfriend... Yes, Li-Lionel is my boyfriend," she stuttered, still holding her hand out for the postcard.

"I like to be neighbourly and make friends with everyone in the street," he said.

Kate raised her eyebrows.

Howard waved a hand at the path along the terrace, which allowed each occupant to access their back garden. All bar her garden had a gate. *I need to get one!*

"I was walking along the path and saw your door was open. The sun was still out, so I wondered whether you had a bottle of wine on the go?"

"No, I haven't," she replied, relieved she hadn't got the bottle out on show.

"Be sure that young chap doesn't rip you off. I could take over. Just say the word."

"That won't be necess—"

"Anything you need doing, love. Decorating, plumbing, or electrics, I'm your man."

"Well, thanks," she said, gesturing towards the door again, hoping he might get the message, give her the card back, and leave.

He studied the words on the reverse of the postcard. "This chap died in 1915. Wooo... Hellooo, dead man." He held the card out to her with a grin on his face, but she didn't acknowledge it or find him funny in the slightest.

"I've got things to do, Howard." She snatched the postcard.

"We must have a coffee or a glass of wine some other time then," he said, looking around the room before finally stepping outside.

She watched as he strolled down the garden and surveyed the branches cut from the fir tree before turning and waving at her. She headed to the kitchen for a drink of water and took two paracetamol. As she locked the French doors, she was aware of her heart pounding and sweat trickling down her back.

Later, unable to fall asleep, a plan formed in Kate's mind as she tossed and turned in bed.

I'll get Jake to put up a gate at the end of the garden. I'll speak to the people at number 87 about the flowers and ask what they know about Howard.

She punched her pillow, unconvinced Howard was just being neighbourly. *I won't say Lionel's name out loud either. Bloody Lionel. Bloody neighbours. Bloody men! So much for a quiet life.*

CHAPTER 18

Lionel had filled her dreams, and when Kate woke, she analysed every aspect of their relationship. Was she that weak and naive to have believed every word he'd told her? He just "forgot" to mention a few important things about his life. The demand to remind herself of that inexcusable and straightforward fact was constant and exhausting. *I can't even yell at him now about it.*

Come on. Don't dwell. Skip instead. She smiled, reminding herself how she'd skipped up the path two days earlier. *I need to regain that feeling.*

She threw on her dressing gown as she headed for the bathroom. Looking into the mirror, she was surprised by her pale complexion. Kate had never been one for cosmetics or having a skincare regime, and Lionel had always teased that she was a natural beauty. After studying her crow's feet and dry skin, she reached for her makeup bag, applied some moisturiser, and pulled out her blusher. She swept the brush across each cheek. *That'll do.*

Despite having a wardrobe full of new clothes, she put on an old comfy jumper and a pair of jeans. *Ugh, I'm so bloated.* It was a mystery why she felt so out of sorts, even without drinking the night before. She hoped she wasn't sickening for something because there was still plenty to do.

Before going downstairs, she stepped into the back bedroom. Apart from dust, a worn carpet, and peeling wallpaper, the room was empty. A theme that ran through the house. *At least the house is all mine, warts and all.* She wrapped her arms around herself and turned a full circle. Even if she didn't feel great, she could start planning and making her to-do list.

She couldn't resist peeping out the window at Jake working in the garden below. Today, he wore jeans and a black T-shirt and lifted heavy branches and fed them into the woodchipper. All her earlier thoughts and the doubts planted by Howard concerning Jake's capabilities had dissipated. There were still plenty of weeds, brambles, fencing, and the shed to clear, but he'd dealt with the fir tree so professionally that they would surely be no problem.

"Fit" wasn't a word she'd ever spoken, but it oddly came into her mind as she studied him. Jake's muscular arms and shoulders lifted the cut branches with ease. She smiled to herself as another seldom-used word came to her. *Hot.*

Was Lionel hot? He perhaps had a more sophisticated, suit-wearing, debonair sort of air about him. He'd have had no clue how to tackle this garden or any DIY jobs inside. The image of him disappeared as Jake bent down to turn off the woodchipper, removed his helmet, and wiped the sweat from the back of his neck. Like a silly schoolgirl, she stepped away from the window and laughed out loud at herself. *This house needs to be a man-free zone for now and maybe forever.*

Once in the kitchen, she flung open the back door and breathed in the morning air, hoping it might clear her head. Jake waved, discarded his safety goggles, and headed towards her.

"Good morning! How are you today?" he asked, leaning one arm on the door frame and wiping his forehead with his other hand.

A tattoo that snaked up his upper arm caught her eye. She hated tattoos but tilted her head to read what the thick black letters spelt. Jake gave a slight cough before removing his arm. She could see the amusement in his eyes.

"I'm... I'm fine." *Stop staring at him.* "Still so damn tired though, and I've so much to do."

"There's no rush, is there? If the house is liveable." He looked over her shoulder. "The kitchen looks okay."

"Yes, it is. Everything's in working order. Dated though. Plenty of old carpets to rip out and flowery wallpaper to remove. The place needs a little TLC. And don't we all!"

A smile spread across his lips again and widened as her stomach growled.

"I need to eat some breakfast. I'm not feeling great... hopefully, not coming down with something."

He stepped a pace back. "Hope it's nothing catching! They say moving house is one of the top three most stressful things in life. Divorce and death being—Oh shit, sorry, Kate. I forgot your Lionel has passed away."

Gosh, I told him that too!

"He wasn't really *my* Lionel, was he?" she said, laughing, pleased with herself for joking about the betrayal. "And anyway, you're going through a breakup yourself, Jake."

"I took mine more on the chin though, I reckon." His eyes met hers again. "No point dwelling, that's what I say."

"You're right... Onwards and upwards."

He nodded. "I'll knock down what's left of the shed next," he said while looking back at the garden. "It's seen better days, for sure."

She hesitated. "And... and any chance you could put up a high fence and gate at the end? A gate that locks."

Jake frowned, and she saw a questioning look in his eyes.

"That damn neighbour, Howard, called round yesterday evening. He waltzed up the garden as bold as brass!"

"Not slighting my gardening capabilities again, was he?"

"Yes, a bit. He offered to take over if I'm unhappy with your work."

"And are you happy so far?"

"Of course! Gosh, you've made easy work of that fir tree!"

"Well, I saw him staring out of his window this morning when I arrived," said Jake, putting his safety goggles back on. "He's an odd bugger, for sure."

"He used to help Betty, the elderly lady before me. But I don't need or want his help." Dizziness caused her to hold on to the back door, and Jake reached forwards.

"Sorry, I'm okay." She felt nausea bubbling in her stomach. "I best go and get something to eat."

"Yes, good idea. You're looking peaky. Do you want me to have a word with Howard?"

"No, it's fine."

"Okay, if you're sure. We'll chat about the garden later if you're feeling better?"

"Yes, definitely, and I've got a few ideas."

Back inside, and after a bowl of cereal and three rounds of toast and marmalade, she felt brighter. After hooking on her jacket, she opened the front door and walked along the terrace to number 87. A young blonde woman greeted her.

"Hello there, I'm Kate. I've moved into number 81," she said, pointing to the house.

"Hi, pleased to meet you. I'm Maxine. How are you settling in?"

"I'm gradually sorting myself out, but there's still plenty of unpacking. Erm, I came around to apologise about any noise from my garden."

"No, it's okay, no worries. It'll be great once it's tidied up. That fir tree was enormous. It was a shame the place got so neglected once Betty's husband died," Maxine said.

"Oh, I suppose the house and the garden became too much for her?"

"That's right. She was quite elderly by that time."

Kate glanced over her shoulder. "A neighbour brought round some flowers for me. Unfortunately, he might have taken them from your front garden." She pointed at the three pink rose bushes.

"Ah, you've met the lovely Howard then! We wondered what had happened to the last few blooms. He's an absolute pain, to be honest. My husband and I steer clear. Most people along the street do, but he was always at number 81 when Betty was alive. Not sure why though. She was a sweet, polite old lady, so perhaps she couldn't get rid of him."

Kate bit her lip before saying, "He's creepy though. He seems to gawp out of his window most of the time and has taken a real exception to my gardener."

"There was a right altercation when an estate agent put the 'For Auction' sign outside your place. We all thought Howard would rip the sign out once the young man had left." Maxine looked up and down the street before continuing. "Between you, me, and the gatepost, the talk is that Howard's an alcoholic, and that led to him splitting from his wife. And losing any custody of his three daughters too."

"I see."

"Best to be blunt with him if I was you, Kate. When he came here, we shut the door in his face, and my husband eventually spoke with his probation officer."

"Probation officer?"

"Yes, I think he calls round... his name's Bill, and he drives a small red car. Howard fails to attend meetings, so he comes to Howard instead. So, have a word if Howard continues to bother you."

"Okay, I will. I best get on. It was lovely to meet you, Maxine, and sorry about the flowers."

"Not your fault, Kate," she replied before closing her door.

As she returned home, Kate resisted the urge to glance at Howard's window. The conversation with Maxine had done nothing to ease her annoyance with Howard. But at least now she knew he was a nuisance to other residents, not just her.

A British Telecom van pulled up outside as she put her key in the front door.

"Hello, Miss Walker?" a man called, leaving his van. "I'm here to set up your Wi-Fi."

She had completely forgotten about the appointment. *My head is like a sieve.*

Kate spent the next hour cleaning and unpacking a few more boxes as the engineer installed her broadband. Once he'd left, she sat at the dining table with her laptop, submitted gas and electric meter readings, registered for council tax, and bought a TV licence.

Meanwhile, Jake had dismantled the old garden shed, pulled up broken fence panels, and tackled some brambles in the far corner of the garden.

She yawned and stretched her arms, satisfied with her morning.

"Shall we have that chat now?" called Jake, waving at her through the French doors.

She watched as he removed his heavy boots and stepped inside.

"You've worked hard," she said, smiling. "You must be ready for a cuppa and some cake."

"Yes please... always partial to a piece of cake."

"Right, you are. Tea and cake coming up."

"I only had to breathe on the shed and it collapsed. The brambles weren't so compliant though." He took off his gloves to inspect his wrists and hands. "I best bring some thicker gloves tomorrow."

She studied his hands, strong worker's hands. *So different from Lionel's who was a penpusher.*

"Did the engineer sort your Wi-Fi out?" he asked, looking over at her laptop.

"Yes, I'm up and running now. I expect the old lady wasn't into computers, so it's never been installed."

"Perhaps we could draw up a plan for the garden? Go online for some ideas?" said Jake.

"Yes, that'd be great."

"I've found a few paving slabs, so I assume there was once a path on the left-hand side."

"Yes, and there's that old metal archway in the cellar I've already told you about."

"Shall I go down there and look at it now while you put the kettle on?"

He retrieved his boots and carried them to the hallway. "In here, is it?" he asked, opening the slatted door to the cellar.

"Yes, there's a light just inside the doorway," she called from the kitchen.

Within minutes, he reappeared, carrying the metal arch. "I'll get you some poison, Kate. Plenty of mice droppings down there."

"Gosh, I thought there might be. I heard some rustling when I ventured down there myself."

He carried the archway out through the back door.

"Is it salvageable?"

"Yes, I think so. It needs a good rubbing down and then repainting. I saw the sideboard you mentioned. I'll get my mate to help me lift it."

"Oh, thank you. I'll bring the tea through to the dining room, Jake. Pencil and paper on the table if you want to start drawing a plan."

He was standing beside the bureau when she walked in carrying a tray.

"This is a lovely piece of furniture. Beautiful mahogany," he said, running his hand over it.

"It came with the house. I need to give it a good polish."

"There's an antique shop in town. It's more like a scrap yard, and I saw a similar-looking bureau there. The same sort of pigeonholes and drawers. Do you mind if I look inside the drawers?"

"No, no, carry on."

She watched him open the four small drawers on each side and tap the wood in various places.

"Aha." Jake removed one drawer, and his hand disappeared inside the space.

She moved closer. "What on earth are you doing?"

"The one I saw had a secret compartment, and maybe this one does too."

"That'd be exciting!"

"There's a little catch inside. My hands are too big, so here, you have a go." He stood to let her sit.

She reached inside. "Yes, I can feel it. Do I have to press or lift it, do you think?"

He leant in closer, and she lowered her eyes and enjoyed the moment of closeness. His wasn't a smell of aftershave. He'd been working hard.

"Lift, probably." He motioned with his hand.

"Yes, I've done it!" she said, grinning triumphantly at him.

"Kate, you're going to be disappointed now if it's empty back there. Nothing apart from spiders."

"Ew, you can take over then." She gestured for him to take her place on the chair.

He sat and reached inside the bureau again. "Yes, yes, a bundle of... a bundle of letters!"

Every letter had a blue airmail label attached to the top left-hand corner.

Jake turned them over to read the sender's name and address. "A Mr Harris in Toronto, Canada," he announced, passing them to Kate before returning his hand to the secret compartment. "Hold on, hold on, there's something else, but it's caught right at the back."

After a few seconds, he produced another letter from the hiding place. It was a letter addressed to Miss Elizabeth Doyle, 81 Whitehall Street. It was unopened and had a King George V stamp and a black ink stamp: Woodstock, Ontario.

CHAPTER 19

William

Jake's in the house, and Kate is all a flutter. She's brought tea and a delicious-looking cake into the dining room. After placing it all down, she fiddles with her hair and turns to see what Jake's doing.

He's sitting at the old bureau and pulls out a bundle of letters from inside. Are they... my letters?

I hear a voice. *"William, you didn't send that many letters or any money."*

"Yes, I did!" I shake my head. "The war slowed down the post."

"Excuses, excuses."

I can see these letters are addressed to Mrs Betty Harris, the lady who lived here before Kate.

But hold on. Jake puts his hand inside again and pulls out another letter addressed to Miss Elizabeth Doyle. Lizzie!

"What? I never saw that letter."

It's strange, but the writing looks familiar to me. I know it from somewhere, but for the life of me, I can't think where!

"I assume you're going to have a good nose at all these letters, Kate," Jake says, smiling and sipping his tea. I can tell he's teasing her again. He seems to enjoy doing that.

"Well, it is my house, so finders keepers. They're all addressed to Mrs Betty Harris, the lady who lived here before me," she says, flicking through the bundle.

Jake takes a piece of cake and, before biting into it, asks, "What about the other one?"

"I'll look at it later." Kate places all the letters back in the bureau and closes it. "Let's talk about the garden instead." She passes him a pencil and paper.

They sit beside each other at the table and stare at a small screen. It's like a typewriter but far smaller and less clunky sounding. Kate puts her glasses on and taps away on the flat keys. They're looking at pictures of gardens and different plants. I've never seen anything like it! The colours are so bright.

Jake moves his chair closer to hers. Yes, they seem very at ease with each other. I wonder if he knows about the baby.

"So, do you want to keep the path on the left-hand side of the garden?" Jake asks.

Kate stares through the French doors. "Yes, I think so... But could we bring it up to these doors?"

"Yes, that's how it once was," I say. "The path was on the left, and Lizzie had a flower bed on the right."

"Perhaps have a flower bed on the right," suggests Jake, glancing out at the garden. "We could curve it into the lawn, so the grass isn't just one long narrow rectangle." He draws a picture on the paper and shows her.

Kate nods. "A semi-circular flower bed... Yes, that would be nice."

I nod in agreement too. "Lizzie had daffodils in the spring and beautiful pink delphiniums and roses in the summer. Kate, you must get some roses!"

"We could plant bulbs ready for next spring," Jake says.

"And delphiniums. And some roses?"

"Are you a keen gardener, Kate?" He takes another mouthful of cake.

They lock eyes and laugh as she says, "I've no idea where that came from. And no, not at all! Maybe hydrangeas along the bottom fence?"

"Yes, that'd work," he replies, laughing at her again.

"Have pink ones just like Lizzie used to have," I suggest. I didn't think Kate could hear me, but she likes my ideas.

"You missed so many springs and summers in the garden with your daughters, William."

Pressure radiates across my chest. "I know, Lizzie. I know."

It's so nice to hear laughter and feel the warmth between two people, and I focus on that, not the voice in my head. Jake's made such good progress in clearing the garden already. It'll be fascinating to see what he does next. He looks back at his drawing, and as he reaches for another piece of paper, I notice a tattoo on his arm. I thought it was only sailors who had them. Thick black letters snake up, but I can't make out what they spell.

He starts a list. "We'll need turf and some fencing panels. Do you want the two-metre-high ones? It'll look odd when the neighbours have lower."

"Yes, somewhat antisocial," she says. "Well, I suggested it because of that bloody nuisance Howard calling round uninvited."

Oh no, has Howard upset Kate?

"Could I have a higher fence just at the bottom with a gate?"

Jake looks concerned.

"I spoke to the lady at number 87 earlier, and apparently, Howard's a right nuisance to everyone in the street, not just me."

"You're sure you don't want me to have a word with him?" asks Jake, looking serious.

She shakes her head. "No. That might make him worse if he thinks it's bothering me."

Despite her refusal of Jake's offer, I think she's uneasy.

"I'll keep an eye on him though," I say, trying to help. "I did the same for Betty."

They both look back at the list Jake is making.

"I'm going to need some topsoil and fertiliser because the soil is poor," Jake says.

"That's fine. Just get what you need. Do you need some money upfront for materials?"

"I'll measure up tomorrow, put an order in, and let you know." He finishes his tea and stands up. "I best get off now. Thanks for the tea and cake. I'll leave you to your mysterious letters."

She watches as he puts his boots back on and packs up his tools. They wave goodbye and smile at each other before he leaves. Kate looks deep in thought as she closes and locks the French doors. She double checks it's locked.

I watch as she retrieves the letter addressed to Lizzie from the bureau and settles down in her comfy armchair. I hope she's going to open it.

"Why didn't you open it, Lizzie?" I ask. "How did it end up right at the back of the bureau drawer?"

"I've no idea, William."

It's dated 31 December 1915, and I stand behind Kate and read along with her.

Dear Miss Doyle,

My name is Charles Bevan, and I hope this letter finds you in good health.

"Blimey, now I remember whose writing it is. My very dear friend Charles. Oh, how I miss him."

> I WRITE TO EXPRESS MY SINCERE CONDOLENCES ON THE DEATH OF YOUR BROTHER-IN-LAW, WILLIAM TATE. I HOPE HIS THREE DAUGHTERS ARE COPING AFTER RECEIVING SUCH SAD NEWS ABOUT THEIR DEAR PAPA.

"What? What?" A familiar tightening shoots down my arm as I read on while suddenly feeling the need to blink back tears.

> I WAS WITH WILLIAM WHEN HE PASSED AWAY. WE HAD ARRANGED TO MEET AS USUAL AT WOODSTOCK LIBRARY. BUT UNFORTUNATELY, HE SUFFERED A HEART ATTACK JUST AS HE ENTERED. I HOPE IT WILL COMFORT YOU WHEN I SAY HE LOST CONSCIOUSNESS IMMEDIATELY, SO HE DIDN'T SUFFER.

Yes, Charles was with me. I remember now. I'd gone to the library to get away from Emillie. We had a terrible fight about money, and she said some awful things about Theresa. And I... no, I don't want to remember what I did.

> WILLIAM WAS BURIED IN WOODSTOCK CEMETERY ON A COLD BUT SUNNY DAY. MANY FRIENDS FROM THE IRONWORKS ATTENDED, AS WE ALL HELD HIM IN HIGH REGARD.

"What? Woodstock? But I'm here at number 81," I whisper between breaths.

> I HOPE THE MONEY WILLIAM TOLD ME HE SENT EACH WEEK WAS OF HELP. HE OFTEN EXPRESSED GRATITUDE TO YOU FOR CARING FOR HIS BELOVED DAUGHTERS, ADA, ETHEL, AND LITTLE DOROTHY. LIKE MANY OF US, HE LONGED FOR THE WAR TO BE OVER AND TO BE REUNITED.

Kate has tears running down her cheeks.

> I SENSE THE DEATH OF HIS WIFE WAS SOMETHING HE NEVER GOT OVER, AND FEAR HIS SECOND WIFE, EMILLIE, WAS NOT ALWAYS AS TRUTHFUL AS SHE SHOULD HAVE BEEN.

"Oh, I wonder what Emillie did?" asks Kate.

I shuffle my feet. "You're right, Charles. Money slipped through my fingers when Emillie was around. I don't know where it all went. But I shouldn't have struck her. I was as bad as my bloody father."

> He intended to reunite one day with his daughters. May he rest in peace now, and may God give you and his daughters the strength to carry on together.
>
> Yours warmly,
>
> Charles Bevan

Kate folds the letter back into the envelope. "That's sad. Why didn't you open this letter, Elizabeth?"

Kate reaches for the cake tin sitting on the shelf beside the fireplace, and fishes out a postcard. Then, looking at the picture, she says, "Hello, William."

The picture is me! I slump my shoulders and a penny drops inside me. A familiar black veil returns and covers my eyes, and once again, there's darkness.

CHAPTER 20

Knowing Jake would arrive early, Kate put the kettle on. *I don't want him to think I lie in every morning.* On waking, she'd felt out of sorts again, but after eating some toast, she perked up.

She was keen to unpack the last of her boxes, do even more cleaning, and walk into town. The fresh autumn breeze would blow away the cobwebs, and she was eager to explore the streets and shops in Shrewsbury.

William Tate, Charles' letter, and Lizzie's sampler had filled her thoughts before going to bed, and she planned to search online later to see if she could find out more.

While sipping her orange juice, thoughts of Jake filled her mind. She shook her head. *For God's sake, Kate.*

In one respect, she was pleased the house and garden were occupying her mind and pushing away thoughts of Lionel. But she needed to stop looking at Jake with rose-tinted glasses, or any man, come to that. Yes, he was friendly, chatty, and seemed to enjoy winding her up, but he'd recently split from his girlfriend.

No, this is a new start. I don't need a man in my life. Sighing loudly, she put out two cups, then headed for the dining room to open the French doors and let in the morning air. The house still had a musty, unlived-in smell despite her cleaning efforts.

She froze as she walked in, and her eyes darted around the dining room as she tried to comprehend the scene. The bundle of airmail letters she'd put back inside the bureau the day before lay scattered all over the floor, each one opened, screwed up, and discarded. Every drawer of the bureau sat out on the fold-down desk. The tin she'd found in the cellar was under the table, and the contents were strewn across the dining table. The postcard with William's picture sat face up on the white marble hearth. She picked up Lizzie's cross-stitch sampler and clasped it to her chest.

Kate sank into her armchair but jumped as Jake tapped the French doors. He shrugged at what he could see, and Kate beckoned him.

"What the devil happened?" he asked, open-mouthed. "Have you been looking for something?"

"I didn't do this!" she snapped.

"So, have you been burgled?"

"I don't know!" Then, spotting her handbag beside her chair, she grabbed it and fished around for her purse. "Everything's here. My cash and my cards."

Jake examined the French doors. "Well, this doesn't seem broken or forced." He picked up an envelope from the floor, one addressed to Mrs Betty Harris.

"Jake, I only opened and read the letter we found addressed to Elizabeth Doyle. I didn't read any of the others."

"And you're sure you didn't—"

She glared at him. "You think I would have left the room like this?" Her eyes welled. "And no, I didn't have a drink last night, if that's what you're thinking."

"Woah. Okay. Calm down."

"Don't tell me to flaming well calm down."

He held both hands up in surrender. "Okay. Okay. So, perhaps someone was searching for something, and it wasn't money. And you're absolute—"

She threw her hands in the air. "How many more times? I didn't do this! The only letter I opened was the one addressed to Elizabeth Doyle."

He stared at her but said nothing more.

As she jumped to her feet, the sampler fell from her lap. "You see me as some ditzy menopausal woman who ransacked the room and then forgot about it?" She knelt and began sifting through the screwed-up pieces of paper.

He knelt beside her. "Hey, let me help you. Nothing to get upset about, I'm sure." He retrieved the tin from under the table and placed the sampler, newspaper cutting, and photograph inside.

"I found those the day I moved in. And things seem to have gone downhill since then. What with Howard and now this."

"And all this stuff on the table was definitely in this tin?"

She rolled her eyes at him.

He retrieved the postcard from the fireplace and studied it.

"His name's William."

"Okay, and he died in 1915." Jake tapped her on the shoulder, making a wooo sound. "Perhaps the ghost of William was here."

She punched him on the arm. "Jake, that's not funny!" Standing up, she snatched the card from him.

"Only kidding. Just trying to lighten the mood."

No. You're immature and insensitive. Since arriving in the house, Kate felt her tears were only ever a second away from the surface, and at his last so-called joke, they flowed.

He stepped forwards, touching her arm, but she brushed it away. "Sorry. I didn't mean to upset you, Kate."

She slumped back in her chair and reached for a tissue. "Should I call the police?"

"And nobody else has a key?"

She shook her head. "I should check every room, I suppose."

"Yes, and I'll speak to the neighbours and ask if they saw or heard anything last night."

Her tears started again, and he placed his hand over hers.

"You don't think Howard did this, do you?" she asked.

"No, surely not... Why would he? And how'd he get in?"

"I... I don't... know."

"Well, if it puts your mind at rest, I'll ask him. We can at least put that worry to bed," Jake said, striding out of the room.

Kate wiped her tear-stained face and followed him, closing the dining room door behind her.

As Jake opened the front door, Howard raised his hand to knock.

"Can we help you?" Jake asked.

"I was wondering how you're settling in and whether there's anything I can do to help." Howard's eyes circled Jake to meet Kate's.

She followed Jake as he stepped outside. Howard had dressed smartly again but still had a cigarette hanging from his lips.

"Well, Kate thinks someone broke in here last night."

"Oh, love. Poor you," Howard replied. "Are you okay? I can see you're upset."

"I'm fine," she snapped.

Jake put his hands on his hips and stepped closer to Howard. "Well, it's strange because no locks have been forced open."

Howard ignored Jake and looked straight at Kate. "Well, that's odd. I'll alert the neighbourhood."

"Don't they use social media to keep in touch?" Jake asked.

Howard shuffled his feet. "No, I like things to be more face-to-face... more friendly-like. I enjoy chatting with people."

You mean, nosing in other people's business.

Kate studied his face. "So, Howard, you knew Betty Harris well?"

Howard glanced up. "Yes, we were friendly."

"So, fancy a coffee, Howard?" asked Jake, "While we try to figure out what's happened here."

Kate glared. *What the hell?*

Jake turned to her, nodded, and winked. Howard stubbed out his cigarette and followed them both through to the kitchen. Jake offered a chair to Howard but remained standing himself. Kate busied herself making coffee.

"So, Howard, should Kate inform the police?"

"Has anything been stolen or damaged?" He leant back in his chair and surveyed the kitchen. "I shouldn't bother."

She passed them both a coffee. "You must know this house quite well if—"

Jake interrupted her. "The thing is, Howard, we found some letters addressed to Betty Harris."

Howard bit his lip and momentarily stared at Jake before speaking again. "Yes, I spent a lot of time here with Betty until she... We were like family. I... I told you that the other day, Kate."

Jake sipped his coffee but kept his eyes fixed on Howard. "No family of your own then?"

Howard scraped a hand through his hair. "Yes, I have three daughters. Okay if I smoke, Kate?"

"Yes, go ahead," she said, turning away. *Ugh. Don't mind me.*

"But your daughters don't live with you?" Jake asked.

"No, they don't. I need a bigger place. Me and the missus... well, it all got rather nasty. Women, eh?"

Oh, excuse me.

"I've just split with my girlfriend," said Jake.

"Met someone else, I suppose?" Howard chuckled and blew wisps of smoke into the air.

Jake ignored the remark. "Did Betty have any family?"

"Um... Well, I thought not, but apparently, she did." Howard paused. "So, are you two an item then?"

"No! No!" Kate said, "I only met Jake a few days ago. He's clearing the garden for me, that's all. And helping me this morning because it's all been a bit of a shock."

"The odd thing is, someone opened all of Betty's letters... the ones we found... and maybe even read them," said Jake.

Howard paused, his eyes flicking around the room. "All very odd. Perhaps that dead man has come back to the house."

"Don't you start with that too, Howard!"

Jake raised his eyebrows at her. "Howard has seen the postcard you found? Yes, maybe ghostly old William has returned," Jake said, nodding slowly. "Yes, maybe he has..."

"I wouldn't bother the police with it," Howard said, casually leaning back in his chair. "I can watch this evening and make sure no one's about."

Oh Lord. "I'm sure that won't be necessary."

Howard gulped down his coffee and stood up. "Anyway, I best get on. Make sure you do an excellent job in the garden for this lovely young lady," he said, smiling and pointing a finger at Jake.

"Well, that was fun... not," Kate said after he'd left. As she scooped up the coffee cups, she looked across at Jake. He was biting his lip. "Well, did he seem guilty to you?"

"Odd though," he replied, scratching his head. "You'd have thought Howard might have asked more questions. Which room were the letters found? Or how we knew someone had opened and read them? Even asked to have a look?"

"And why did you ask if he used social media?"

"Kate, it's amazing what you can find out about someone there."

Kate shuddered. "The man has issues. He's got a probation officer, and his daughters don't or can't visit. So, I don't know, Jake. I'm not sure we're any the wiser. But I don't want him in my house again!"

"I thought it might unease him if we were friendly."

Kate shrugged. "Howard gives me the creeps, never mind William, my dead man."

"So, I'll get back out to the garden. I've still plenty to do," said Jake.

"I'll call the police," she said. "And I'm sorry I got upset and snapped at you. I know you were only trying to help."

"This morning's been a shock, so don't worry. And anyway, I'm used to being shouted at by women."

She immersed herself in his eyes and saw warmth and openness. *Stop staring at him!*

"Anyway, I'm going to have a quiet day, look online for stuff for the house, and do some research on one of those family tree websites."

"Yes, keep your mind busy. My mate's calling later, and we'll see about getting that sideboard up from the cellar. And I could show you the antique shop in town."

"Yes, yes, that would be nice."

"The police will probably only log your call and give you a crime number."

"But at least it'll be on the record, Jake."

CHAPTER 21

That night, Kate sat bolt upright in bed on hearing any creak, car engine, or owl hooting. She'd crept downstairs twice in the early hours to make a hot milky drink, hoping it'd help her sleep. Leaving the dining room door open gave her a view inside from halfway down the stairs. Kate had mulled over every explanation of why the letters were all over the floor. It was stupid to think a bird might have flown down the chimney or she hadn't secured the door. Jake was right about the police; they'd just given her a crime number. Her explanation that someone had opened and read a bundle of letters she felt gave the constable a good laugh.

"So, no sign of a forced entry and nothing taken?" he'd asked three times.

She'd kicked herself for mentioning that perhaps the house was haunted.

Kate laid out William's postcard, the wedding photograph, newspaper cutting, Charles' letter, and Lizzie's sampler in front of her. She scrutinised each before switching on her laptop and pulling a notebook from the bureau. She wrote the names John and Mary Doyle, followed by all the initials on the sampler. On another page, the names on the wall in the hallway: Ada, Ethel, and Dorothy. Finally, the date from the postcard, 12 December 1915, which she underlined.

After putting on her reading glasses, she googled births, marriages, and deaths, and numerous websites popped up. The first one had all these records plus census records up to 1911. Several birth records appeared, but only one was registered in Shrewsbury for Ada Tate. She double checked the date of the Oriental Bazaar and decided that Ada Tate, born in 1899, would be about right.

For Ethel and Dorothy Tate's births, two online records jumped out at her: Ethel Tate, born in 1907 and Dorothy, born in 1910. Kate sucked on the end of her pen, thinking about what to do next. Then, clicking on the 1911 census, she searched for Ada Tate, born in 1899, and zoomed in on the document. Ada lived at 8 Marine Terrace with her two sisters, her mother, Theresa Tate, and William.

Kate smiled to herself and wrote the information in her notebook. Next, she checked the marriage records, typing in William Tate around 1899, seeing as that was the year Ada was born.

"Bingo!"

The record was for the last quarter of 1898, and Kate held her breath looking for his spouse's name: Theresa Doyle.

She picked up the sampler and focused on the embroidered T, the letter that was brighter than the others.

"T is for Theresa!"

Taking off her glasses, she looked at Jake and caught his eye as he tackled some brambles. He was wearing far thicker gloves than on previous days and lifted his hands to show her. After lifting a heavy clump into his wheelbarrow, he approached the house.

"Everything in its place this morning?" he asked, poking his head around the French doors.

"Yes, thank goodness." *No need to tell him about my sleepless night.*

He studied the lock and key in the door. "I'll fit a new one here for you anyway to be on the safe side."

"I'd be grateful if you would. I'm online trying to learn more about the people who lived here."

"Genealogy website?"

"That's right. I've found Ada, Ethel, and Dorothy Tate on the 1911 census with their parents, William and Theresa."

"William from the postcard?"

"Yes, and the three girls' names are the ones I've seen written on the wall in the hallway."

"Wow. Under the blinding green wallpaper?"

"Under the flowery one beneath that."

"A mate of mine researched his family online and wanted to do mine. I told him not to bother. My old man was a total waste of space."

"Oh dear."

The tattoo on his arm caught her eye again as he fiddled with the door. The black letters spelt Madden.

"So, the tattoo is your surname."

He pulled his sleeve up. "Yes, a moment of madness in my youth! My mum, God bless her, called my dad 'Mad Madden'. I thought that was cool, but he was a right sod and buggered off before I was born."

"I'm sorry to hear that, Jake."

"No, don't be. I'm sure I'm better off without him. What about you... any family?"

"No, I lost both my parents within a matter of weeks. Mum had a heart attack, and Dad gave up and didn't want to continue. He died six weeks later."

"That's sad. You've no brothers, sisters, or friends left in Warwick?"

"Well, there was Lionel." *Shit. Why does his name always pop into my head?* "No, it's just me."

A momentary silence hung as she held his gaze before holding up the sampler towards him. "I think I've found out what the T stands for here. Theresa."

"You're a budding detective. And who was Theresa?"

She picked up the picture of William. "His wife. Amazing what you can find out online these days."

"Don't go typing in my name. I'm from a long line of wrong'uns," he said, winking at her.

She laughed, glad Jake was around, keeping her mind off the break-in and sleepless nights.

"Are you feeling better today, Kate?" he asked, leaning on the door.

His T-shirt rose, and she tore her eyes from his toned stomach.

"Yes, I'm fine. I must have eaten something that upset me. I'm going to take a walk into town later."

"Perhaps we can call in at the antique place I mentioned?"

"Yes, that'd be great. I want to find frames for this sampler and wedding photograph."

"Maybe late afternoon?"

"Yes, that suits me."

As Jake closed the door and returned to the garden, she couldn't get over how helpful he was and how much of the garden he'd already cleared. The shed and most of the brambles and nettles were gone. He had sanded down the old metal archway, and he'd taken delivery of paving slabs and topsoil.

She returned to her laptop and typed in the name Theresa Doyle.

"Wow."

There was a birth record in 1880 and a death record in 1912.

"Oh no. Theresa died aged thirty-two. Those three girls lost their mother when they were all very young. Dorothy was only two."

Kate felt a lump in her throat and reached for a tissue. *Don't be silly. These people were not your relatives, and they're all long dead.*

She bit her lip and returned her attention to William. It surprised her to see a ship's passenger list in 1912 come up after typing in his name. The record showed he'd travelled from Liverpool to Canada aboard a ship called Lake Manitoba. The same year Theresa died.

The name of the passenger below caught her eye: Emillie Tate, wife. Did he marry again? Did he leave his daughters with Elizabeth? And that's why their names were written on the wall here?

"What an absolute arse!"

Next, checking the 1911 census for Elizabeth Doyle, she noted that her occupation was a lodging housekeeper at 81 Whitehall Street.

"This place was a B&B back in her day!" Questions buzzed around her head as she stared at William's picture. "Did you leave Ada, Ethel, and Dorothy in this house?"

I wonder what happened to the girls? Especially little Dorothy.

1952

Dorothy waited in the church hall, holding her baby close and occasionally stroking her pink cheeks with the small brown teddy bear Ada had given her. She stared at her daughter's face, determined to remember every bit. She looked up as the door opened and a slim woman with glasses perched at the end of her nose walked in. Dorothy bit her lip.

"It's all for the best, Miss Tate," she said as she approached with open arms.

That's right, emphasise the "miss", why don't you.

Dorothy held her baby closer and kissed her forehead. "No, please, a little bit longer. Just another five minutes."

"Her new parents are waiting in Father Kelly's study."

Oh yes, the sanctimonious Father Kelly.

"All the paperwork is complete, miss, and you know it's for the best. He's told me about your situation, and it's plain to see that she would be better off with a good Catholic married couple."

The baby let out a little whimper. Dorothy had a lump in her throat and struggled to speak but rocked her baby and cooed instead in the hope of getting a few more precious seconds.

The woman touched the baby, putting her arms over Dorothy's. "Come on now, come on."

Dorothy tried to hold on until her fingertips eventually fell away.

"Father Kelly will come and pray with you and forgive your sins."

Dorothy fell to the floor, clutching the small brown teddy bear.

She called out to the woman, holding out the bear. "Can she keep this?"

But there was no reply, and she let her tears flow until she could cry no more, and the bear was damp. Another woman came in, lifted her from the floor and escorted her to the door without saying a word. Dorothy clung to the bear as she staggered home in the pouring rain and felt like everyone in the street knew she'd given her baby away.

The pain gnawed at her, and she spent months walking around town peering into prams, hoping she would recognise her daughter. She was convinced the child would have the Doyles' dark wavy hair.

While working behind the bar at the Malt Shovel, she put on a face, then went back to her room to cry.

The Catholic Church dealt with the situation efficiently. They persuaded her that, as a Catholic, she'd committed the ultimate sin. And with the lack of financial support and a suitable home, they'd offered her an alternative.

1954

Ada Powell sat on one side of Dorothy's bed, and her sister Ethel Jones sat on the other. Whatever the doctor had prescribed had at least made Dorothy less agitated. Ada's son, Gordon, appeared at the door with a tray of sugary tea.

"How is she?" he whispered.

Ada took a cup. "The same... the same, but more peaceful."

Dorothy had spent the past two weeks in the small bedroom above the Malt Shovel pub and had not eaten for a fortnight. Her arms had flailed some days, and she'd shouted at her visitors. She'd shooed away Father Kelly angrily whenever he called to offer prayers and comfort. A weariness had thankfully descended now, and her chest was barely rising. From below, Ada heard chatter and laughter as life continued: tankards of ale drawn, card games won and lost, and men telling saucy jokes.

"Life goes on no matter what, Ethel."

Ethel nodded as she stroked Dorothy's pale hand. "I'm sure everyone is missing little Dorothy. She was always so lively behind the bar and could persuade most customers to have another drink."

"Oh, Ethel, it's funny how we still call her little Dorothy. It was Da who started it, but he didn't hang around to see her grow up, did he?"

"Time to let it go, Ada. He's been dead forty years."

Ethel reached across the bed and held Ada's hand too, so they made a chain of hands like they often did as children.

The day before, the doctor had said Dorothy's heart and lungs were failing, and her liver shot. "Too much alcohol" were his parting words. He wasn't telling them anything the family didn't already know. But they knew she drank to forget that her baby had been taken from her.

"Is she lingering, do you think? Waiting for someone else to come and say goodbye?" asked Ethel.

"Maybe. I rue the day that bastard Sean Madden walked into this pub." Ada crossed herself.

"You're turning into Aunt Lizzie, Ada! Remember, she always crossed herself when she swore."

They both smiled.

"I'm so glad she's not here to see this," said Ethel. "It would have broken her heart to lose Dorothy. Forty-four is no age."

Ada nodded. "We warned her off that Sean Madden, but I think she was flattered by a younger man's attention. Even when he disappeared for weeks, she'd welcome him back." She wiped her eyes as they welled. "Dorothy went through hell because of the Catholic Church. Thank God I met my Harry. I'm blessed to have Gordon, Dot, Mildred, and Joyce now."

Gordon smiled, picked up the tray and cups, and left the room. They lowered their heads and prayed for Dorothy's soul as her chest stopped rising, and she passed.

"She's with Ma and Aunt Lizzie now," Ada said, kissing Dorothy's forehead.

"Let's hope that sweet little girl is safe and well somewhere. Should we have done more, Ada?"

"I'm not sure," she replied, wiping away a tear. "The pub was no place for a baby. Harry can't work anymore because of his arthritis, so money was and still is tight."

"And none of us is getting any younger," added Ethel.

Ada nodded.

"And now you have your lovely grandchildren, Ada. Clive, Jean, Lynn."

"I do, and I want to spend time with them. Let's pray that Dorothy's little girl is safe and enjoying life... and that we did make the right decision."

Ada placed rosary beads in Dorothy's hands.

CHAPTER 22

Aileen Thompson parked beside the Abbey Church and walked towards Whitehall Street. A feast of scarlet, yellow, and brown leaves blew across the church grounds and followed her, and the relentless autumn breeze urged both her and the leaves forward.

She retrieved her gloves from her coat pocket and glanced at Abbey House, a grand Georgian building. She'd visited this part of town often during her life. *But was Dorothy still alive? Was she still living just around the corner on Whitehall Street?*

There was always a midnight Mass on Christmas Eve at the Abbey Church. In the eighties, she and her friends fell out of the pub nearby and went to the service with tinsel tied around their heads. *Was Dorothy in the congregation? Or celebrating in the pub?*

Her adopted mum would have hated Aileen going from a pub to a church, but what she didn't know didn't hurt her. Her Catholic faith had been important right up to the point of her illness. But once dementia set in, her mother had no idea who the priests were that prayed at her bedside. Aileen shook her head to dispel the painful memory of her mum swearing at them.

Her mum was at peace now. And watching her disappear bit by bit until she didn't even recognise her only daughter had ripped Aileen's heart out. Her mum had known very little about Dorothy, only that she was unmarried. It seemed like a betrayal to find out more until now. But what was she hoping to achieve? She didn't want to call Dorothy her real mother or birth mother, and wondered whether there was ever a good time to pull skeletons out of the cupboard.

She turned into Whitehall Street, her mind mulling over the idea she should sell the family home. Sixty-three years she'd lived there, but now it seemed cavernous. Every room held memories, and at the moment, the sad ones brushed aside the precious ones. Aileen had taken sick leave from work, stopped calling friends, and cut herself off, trying to deal with her grief and loss of direction. But she'd woken that morning, hearing, "Best foot forward, Aileen." A phrase her lovely mum often used.

She retrieved a scrap of paper from her pocket to recheck the name and address she'd copied from her adoption file. She turned her collar up as she walked up Whitehall Street, noting each number. A huge part of her hoped the ravages of time had obliterated number 81. She passed a terrace of six tiny houses, and at one end, the occupant had built an extension and matched the bricks to those used in the original house. The house at the other end was now a printing shop. Then came a terrace of bay windows, and glancing across to the other side, she realised all the houses had been there for a long time. She could see more 1950s houses ahead, with their fake Tudor frontages, so the council had knocked some places down.

Her eyes widened as she reached 81. It was a well-kept terraced Georgian townhouse.

"No. This can't be it." Her eyes flicked from the piece of paper and back to the house. From reading her adoption papers, she'd expected something smaller, something the council would tear down. Maybe the details in her file weren't accurate. Or they had renumbered the street.

However, the window style matched Abbey House; she reasoned that this had also stood for over a century.

She looked up at the bedroom window. *I wish I'd been born here and not above some seedy old pub in the middle of town.* But her life had been good, with a successful career at the bank and parents who loved her, so why did reading and learning about Dorothy trouble her so much?

Last night, armed with a glass of wine, she'd finally read her adoption file that had been in her possession for weeks. The character assassination that a Catholic priest had written had reduced her to floods of tears.

"Can I help you?" called a lady at the door.

"Oh, oh no... it's fine. I'm just being silly."

"Are you sure? You're looking a little lost."

———•———

Kate walked down the path, pulling her hood up as the wind whistled. "Are you looking for someone?"

The woman passed a scrap of paper towards her. "My birth mother grew up in this house."

"Wow, that's interesting." Kate looked at the paper. *Dorothy Tate!* "I'm Kate, by the way." She held out her hand.

"I'm Ai-Aileen, Aileen Thompson," the woman replied, shaking Kate's hand.

"Have you come far, Aileen?" Kate asked, still holding the paper.

Aileen pointed down to the bottom of the street. "No, not far. I've parked my car down there by the Abbey Church."

Kate beckoned her. "Seems a shame not to have a peek inside now you're here."

"I wouldn't want to bother you." A gust of wind caused Aileen to step forwards.

"It's no trouble, and we should get out of this damn wind. You can tell me all about Dorothy."

Aileen paused for a moment. "Well... well, that's kind of you."

"I was just going to make some tea for the gardener anyway, so please come in."

The names written on the wall in the hallway were hopefully too small for Aileen to notice. *I need to tread carefully.* "Make yourself comfy in the armchair in the dining room."

After waving to Jake that a fresh cup of tea was on the kitchen window ledge, Kate carried tea and cake to the dining room. Aileen had removed her coat and stood in the middle of the room.

"Kate, the fireplace is stunning, and the cornicing."

"Yes, there are lots of original features in the house. It's going to keep me busy for sure."

Even as she sat down, Aileen's eyes continued to drink in the room. She perched on the armchair, pushing back her dark wavy hair. But it was her eyes that caught Kate's attention. Their rich, velvety brown popped out despite the tired circles beneath them.

"Aileen is a beautiful name," she said, passing over a cup of tea and a generous slice of lemon drizzle cake.

"Thank you. Irish origins. I believe it means bright, shining light." She sipped her tea. "Well, that's what Mum told me. Not that I feel like one at the moment."

She noted the scepticism in Aileen's voice just as Jake appeared outside the French doors, doing a silly jig and puffing out his cheeks at the size of the slab of cake she'd left out for him. She couldn't help laughing.

"Ignore Jake. He thinks he's funny. But he's doing a good job, so I'll put up with him for a little longer. Believe me, it was like a jungle out there four days ago."

"Sorry," he mouthed on spotting she had company.

"It is quite a large piece of cake, but delicious," said Aileen after a bite. "The house isn't quite what I was expecting."

"It all needs a thorough cleaning, and a few sash windows are impossible to open. And don't get me started on the decor. You must have noticed the awful lime green wallpaper in the hallway. It's almost blinding!"

They laughed, and she sensed Aileen relax and sit back in the chair.

"So, what made you want to find this house?" Kate asked.

Aileen's eyes filled, and she reached for a tissue from her handbag. "Please excuse me. The slightest thing sets me off these days."

I know that feeling. "I'm so sorry. I didn't mean to pry."

Aileen dabbed her eyes. "I think Dorothy was... well, to put it politely, a fallen woman."

Kate bit into the cake, unsure what to say next.

"I'm adopted, you see."

"And have you only just found that out?"

"No, I always knew. Mum and Dad passed away recently, and the time seemed right. I wasn't sure this house would still be standing."

"How did you know the address?" asked Kate, pouring more tea. "From your birth certificate?"

Aileen shook her head. "I sent for my adoption papers after Mum died. I picked up the courage last night to read through them."

She passed a cup to Aileen. "More cake?"

"No, thank you. In the file, there were statements from various people."

"Was Dorothy very young?"

"No, no, that was the surprise. She was forty-two."

Blimey, that's the same age as me. "But no husband?"

"They gave my father's name, but it looks like he did a runner when he found out Dorothy was expecting. Her family were Catholics. The church handled the adoption. A Father Kelly wrote a derogatory description about my moth—Dorothy's character."

"I'm so sorry, Aileen." Kate paused and took the teacup from Aileen's shaking hand to put it on a side table. "What year were you born?"

"1952. And I've heard awful stories of adoptions the Catholic Church did back then." Aileen dabbed her eyes.

Kate nodded. "Bit different these days. But being a single mother in the fifties was harder, especially with no husband to give financial support."

"It... it was all such a lot to take in."

Kate moved her dining chair closer to Aileen. "And perhaps this is all too soon after losing your mum?"

"Yes, you're right." Aileen finished her tea and cake in silence before standing up. "It was very kind of you to invite me in, but I best be heading home now."

"You can stay a little longer if you like... until the wind dies?" *She won't return if I don't tell her something about what I've found in the house.*

Aileen shook her head. "I won't take up any more of your time." She reached for her coat. Following Kate into the hallway, Aileen glanced into the front room and up the stairs.

"Can I show you this before you leave?" asked Kate.

"I don't need to look upstairs. I'm sure you've got things to do."

"Look what's written on the wall, just here," Kate said, pointing. "I couldn't resist pulling off some layers of this awful wallpaper, and—"

Aileen fumbled in her handbag and popped on her glasses. Stooping down, she stared at the lines and the names written. Dorothy at the lowest level, then Ethel and Ada at the tallest. She touched the name Dorothy with two fingers and then brought them to her lips. "Dorothy was so small... two or three? And she had two sisters?"

"Yes. It looks like the girls measured their heights back in 1916." Kate smiled but saw Aileen's hands trembling. "I'm so, so sorry. I didn't mean to upset you more."

"No, no, it's wonderful," Aileen replied, half laughing, half crying.

"Can I take your number, Aileen? Just in case I find anything else in the house."

"Oh, okay."

After adding Aileen to her few contacts, Kate instinctively hugged Aileen.

After a final wave goodbye, Kate headed for the kitchen to make another coffee for Jake, who was mixing concrete and laying paving slabs.

"Has your friend gone?" he asked as she passed the mug to him through the window.

"I've never met her before! She was outside looking at the house and seemed lost."

"I see."

"She's started searching for her birth family. Her mother was Dorothy Tate."

Jake's eyes widened. "Wasn't that one of the…"

"Yes, one of William Tate's daughters."

"Did you tell her everything you've found in the house?"

"Not yet. She was pretty upset about what she read in her adoption file, so I'll wait until I know more."

"Oh dear. Does she know who her father was?" he asked, sipping his coffee.

"There was a name in her adoption file, but he didn't hang around. Oh, sorry, Jake. I forgot your dad did a runner too."

"Ah, forget it. I'm long over not having a father figure. Anyway, thanks for the coffee. I best get back to my concrete mixer," he said, turning away.

"Still okay to show me that antique place in town later?"

He turned back and smiled. "My mate can't make it here until tomorrow, so the sideboard will have to wait… but yes, give me a shout when you're ready to go."

Returning to the dining room, she opened up her laptop to research a design of wallpaper that might suit a

Georgian house. But her head was buzzing with Aileen's visit, and she soon returned to genealogical websites.

She paused momentarily before typing in the name Dorothy Tate, born in 1910. A record popped up, and Kate bit her lip. Oh no. Dorothy died in 1954, just two years after Aileen was born. She shut her laptop, wondering why she was getting so emotional about people who had nothing to do with her. *Ugh, I need some fresh air.*

She sighed and waved at Jake to get his attention. "Shall we go into town now?"

CHAPTER 23

"Well, I... I think you're bloody... un... unreasonable," Howard spat.

"Howard, you're not supposed to contact me."

"I want to see my girls."

"But you've broken the court order. You're breaking it now!"

"Things just aren't going my way at the moment."

"So, I take it the old lady didn't leave you her house then?"

He could sense the "I told you so" in his ex-wife's sanctimonious tone. "I'm... I'm goin' to bloody con... contest the—"

"Have you had a drink today?"

"Nah, I haven't. Course not," he replied, placing his whiskey glass on the side table. "Some bleeding posh cow's moved into the house now."

"You're a fool. Contesting a will could take years!"

The temptation to hang up on his ex-wife grew.

"And anyway, that's all beside the point. You're not allowed access to the girls until you stop dri–"

"Yeah, blah, blah. I don't know why you took that fuc–flaming restraining order out in the first–"

"We've been through this, Howard. You know why. You put me in the hospital last–"

Spotting Kate and Jake leaving number 81 distracted him from the conversation. *Those two look very cosy.*

"But... Ok, I'll speak to Bill again."

"Yes, do that. It's the only way forward."

Howard hung up. He'd have to cut out the drinking to see his daughters even on a supervised footing. Since Kate moved into number 81, the golden liquid had become his best and constant friend once again. The occasional cold shower and clean shirt enabled him to call on her, but he sensed Jake was getting his feet under the table. *Yes, I need to up my game.*

Bill, his probation officer, wouldn't be happy; Howard had feigned illness to get out of their last session. But lifting himself out of his armchair and engaging with life seemed impossible right now. *I'm not sure I'm ready to climb that mountain.*

As he watched Kate and Jake walk to the end of the street, he downed his whiskey and scooped up his keys from the side table. Once outside, he placed a hand on a lamp post to steady himself. He lit a cigarette, inhaled before launching into the road, and failed to spot a blue Mini approaching. He gestured rudely as the driver beeped her horn and waited for him to cross. On reaching number 81, he glanced up and down the street. There was no one in sight.

He fumbled with the key until the door clicked open. *The daft cow hasn't changed the locks.*

"Hellooo?" he called on entering the hallway.

The house was silent, and he headed for the dining room.

"Now, where are those bloody letters again from that so-called nephew? I should have taken one with me the other night when I was here."

After plonking himself down in front of the bureau, he opened it. The bundle of letters was inside the small drawer on the left. He slipped the top one out and put it into his pocket. *I'll write and ensure that blasted nephew knows there is another and more recent will somewhere.*

"Maybe a letter from me might prick your conscience, you bastard. I was more like family to Betty than you ever were," he said, slamming his fist on the drop-down desk.

He replaced the letters, inhaled his cigarette, and leisurely blew the smoke upwards. *How come Kate found these and I never did? Well, it's not over yet, my lady.*

He stubbed his cigarette out on the desk and then flicked his wrist. The stub landed in the iron basket of the fireplace. "Great shot, Howie!"

Returning to the hallway, he paused, held his left wrist with his right hand, and tried to focus his vision on his watch. *How long have I been here?* Then, steadying himself with the banister, he climbed the stairs, one at a time.

I'll search everywhere again if I have to.

The door to Kate's bedroom was open, and the view diverted him from pulling down the attic ladder. *She's an attractive woman. I'm more her age than that Jake!* Drawn to the line of her colourful perfume bottles, he couldn't resist spraying a couple into the air and breathing them in.

He caught a reflection of himself in the wardrobe mirror and passed his fingers through his lank, greasy hair. *I need to smarten myself up.* Then, sighing and gazing in the mirror, he sat on Kate's bed.

"Shit. I'm a flaming mess," he said, examining his ruddy complexion and bloodshot eyes.

He couldn't resist opening her wardrobe before he left. Kate's colourful clothes hung inside, and he ran his fingers down a silk blouse before spotting several designer labels. *Reckon she's got a bob or two.*

His thoughts disappeared as he heard a car door slamming in the street. Standing back from the window, he stretched his neck to see outside.

"Shit, shit."

Bill, his probation officer, was getting out of his car. He carried a leather briefcase, wore a smart navy suit, and marched towards Howard's flat.

Once back in the hallway, Howard opened the front door, inch by inch, before slipping outside and scurrying down the path. His head was pounding. *He's going to give me a right kick up the arse.*

"Bill... I'm... I'm just coming!" he called.

Bill turned, his eyebrows raised, as he said, "Howard, we had a meeting yesterday, but you didn't show up or call the office. And what are you doing over at number 81?"

"Oh, sorry, mate. I wasn't feeling great."

"Can we speak now then?"

"Yes, of course."

Howard fumbled getting the key in his flat door and could sense Bill's eyes drilling into the back of his head. As they entered the living room, Howard spotted and kicked an empty whiskey bottle. The bottle spun a few times before settling just under his armchair.

Bill pushed aside newspapers and takeaway menus before sitting on the sofa. He raised his eyebrows and wrinkled his nose as he scanned the room. "I can see things are getting on top of you again," he said, taking a file out of his briefcase. "Perhaps occasionally opening a window might help?"

Okay, okay, you sarcastic bugger. "I'm managing just fine." He offered a cigarette to Bill.

"No, I don't smoke, Howard," Bill replied curtly.

"No, you wouldn't," Howard said under his breath.

"It's of the utmost importance that you keep to our sessions, Howard," Bill said, retrieving papers from his briefcase. "Anne's told the police she's seen you on her road. And that you've been calling her."

"Can I get you a coffee, Bill?"

Bill ignored the question. "You know that the restraining order states you're not authorised to go within ten miles of her or the children."

"I know, I know, and she's a right sarcastic bitch on the phone."

"You're not to ring her either!" Bill said, sighing.

"I had a bit of a setback. I thought I was coming into some money."

"Is this the business with the house opposite?"

"It should be mine."

"But the lady who died was not a relative, Howard. So why on earth would she leave you her house?"

I'll get it. You watch this space, mate.

"Are you claiming all your benefits? Housing? Job Seekers?"

"Yes, of course, but who the hell's gonna employ me?"

"And what about your AA meetings? Are they helping at all?"

He's seen the bloody bottle for sure. "Yep."

"But I'm told you've stopped attending. It's important, Howard, for you to move forward. You could talk to others who are struggling with alcohol."

"What good does talking to strangers do? They all drink far more than me anyway. I've been busy doing odd jobs for neighbours."

Bill's jaw dropped. "And purely voluntarily, I assume. No cash in hand?"

"I'm just trying to be neighbourly, and I thought it might make a good impression on my job applications. I'm helping the lady who's just moved into number 81."

Bill strained his neck to stare out of the window. "Number 81? The one you thought was going to be left to you?"

Howard turned away, not wanting to meet Bill's eyes.

"Not making a nuisance of yourself, I hope?"

"No, we're getting on fine. She's a right looker—"

"This is hardly the time to be chasing another relationship. Unless things improve, you won't even get supervised visits with your daughters."

"Yeah, yeah." *All right for you to sit there with your fancy suit and briefcase.*

"And I'll have to update my report about..." Bill's eyes swept around the room again. "About your living conditions."

Good job he hasn't seen the kitchen.

CHAPTER 24

Jake waited by his van, and as Kate came down the path to meet him, he wished he wasn't still wearing his heavy-duty boots and muddy trousers. At least his puffer jacket was clean and covered the faded black Bruce Springsteen T-shirt he wore beneath.

Her bluey-green eyes met his as she finished buttoning up her red woollen coat. She placed a knitted, navy bobble hat on her head. "I see the breeze hasn't died down any," she said, pulling up her collar and distracting him from thinking how lovely she looked.

"We could go in the van if you'd prefer?"

"Jake, I've been here for four days and barely left the house. Let's walk."

"Yes, you're still looking pale. The fresh air will do you good."

"Still don't feel quite myself, to be honest, especially in the mornings." She bit her lip.

Howard stood in his window talking on the phone as they set off. *I don't like the way he calls round to Kate's uninvited.*

"So, what made you pick Shrewsbury for your fresh start?" he asked, hoping Kate wouldn't spot Howard.

"A regular guest at my old B&B came from here and told me lots about it. But, to be honest, it was very much a spur-of-the-moment decision."

"After a bottle of wine?" He laughed.

She stopped walking and punched him on the arm with a smile. "You've got the wrong impression of me, Mr Madden. But yes, maybe. I saw the house online and put a bid in. Didn't even come and see it."

"Wow, a bold move." *I'm glad you're here.*

They walked past the Abbey Church, under the railway bridge, and towards the English Bridge. They battled against the wind and laughed as they began walking across. Kate stopped at the crown of the bridge to read a bronze plaque.

"The original bridge was completed in 1774 but dismantled and rebuilt in 1927, using all the original stone. Its gradient halved, and its width increased, Queen Mary declared it open."

Jake stood close to her to hear, pleased to see her cheeks were pink now, and even though her eyes watered from the wind, they sparkled.

"I've lived in Shrewsbury my whole life and never stopped to read this plaque." He shoved his hands in his pockets.

"Well, you won't be much of a tour guide!"

"I suppose it was just horse and cart back then... no flash BMWs."

She nodded. "My new car was another spur-of-the-moment purchase."

"So, you're an impulsive woman?"

Kate looked serious. "I didn't use to be."

They walked on, and because he didn't want to talk about her ex, Lionel, he changed the subject to antique furniture and Belfast sinks. *I hope she asks me to help renovate the house's interior.* "This is Wyle Cop. It'll be even more fun walking up here, Kate." He fought the urge to link arms but slowed his pace to keep alongside her.

"Woah, this is a proper hill," she said, panting. She stopped at the top of the cop. "Beautiful," she said with a smile as she admired the Tudor buildings on either side of the cop.

They paused halfway along High Street, and he pointed to a sign. The narrow passageway with black-and-white buildings on either side were only feet apart.

"Grope Lane!" Her face lit up with laughter. "So, this might have been a place where—"

He grinned. "Yes, a sort of medieval red-light district, perhaps?"

"Or it was so dark in medieval times they had to feel or grope their way up the passageway."

"I prefer the first explanation," he said before walking on.

"Me too!" She caught him up and shoved him in the back, laughing. "You're not such a bad tour guide after all."

Passing the market square and the statue of Clive of India, they turned left and faced the clock tower.

"That's the market hall," he said, pointing. "A blot on the landscape, my mum always used to say. There was an ornate Victorian one before, but they knocked it down in the sixties."

"Yes, sixties architecture has a lot to answer for. It's just a tower of red bricks with no character." Kate made a sad face.

They turned right into Mardol, and Jake stopped halfway along. "This is your Hills Lane. Why don't you have a walk along? I'll come back and meet you after I've been to the hardware shop."

"Okay." She was already peering into a gift shop window at the top of the lane as he crossed the road.

Jake had ordered most of the stuff he needed for her garden online to be delivered or collected. Earlier delivery slots had been available, but he'd chosen later ones to draw the job out. He'd tried to reason with himself that he was doing it because he'd have less work with the winter coming. But he knew he was kidding himself.

He came out of Birch and Sons carrying the new door lock and headed back to Hills Lane. He was familiar with the cobbles, repaired over the years but still holding great charm. A Tudor building stood on the left-hand side, leaning forwards in parts and backwards in others. And on the right, a terrace of three-storey houses, all with brightly painted doors, curved around the lane.

He spotted Kate standing outside them, but looking over at the other side. Strands of her hair had escaped and fluttered over her face, and he smiled as she tried to recapture them and tuck them back under her hat.

She smiled as he approached, and they stood side by side in silence, looking around.

"This is it then, Kate."

She had a beautiful but distant look on her face, and he struggled to stop staring at her.

"It's a lovely lane, Jake. Plenty of history. I can imagine people going up and down the cobbles, horses, the coalman, rag-and-bone man, and neighbours in and out of each other's houses."

He said nothing but noticed another strand of hair escape from underneath her hat. The wind was whistling around the corner from Bridge Street, and he fought the urge to push back her hair and wrap his arms around her. *For Christ's sake, you've only known her for a few days, and I'm enjoying being single, remember?*

"But do you think the door numbers now would be the same as they were back in 1916?" she asked, looking at him.

"What—? What? Sorry."

"Am I boring you, Jake?"

Shit, no. Far from it!

"Lizzie's sampler said 84 Hills Lane, but there isn't one."

"This car park wouldn't have been here, but Rowley's Mansion... I think that would have been here," he replied.

"Yes, there could have been loads of houses occupying this space originally."

"Look at the houses on the other side, Kate. One's a hairdresser's now, a solicitor's office, and a nightclub in that building. So hard to know what the lane might have looked like in the 1900s."

"Yes, the Doyle house was more than likely on the demolished side. By the way, I picked up this from the gift shop." She pulled a small book from her handbag. "It gives a little history about the town... so I might learn more about how the town's changed."

"What's next, Inspector Clouseau? Or is it Miss Marple?"

"Stop it! I'm crackers, aren't I?"

"No, not at all. The items in the house are intriguing, and it's odd that Aileen should turn up just a few days after you found them. She seems like a nice lady."

"Yes, she does, and everything I've found in the house belongs to her. And I need to tell her about them, but I want to find out a bit more first." Kate looked up and down the lane.

"You're feeling sorry for her?"

"I am. Yes, I am a bit. Must be very strange finding out you're adopted." Her eyes teared. "This damn wind is making my eyes stream."

He wasn't fooled but said, "Look, the antique shop is just around the corner. Let's get there before they close."

Jake enjoyed the walk back to Whitehall Street because Kate had been like a kid in a sweet shop in the antique place. She'd bought an old wooden frame to mount Lizzie's sampler and a brass cameo frame for Theresa and William's wedding photograph.

"Oh, that was wonderful, Jake! The sort of place you just never know what you might find. Next time, let's go not so close to closing time. We have a front parlour to furnish."

Jake turned away so she didn't see the broad smile on his face as she'd included him in her next visit. As they reached the bottom of the street, he asked, "Do you want me to fit this lock for you before I go?"

She clasped her hands together. "Would... would you?" *Were the opened letters still unnerving her?*

He left just after seven but sat in his van for a few minutes before driving off. He'd enjoyed spending more time with her and was glad he'd fitted a new lock on the French doors. Reassured at seeing Howard's curtains drawn, he set off. *He's up to something, but I can't put my finger on it.*

CHAPTER 25

William

Crossing the English Bridge feels like old times. The water from the Welsh mountains still rushes under the stone arches. The shops on Wyle Cop are far more colourful than I remember, and the prices confuse me. Where have the shilling signs gone? And I can't believe how many cars and lorries cross the bridge. The black-and-white buildings still stand along High Street and Mardol, and it's a comfort to see them.

I'm in Hills Lane now and feel sad at how much it's changed. I barely recognise the place apart from the cobbles. The Tudor building at one end is a shop selling gifts and colourful books about Shrewsbury. In the window, I can see plates decorated with the town's coat of arms and even thimbles with the three loggerheads painted on them. Theresa and Lizzie would have loved one of them when they were sewing.

The Gullet Inn has gone. It would have been nice to have popped in for a tankard of ale and see familiar faces. I'm sure the landlord, Charlie Hughes, would be there cracking jokes from behind the bar. That old devil Peddler would be sat in the corner taking bets or orders for scrap metal or rags.

It's lovely to see Kate and Jake in the lane.

The warm red coat Kate is wearing would have suited my Theresa a treat, making a lovely contrast to her dark hair. Jake's eyes are full of warmth and amusement.

"This is the Doyle house," I say, pointing.

They're talking about houses being demolished, and the Doyles' house seems to stand alone. There's a vast space next door and shiny cars regimentally parked up. I scratch my head, wondering why someone has painted white lines on the ground and why all the cars have small tickets displayed in their windows.

Where have the people and houses gone from this side of the lane? I cross over to the other side and gaze through the window of Peddler's house. There are shiny mirrors on the walls and padded chairs in front of each one. I step inside, and a lady is having her hair washed, and shelves are stacked with bottles. It's soap or maybe perfume. In the bedroom upstairs where Peddler's four children slept, there's a couch, clean white towels, and candles that smell very sweet. It's all very odd.

I head back to the Doyles' and gesture to Kate and Jake, but they turn and leave, which is a shame. I don't understand why they don't want to come inside.

It's nice to be back. The house looks the same: two rooms downstairs and two up. Voices and memories circle me. I hear John Doyle declaring his never-ending love and watch as he slips his arm around Mary. Even though the meal on the table is sparse, there's laughter. It's rabbit meat and vegetables swimming in a thin broth. Patrick and James are bolting their food, probably to get back outside to play football. Lizzie checks the younger ones clear their plates and is the first to tidy up and make Ma and Da a cup of tea. And dear, dear little Bridget. Stew trickles out of the corners of her mouth because she's eating and chattering.

"Yes, we always welcomed you with open arms, William. Shared whatever we had."

I turn. "Lizzie?"

Another voice distracts me. A familiar, sweet tone.

"Got summat for me, mon?"

I could never resist her, and I search my pockets for a coin, a penny, or a sixpence.

"Sorry, not today, Bridget." I turn my pockets inside out to show her.

But now she's not the four-year-old with a cheeky grin and big eyes that make everyone's hearts melt. She's a small body curled up and blackened on the floor. I cover my face, not wanting to see.

I remember that day so clearly. Mary sobbing, "She was just dancing." The words repeat over and over in my head.

I don't want to see or hear anymore. I don't want to relive the day little Bridget was taken. Theresa and Lizzie held onto their faith, but not me. No, not me.

Yes, that was the day I closed myself down. What good did praying ever do? God could have taken my father, a violent brute of a man. I look up. "But no, you took our little Bridget."

Going back outside, I gasp, seeing my darling Theresa skipping down the cobbles towards me. The wind balloons her skirt, and her bonnet blows off. I laugh and put out my hands to catch and swing her around. But no, she calls out.

"It's hard for everyone to forgive you."

Like an autumn breeze, she rushes past me and disappears.

I'm back at number 81.

Jake's not here, but Kate's sitting in the parlour. She has her typewriter thing on her lap and is looking at a screen. Lizzie's sampler is beside her, and the letter T is still brighter than any of the other letters.

Kate's writing in a notebook.

"I can tell you what all those initials stand for," I say, looking at the sampler.

She puts on her glasses. "Let's see what I can learn about the Doyles."

I'm not sure what she's looking at, but the screen is lit up, and she picks up her pen and writes:

From the 1891 census:

John Doyle (father), Mary Doyle (mother)

"Oh, and then it gives their children. Elizabeth Doyle was the oldest, then Theresa and Patrick."

I want to leave the room and not see the names she's writing, but it's like an itch that needs to be scratched.

I look over Kate's shoulder. "You're missing Ann, Mary, James, and little Bridget." The words strangely slip from my lips. "Ann and Mary died in infancy from scarlet fever, which was rife in the town."

"Aha," Kate says, and her pen is poised.

> ON THE 1911 CENSUS, JOHN, MARY, AND PATRICK DOYLE ARE THE ONLY ONES LIVING IN HILLS LANE.

She holds her finger on the screen. "Oh no. It says they had seven children, but only three lived by 1911." She picks up the sampler. "So, I'm missing an A, M, J, and a B."

Kate sucks on the end of the pen and then types furiously on her thing. "So, on the 1901 census, those names don't appear... so did they die between the 1891 and 1911 census?"

There are tears in her eyes as she writes:

> JAMES DOYLE DIED AGED NINE, AND ANN AND MARY AGED ONE, AND FINALLY BRIDGET DOYLE AGED FOUR.

Kate looks pleased with herself now she's matched all the initials on Lizzie's sampler. A weight descends on me, and I reach for my Woodbines and light up, hoping a smoke will calm me.

Kate picks up the sampler. "By 1916, Lizzie, when you stitched this, only you and Patrick were still alive."

"Oh yes, dear Patrick. He worked on the railway. I wonder if he ever became an engine driver."

Looking back at her notebook, Kate shakes her head and says, "So, Mary and John lost four of their children."

As she writes, I can feel her sadness.

"*Death spared no family.*" Lizzie is standing by the fireplace, holding her Bible.

The last time I saw those well-turned pages was when Theresa passed.

Mine and Theresa's bedroom appears. It's dimly lit, and a shard of daylight is moving slowly up the bed. I cover my eyes, not wanting to see the face on the pillow.

"*It was just Theresa's time, William.*" Lizzie crosses herself.

"But four of John and Mary Doyle's children never grew up! How can you say it was their time?"

"And you left the three daughters you had, and never saw them grow up."

"My precious son John Rupert didn't reach his second birthday either. He didn't have the chance to grow up. How could you still believe in God, Lizzie?"

She crosses herself again. *"Oh, be quiet, William."*

I turn away.

"Shit. What on earth's the matter with me?" Kate asks, wiping her eyes and distracting me from my thoughts.

"Theresa was like that when she was expecting. Cried at the drop of a hat."

"Poor Lizzie." Kate drops her glasses down from her forehead and types on her thing again. She writes:

Lizzie died in 1935 aged sixty-two.
Never married.

"You never married?" I ask, looking back at Lizzie.

"Ha, I was looking after your daughters. God bless them."

I clutch my arm as it aches, and heat spreads across my chest. I know Lizzie always speaks the truth. Perhaps I was ill like she suggested at the time I left England.

Kate turns back a page in her notebook, but I rip my eyes away. She knows more about me than I thought. What on earth will she think of me now? I look down at my feet, but the names and dates jump from the page and swirl in front of me, urging and teasing me to look.

"So, William," Kate says, "Theresa died, and you went to Canada with someone called Emillie." She looks back at her screen. "Oh, and here we go... There's a marriage record, and you married after being in Canada for a month. Your wife was barely cold, and you left your daughters behind. What an arse you were!"

I cover my ears, not wanting to hear her words.

"And did Lizzie Doyle look after your daughters?" she asks.

Lizzie nods her head. *"Ada never forgave you, William. She needed you. They all did."*

"Typical bloke, leaving all his responsibilities to the womenfolk," says Kate. Her face is tear-stained, and she picks up a cushion and punches it for some reason. "Men! They're all the bloody same. I'll never forgive you, Lionel, and I'm damn sure Dorothy and her sisters never forgave you, William."

I lift my hand to my forehead. "But... but you haven't heard my side of the story."

Lionel, whoever he is, has undoubtedly upset Kate. I wait for her to calm herself, concerned about her constant crying.

"Sure this Lionel chap ain't worth all these tears, Kate," I say as she stares straight at me, still sniffling.

Lizzie throws her hands in the air. "*Ha, you should have seen all the tears you caused, William.*"

"I'm sure Dorothy and her sisters never forgave you." Kate's words repeat over and over in my head. Louder and louder. And a pain shoots down my arm, and I can't help wondering if Kate is stuck in the past, like me. Not just her own, but mine too.

CHAPTER 26

The following day, expecting Aileen to arrive soon, Kate set out a tray of tea and cake. She'd not slept well after all the crying the night before, and she'd ignored Jake's concerned looks as he'd arrived and she switched off from his usual early morning chatter.

She'd thought she was all cried out over Lionel, but it seemed not. Finding out about the Doyles and what happened to Aileen's mother and her sisters had added more tears. She felt drained and hollow somehow and considered making a doctor's appointment. *I just don't feel right.*

For weeks, she hadn't looked at the text Lionel's wife sent but needed to reread it this morning to remind herself of his deception and that he was dead.

> HELLO. THIS IS MONICA, LIONEL ATTWOOD'S WIFE. JUST LETTING HIS WORK CONTACTS KNOW THAT HE SADLY PASSED AWAY AFTER SUFFERING

A HEART ATTACK IN FRANCE LAST WEEK. PLEASE REPLY FOR DETAILS OF THE FUNERAL.

A knock at the door distracted her, and after checking who was there by looking through the living room window, she smiled at seeing it was Aileen. *Glad she's here. It'll stop me from thinking about my problems.*

"Thank you. Nice of you to invite me over," she said, stepping into the hallway.

"Oh, thanks for coming. I hope you didn't mind me texting you quite late last night."

"No, not at all, and what you said all sounds very intriguing."

"Here, let me take your coat," said Kate. "You remember Jake?" She gestured towards him as he stood in the kitchen doorway.

"How's the garden coming along?" Aileen asked.

"Think you'll be pleasantly surprised. Shall I put the kettle on for you, ladies?" he replied, smiling at them both.

Kate bristled slightly at his offer. *Make yourself at home, why don't you?*

"Yes, please, and we'll go to the dining room." She noticed Aileen's eyes were drawn to the names on the wall as they passed by.

"I expect you'll be painting over this," Aileen said, placing her hand on the letters that formed the name Dorothy.

"Well, well... we'll see," stuttered Kate.

"Are you okay?" Aileen asked. "You're looking a bit peaky."

"I've felt off-colour since I moved in here, to be honest." *Please don't ask me anymore.*

"You've found out more about my birth family, I gather?" Aileen followed her into the dining room.

"Yes, that's right."

Jake appeared, carrying a tray of teacups. "Miss Marple has nothing on Kate."

She glared at him. *Hold your horses. Typical man... with no idea how upsetting this might be for Aileen.*

He laid the tray down and then sat beside Kate. "You don't mind if I listen in?"

"Of course not." Aileen settled into the armchair.

After pouring tea and chatting about the weather, Kate opened the tin she'd left on the table. She passed the postcard to Aileen and watched as she examined both sides.

"Who is it?" she asked, holding up the picture side of the card.

"His name's William Tate, and I think... well, I'm pretty sure, Aileen, that he's your grandfather."

"It's amazing what you can find out online these days," Jake added.

Kate knocked his elbow and mouthed, "Sssh."

Aileen sipped her tea. "But where did you find it?"

"It was inside this," Kate replied, lifting the tin. "I found it in the cellar the first day I moved in."

"Been there for donkey's years, I reckon," said Jake.

"He died in 1915?" Aileen put her hand to her mouth. "But how old would Dorothy have been then?"

"She was five," replied Kate. "Her mother died three years earlier."

Tears welled in Aileen's eyes, and she reached for a tissue from her handbag. "I thought I might need these today. Poor Dorothy lost both her parents by the time she was five?"

Kate nodded but passed William and Theresa's small black-and-white wedding photograph to Aileen, hoping that seeing their happy faces would lift her. Instead, a single tear trickled down her cheek.

"My grandmother?" she asked, half smiling at Kate. "I have her dark wavy hair."

"Yes, you do, Aileen. Theresa was a beautiful lady, and they looked very in love," she said, moving her chair closer to Aileen.

Jake took another piece of cake. "I'll leave you two to it."

"Sorry to blubber."

"He doesn't mind," Kate said. "But I'm sorry for making you cry."

"Dorothy had a tough life," Aileen said, dabbing her eyes.

"Show her the needlework thingy," Jake suggested before leaving the room.

"Do you want to see more of what I've found? We can leave it to another day, if you'd prefer?" She placed her hand over Aileen's.

"I'm... I'm just being silly."

"No, not at all," Kate said, unfolding the sampler and placing it on the table.

"Gosh, that's beautiful."

"It's almost a hundred years old and belongs to you. Each initial represents someone on your grandmother's side of the family. I've bought a frame to mount it in."

"That's so kind of you. Is... is the T for Theresa?"

"Yes, it is!"

Aileen smiled. "It's strange how the letter T is still much more vibrant than the others," she said, running her finger over it. "And the name stitched at the bottom? Who was Lizzie Doyle, and is this... Hills Lane in town? Sorry, Kate, I'm babbling, but my head is full of questions."

"It's okay. I looked online at a genealogical website, and Lizzie... Elizabeth was your grandmother's sister, and I think she bought Dorothy and her sisters Ada and Ethel up in this house. The Doyle family lived in Hills Lane in the late 1800s and early 1900s."

Aileen bit her lip and pulled out another tissue. "That's amazing. I've walked down Hills Lane many... many times not knowing." She studied the small photograph again.

Kate noticed a distant look in Aileen's rich, chocolatey eyes. "You look very similar to her," she said, dipping into the tin again. "This is a newspaper cutting. Dorothy isn't mentioned, but Ada is. They attended a church fundraising event in 1916. They all dressed up in Oriental costumes."

"Sounds fun!" said Aileen as she began to read it. "It's written in such nice, polite English, isn't it?"

"It's different from how they write about things in the paper these days."

"Oh, this is such a lot to take in." Aileen reached inside her handbag. "And I wanted to show you these." She pulled out some official-looking papers and gave them to Kate. "These are from my adoption file."

"The horrible letter you said a Catholic priest had written about Dorothy?"

"Yes. According to him, she drank heavily, and my father was a right fly-by-night!"

Kate was relieved to see Aileen say the words with a wry smile.

The typed documents were discoloured and faded in places, and she couldn't help but notice that certain letters jumped above others. *An old typewriter, I expect.*

She read that Aileen's mother, Dorothy, could not give her baby a good life as she was unmarried.

"Dorothy was forty-two when she had you? Not a young unmarried girl as you might have expected," said Kate, looking up.

Aileen nodded.

Kate read the statement that a Father Kelly had written in 1952.

> Miss Dorothy Tate is an unmarried woman about to give birth. Adoption must be made through the Catholic Children's Society in the child's best interest. The shame Dorothy has brought on her family is regretful. In time though, she will realise this is the best course of action and soon get over it.

"Good God. She'll soon get over it?" Kate shook her head at the words.

> Miss Tate is a barmaid at the Malt Shovel in the town and rents a small room upstairs. This is not the sort of place to raise a child. In the doctor's opinion, Dorothy drinks too much and will not live many more years.

"Do you know when Dorothy died?" Aileen asked.

"I do." Kate checked in her notebook. "She died in 1954."

"Just two years after I was born?"

Kate fought her tears as Aileen's face crumpled again. She looked out over the garden for a moment before reading again.

> A Mr Sean Madden, known locally as Mad Madden, is reportedly the baby's father. He, unfortunately, is a young man with a questionable character. He is currently under suspicion for several thefts in the town and of being involved in a recent brawl in the Kings Head.

She gave in to her tears, and Aileen reached over with her hand as Kate said, "Poor Dorothy... she'd lost both parents by the time she was five, pregnant at forty-two, and then her baby was taken away by the Church."

"Lord, don't you get upset too. Having the nickname Mad Madden doesn't conjure up the picture of an upright citizen or a good father, does it?" said Aileen, half laughing.

"Mad Madden," Kate mouthed, her eyes meeting Aileen's and then drifting out into the garden where Jake was digging a hole to position the metal archway along the path. *That's Jake's surname... Wasn't that the name Jake gave his father?*

"You okay?" asked Aileen.

"Sorry... sorry. What were we saying?"

A cheeky smile spread across Aileen's face. "You like him, don't you?"

"Who? Jake? No... no, of course not. I barely know him, and anyway, I've given up on men."

"That's sad. You're still young!"

Kate laughed. "I'm menopausal! And just so damn tired all the time. And Lionel was the last straw."

"Lionel?"

"I won't bore you with the details."

"Jake seems like a nice chap, Kate. I never had much luck with men. Probably in the genes, I expect."

They both laughed.

"Jake's cheeky smile charms everyone. Even us older women. But he's probably as unreliable as the rest of them. Gosh, Aileen, I sound a right bitter old cow." Not wanting to get on the subject of Lionel, Kate asked, "I wonder why Dorothy's sisters didn't help?"

"They had families of their own by then. Perhaps times were just hard? Have you discovered anything else about William, my grandfather?" Aileen stared at his picture.

"After Theresa died in 1912, he appears on a ship's passenger list heading for Canada, and soon after his arrival there, he remarried. Someone called Emillie Rogers."

"What? Well, he didn't hang around! He left his daughters?"

"Seems so. Your grandfather has a lot to answer for."

"And you think Dorothy and her sisters stayed with Aunt Lizzie?"

"I assume that was the case. I can't check on the 1921 census as it still needs to be put online. They're only published after a hundred years have passed."

"But Dorothy's name is written on the wall here, and it sounds like they went to this church fundraiser in 1916," Aileen said, picking up the newspaper cutting.

"William died in 1915, and they received this postcard," added Kate. "Sending mourning cards was a thing back then."

"What about the sampler? Wonder why Lizzie stitched it?"

"In memory of her family, maybe?" Kate passed her notebook to Aileen to show her the names of the Doyle family. "Some died at a very young age."

"In those days, I suppose a lot of children died in infancy."

Kate stood. "I think it's time for some more tea, Aileen."

William

I'm in the dining room, and there's a woman here with Kate. I'm listening very carefully to what they're saying and trying to block out the voices in my head.

Seeing Aileen is like seeing Mary Doyle, Theresa, or my daughters. It's not just her hair but her eyes and voice.

They're saying I'm Aileen's grandfather, and I'm struggling to take this in. But Aileen does have the Doyle hair.

But I hear that Aileen was adopted. Kate reads aloud what some flamin' Catholic priest wrote about my little Dorothy.

I look up. "Ha, do you see? Catholic priests were never holier than holy."

I'm sad to hear that Dorothy turned to drink. Who the hell was this damned Sean Madden? If I ever get hold of him... well, I'll give him what for.

"But you're not violent, William."

My shoulders sag. "Lizzie, I hit Emillie."

"You know that she didn't post most of your letters."

"The money orders? How do you know?"

"God is all-knowing."

And my sweet little Dorothy died soon after Aileen was born. Why didn't Ada and Ethel help her?

"Time moves on, William. They had their children. Ada had grandchildren. Times were hard, and another war had not long ended."

"Goodness me, another war?"

Kate is telling Aileen how I boarded a ship soon after Theresa died. They both know about Emillie. I can see the tears in Aileen's eyes as she hears about it.

"Show her the letter that Charles wrote," I suggest. My granddaughter might not think so poorly of me. "I didn't know Emillie wasn't sending the money every week."

What more can I say in my defence? Theresa was always the strong one. Girls always need their mothers. I was weak. Perhaps I was ill?

"You always wanted me to see a doctor, Lizzie," I say, looking around the room for her.

"You wouldn't listen to anyone but Emillie." Lizzie is standing by the French doors with her arms folded and waiting for an explanation. My explanation.

"I was a fool. I didn't know how to care for three daughters. Emillie led me on. I couldn't carry on without my beloved Theresa."

Lizzie has gone.

"What do you want me to say?" I call after her.

CHAPTER 27

It was almost five o'clock before Aileen left, and as Kate hugged her, a sense of satisfaction descended; the items she'd found were now with their rightful owner. The day had been delightful, and the sadness about Dorothy's life was eventually replaced with their laughter at getting to know each other. Although Kate was younger than Aileen, they had bonded over their love of travel and the Great British Bake Off.

Aileen spoke about caring for her late parents and her job at the bank but didn't ask too many questions when Kate finally explained about Lionel. She felt she'd at least made one friend in Shrewsbury now, and they'd arranged to go out for dinner the following week.

Kate swung open the French doors to catch the last of the late autumn sun. After pouring herself a glass of wine, she sank into her comfy armchair and smiled.

Jake had left early and had been vague about why, but she'd guessed it might have been something to do with his house sale. She'd wanted to ask but had held her tongue. She didn't think he'd be around much longer with only the turf to lay and some bulbs to plant. The winter was coming, so he'd advised waiting for the spring before purchasing the other plants they'd discussed. She hadn't decided what job to do next in the house and felt a few quiet days would do her good. *I'm going to miss his company.*

She hadn't said anything to Aileen or Jake about the name Mad Madden, but it gnawed at her as she sat thinking and admiring the garden. The fencing was up, the metal archway in place, and the gate at the end just needed a bolt on the inside. The flower beds were all marked out, and she was amazed at how different it all looked.

So, was Madden a common name? Could there have been more than one good-for-nothing Mad Madden in the town? She reached for her laptop and an airmail letter floated to the floor. *Damn, I forgot to show Aileen Charles' letter. I don't want her thinking her grandfather William was all bad. Charles and his work colleagues liked him.*

She placed the letter back on the table and wondered how it ever ended up hidden and unopened, along with all of Betty's letters inside the secret compartment. Putting her wine glass down, she turned on her laptop. She typed Sean Madden into a genealogical website and thought about Aileen and Jake. Aileen was born in 1952, but how old was Jake? Mid-thirties? Maybe he was born in about 1975. There was quite an age gap. What year might Sean Madden have been born?

The 1911 census was the latest online, but she noticed a 1939 record available at the onset of the war to supply national identity cards and ration books. There was no record of a Sean Madden living in Shrewsbury, but several other Maddens. A common surname in the town, perhaps.

A link at the top of the page caught her eye, and she smiled. The website offered DNA tests, but how could she ever persuade Aileen and Jake to take a test without them thinking she was crazy? But knowing the coincidence of the name would eat away at her, she pressed the "buy" button and looked up from her screen. Something in the metal basket of the fireplace caught her eye, but as she was about to take a closer look, she spotted Howard walking along the path at the back of the terrace.

On spotting him, she held her breath, eased herself off her chair, placed her laptop on the floor, and stepped towards her door. Just as her hand landed on the door handle to pull it shut, she glanced up to see him standing just outside. *Shit, what does he want now?*

"Oh, enjoying a glass of wine, are we?" he bellowed. His cheeks were purple and, as usual, a cigarette hung from his right hand, but he had dressed smartly.

"Howard, you made me jump," she said, stepping outside, hoping to stop him from crossing her threshold. "Did you want something? I'm rather busy at the moment."

"You did say to pop around anytime."

No, I didn't.

"And looks like I've timed it just right," he said, gesturing through the half-opened door towards the wine bottle. He stubbed out his cigarette on the house wall, flicked it past her straight into the basket in the fireplace, and came inside.

Shit. Shit. She coughed as his cheap aftershave wafted over her.

"Garden's coming along, I see." He pulled out a dining chair for himself. "Expect he's charging you a fortune."

"Jake's hourly rate is reasonable, and I expect him back here any minute."

"Who was the dark-haired lady that was here today?"

You don't miss a thing, do you?

"Her family used to live in this house." *Not that it's got anything to do with you.*

"I can tell her plenty about this house," he said, taking the half-full glass of wine she'd poured for him. "Betty said she'd leave it to me."

Kate remained standing, but her eyes were drawn to the fireplace and the two cigarette butts. She picked up her phone and clicked on her contacts.

"I was good to Betty. Looked after her, if you know what I mean."

Kate stared at her phone, not acknowledging what he was saying.

"This house was left to me as a home for my three daughters."

"But I bought it at auction. The owner was a Mr—"

"Yeah, some flaming bloke from abroad got it. He said he was Betty's nephew. But he was a bloody con artist, that's for sure."

She perched on her armchair and texted Jake. "Well, I'm sorry about that, but my house purchase was perfectly legal," she said, looking up.

Howard's face had reddened more, and beads of sweat had formed on his forehead.

"The house wasn't Mr Harris' to sell," he yelled, moving forward on his seat. "Betty, like all fucking women, lied to me."

"No need to swear, Howard. I suppose family always comes first." She stood again and stepped from side to side. "I'd like you to leave now."

"Families, eh? You can't pick 'em. Mine don't even want to know me. But if I settled down. Nice house, a good woman." He looked her up and down.

"Sorry, but it's nothing to do with me. I'd like you to go." Kate tried to ignore the heat radiating to her face and the sweat trickling down her back.

Howard remained seated but held up his emptied glass towards her. "Top it up, love."

She tapped the "send" button on her phone again before taking his empty glass and glaring at him in disbelief. As she passed it back with only a tiny amount of wine, he lifted it and stared as if he was about to make some sarcastic comment. Instead, his eyes met hers, and he shook his head at her.

"Finish that and leave, Howard." She clutched her phone to her side, willing Jake to ring.

"Somewhere in this house, there's a more up-to-date will."

"Look, it's getting late, Howard, and I've got things to do." *Come on, Jake.*

Relief swept over her as Howard stood up and placed his glass on the table. "I searched everywhere," he said, waving his arms. "I searched in every flaming room and inside this bloody bureau several times." He moved towards it and opened the drop-down desk. "And you come along and find some fucking letters in here. Letters I'd have destroyed, given the chance."

"Stop swearing, and if you don't go right now, I'll call the police."

He turned away from the bureau to face her, his eyes scouring the room. "All the letters from that flaming nephew were in there all the time." He wiped his forehead with the back of his hand.

She took a step backwards.

"Kate, my dear, just tell me where you've put the will," he whined. "Just hand it over, then we can be good friends."

"There... there wasn't anything else in the bureau apart from letters. But I'll speak to my solicitor in the morning."

"I've already written to Mr Harris, the so-called nephew, but he hasn't bloody well bothered to reply. Surprise, surprise."

"How... how did you know where he lived?" As the question left her lips, the answer hit her. She glanced at the two cigarette butts again and then back at her phone.

"I got his address when I saw all his letters in the bur—" The realisation of what he'd said spread over Howard's face.

"It was you who broke in?" She tapped "call" on her phone.

"Look, we're neighbours. We shouldn't be falling out over a missing will." He knocked the phone out of her hands. "We don't need to call anyone, do we, Kate?" he said, winking at her before lifting his hand as if about to stroke her face.

She brushed his hand away.

"You have an expensive silk blouse in your wardrobe. Why not put it on, and we could go into town? Have a nice meal... and more to drink."

"What? You've... you've been upstairs in my wardrobe?" *Oh my God.*

She circled behind him and pointed to the door with her back to the fireplace. "Get out! Get out!" she shouted with her hands tightened into fists.

He turned slowly and stepped towards the door but swerved, and two enormous hands landed heavily, digging into her shoulders. She wanted to scream, but her mouth was dry. Using both hands, she tried to dislodge his grip.

"Please, Howard... let me go. We can sort this out."

"Yes, I think we can, and after all, what do you need with a three-bed house?"

He released his hold, and she exhaled. Her heart hammered against her ribcage as she said, "Yes, let's sort it out tomorrow."

"We could both be happy living here," he said, holding her gaze.

Are you nuts? She turned towards the French doors. *If I can get outside, someone might hear me shout.*

But his hand landed on her left shoulder, forcing her to face him again.

Shit. Humour him.

"Yes, this is a beautiful house. I... I'm certain your daughters would love living here."

It was just a gentle shove at first, almost playful. But with each step forwards, his sickly grin widened.

"Howard, please." She lost grip of one of her shoes, and he kicked it aside and shoved her again.

"But I reckon you're more into that Jake bloke." He shoved again.

Howard's sweaty face and yellowing teeth were inches away, and he reeked of cigarettes. His towering frame bore down, and she clasped her hands over her head. Every muscle in her body tightened; she couldn't speak or swallow. Black dots danced in front of her eyes. She cowered and, finally, blackness.

CHAPTER 28

William

I can't believe it. Howard is leaving. He picks up his glass and the half-empty wine bottle, closes the door behind him, and doesn't look back.

"For Christ's sake, Howard," I call after him, "You can't leave Kate just lying here."

Her head rests awkwardly on the hearth, and a cut at the side of her head is oozing blood, which contrasts starkly with the cold white marble hearth. One shoe lies on the far side of the dining room where that animal, Howard, kicked it, but the other still clings to Kate's twisted ankle.

Poor Kate. I could do nothing to protect her from his cruel words or the pushing and shoving. She looked so vulnerable, cowering just like my mother used to do.

"You're gonna be all right, lass," I say as I sit beside her.

Her eyes are closed, but not tightly, and occasionally flicker. She's pale, but I know she's not dead because I've seen plenty of that. Her hands and feet aren't mottled, and there's no sign of a yellowing, death-like pallor.

One of her arms lies protectively across her abdomen.

"Keep safe, little one," I whisper and put my hand over Kate's.

Concerned she might be cold, I take off my jacket and place it over her. It's a thick tweed, so it'll hopefully keep her warm. Her blouse has slipped, and I wish I could cover her shoulders and give her some dignity. I wince at the purple marks appearing there now—finger marks from that bastard, Howard.

"Excuse my language, Kate."

It pains me that I could no more protect Kate than I could my beloved mother.

Father was the same. With him, a punch to the stomach or a swiping slap across Mother's sweet but defeated face was always the final blow. But with Howard, it was that one last shove. Did he intend to hurt Kate? Did he expect or want her to fall and crack her head on the hearth?

But no matter, he's left her lying here bleeding, and that's unforgivable.

I urged her to scream or shout because the neighbours might have heard. But it was like words or screams stuck in her throat. The colour drained from her face, and I saw the disbelief and fear in her eyes. She couldn't understand what was happening, what Howard was saying and implying.

It shocked me too. Did Howard think Kate would hand over this house? Her house? That she'd let him live here too? Did he imagine she liked him, romantically? She's done nothing to encourage that, I'm sure.

Kate bought the house fair and square. And goodness knows how much it cost! She must be far better off than ever I was, yet she has no man to support her. Things are just different.

It's not Kate's fault that Howard lost his wife and three daughters because he drinks far too much, making him irrational. Violent? Alcohol is his easy way out.

"Yes, William, what sort of man takes the easy way out?"

I throw my hands in the air and recall how badly Kate and Aileen thought of me. They knew I'd walked out on my family and passed all my responsibilities onto Lizzie. She cared for and guided my girls.

"*Yes, any decent father would protect his children.*"

"And then I married Emillie so soon after—"

"*It was all so quick, William... so rushed.*"

"Hope you don't mind, Kate, but I need a cigarette." I light up a Woodbine, hoping to dispel the voice in my head.

Smoking always helps when I feel... How do I feel right now? Did I take the easy way out of my situation just like Howard's doing now?

"*You avoided the situation.*"

"I know, Lizzie... I know."

It's pitch-black outside, and I wonder if Kate can hear me. "If I talk, it might help us pass the night a little quicker." I move a little closer to her, still worried she might be cold.

"I first saw Theresa running towards the Gullet Inn. When I saw you skip up the path to the house, you reminded me of her. She was always skipping or running up Hills Lane to meet me. I loved her the moment I saw her. Dark curls framed her face, and her eyes... well, they were dark velvety pools."

I smile and picture Theresa whilst blowing my cigarette smoke away from Kate.

"She'd come to the Gullet to tell her two brothers, who were playing just outside, that their dinner was on the table. Then, one evening, I allowed her to go before me as she entered the inn. She was looking for her father."

Kate's eyes flicker, and I wish the sunrise would hurry up. But I carry on talking to Kate.

"Back then, women were the backbone of most families, and the Doyle women were the same... straight-talking with a talent for making their menfolk feel they were in charge. But no, the women controlled most things, including their husbands' pay packets. I handed mine over to Theresa every Friday without fail."

I chuckle and remember how I always took a few coins out before I got home. Theresa probably realised, but she wasn't one for moaning about her man having a drink or two.

"So, Kate, where was I? Yes, John Doyle sprung from his seat whenever he saw Theresa enter. He wouldn't have wanted the grief from his wife if he was late for his dinner. Mary Doyle was always fussy about her family being around the table together."

The wind outside rattles the French doors, and I wish Kate wasn't so close to the fireplace; there's a hell of a draft coming down the chimney. I move my jacket slightly higher, still worried she's getting cold.

"I'd seen John Doyle in the Gullet before, and I made a point of striking up a conversation with him the night after I first saw her. I found out her name... and that she was unmarried. I hung around the lane for hours, hoping to see and bump into her again. She was coy. A smile sometimes... and some days, she'd ignore me completely. She'd turn many a man's head when she came into the Gullet looking for her da. I was lucky to win her affection. Yes, very lucky indeed."

I nod thoughtfully.

"Theresa was the strong one, you see, Kate. Theresa had her Catholic faith."

Kate's eyes open for a moment before fluttering closed again.

"Someone will be here soon," I say, trying to reassure her. "The Doyles welcomed me with open arms. They asked no questions. Why was I renting a small room in Bridge Street when my parents lived in a big house? Or why didn't any of my family come to the wedding?"

I sigh and can see all the Doyles in my head. John and Mary teasing, sometimes bickering, but always with love in their eyes. Patrick kicking a ball and his determination to drive a train one day. James and little Bridget full of fun and mischief. Lizzie and Theresa... the image of their mother, with the same flowing hair and inner strength to keep going.

I stub out my Woodbine, seeing Kate's eyes flicker again.

"We lost our little Bridget. It was terrible, but this isn't the time or place for that now when I'm keeping you company. Theresa was carrying our Ada at the time, a few months gone. I won't give you the details, Kate, but this wasn't long after the wedding. I don't want you to think even worse of me... but we were in love. I'm sorry, so sorry. I'm weak. Very, very weak."

"Finally, you've said it."

"Theresa and Lizzie were strong. Even Ada had more strength and fire than me. I walked away and lost everything I'd ever loved. And I've paid for it. I'm still paying for it. I suppose that's why I'm here... still here. Oh, Kate, wait a second. There's a torchlight moving quickly up the garden path. The sun hasn't risen yet, but someone is here. Yes, yes, my dear, you'll be all right. Jake's here. He's a good man, and he'll help you now."

CHAPTER 29

Aileen cursed as she tried to defrost her windscreen and get going. Her phone ringing at five had woken her with a jolt and left her with a muzzy head. She'd been surprised the call was from Kate's phone, but it was Jake's concerned and gabbling voice at the other end.

It was still dark as she pulled outside number 81 and spotted him in the front room window. He opened the front door as she hurried up the path. His usual broad smile and cheeky eyes were gone, and he looked pale and tired.

"Thank you for coming, Aileen. I wasn't sure who else to ring. I'm not sure Kate knows anyone else."

"What on earth has happened?" she asked, stepping inside.

"I found her this morning at about three thirty. Just lying... just lying on the floor in there," Jake said, gesturing towards the dining room.

She followed him inside, and as she entered the room, her eyes honed in on the dried blood on the hearth.

A young policewoman stood in one corner and looked up from her notebook. "I'll be on my way, Mr Madden, now your friend is here, and I'll be in touch."

Jake nodded as she left, but his eyes remained fixed on the fireplace. "Sorry to have called you so early, Aileen. Kate had no security code to access her phone, so the police let me call. You were the only person I could think of."

"No, I'm glad you called. Kate has been so kind to me, so the least I can do is help her now. She'd banged her head, you say. Was she conscious when you found her?"

"Barely." Jake stood in the middle of the room, wringing his hands and staring at the bloodstain again.

"I'll fetch a bowl of boiling water and wash that down," Aileen said. "I assume the police have finished?"

He nodded and sank into the armchair. "Yes, they were here soon after the ambulance set off. I had to give a statement..."

Aileen watched as he seemed to lose his train of thought.

"I threw my coat over her and held... held her hand. She looked so fragile, vulnerable somehow."

"I'm sure you did all you could. How come you were here so early?"

Jake stood again and threw open the French doors. The chilly morning air rushed in and made Aileen shiver and fold her arms across herself.

"It must have been a shock finding her like that."

He breathed in deeply several times and stretched his arms up in the air. "The paramedics were here damn quick. They bandaged her head and put on one of those neck brace things and a line into her hand. I hope she'll be okay."

"Why not sit down again? I'll make us some tea. You're exhausted, and you've had a shock."

He closed the doors and sighed. "I shouldn't have turned my phone off last night. It's all my fault."

"I can't see how any of this can be your fault. Kate tripped or fainted, I expect."

"But she texted me that Howard was here again. She texted me three times and tried calling me. I showed the policewoman all my texts because I'm damn sure he had something to do with this."

"Who's Howard?"

Jake flung his hand forwards. "You know, the bloke that lives opposite. He's a right... a right slimy git."

"Sorry, Jake, I haven't met—"

"If he's hurt her, I'll bloody well flatten him."

"Calm down, Jake. She'll be okay."

He stared out over the garden. "He's called on her a few times uninvited. Bought her flowers the day she moved in and was narked that I was clearing the garden for her." He held his head in his hands. "My ex kept calling and texting me last night, and I didn't want to speak to her because—"

Aileen studied his face while waiting for him to continue. "Because what?" *Do you care about Kate?*

"She was ranting about wanting us to get back together. I always keep my phone on. But I switched it off. I was so confused and couldn't find the words to tell her that—"

"You must have switched it on again though?"

"I was restless, tossing and turning all night and just thinking. I put it back on at about 3 a.m. and couldn't believe it when I saw Kate had... I just knew I had to get here damn quick."

Aileen drew up a dining chair and sat opposite him. "Because you care about her?"

His eyes widened and held her gaze, but he didn't answer her question. "There was bruising on her shoulders. Her blouse was skew-whiff, and I just wondered if Howard or someone had—"

She reached out for his hands. "Oh no, how awful, but the police will sort it out."

He glanced away and pointed to the other side of the room. "And one of her shoes was over there." He ran his fingers through his hair.

"What? What is it?" she asked.

"The French doors were unlocked when I arrived."

"Maybe she didn't have a chance to lock them before she fell or passed out. She told me she hadn't felt well since she moved in here."

He raised his eyebrows. "Or someone caused her to fall. I think she would have locked them. I've only just put a new lock on for her after—"

"After what?"

"I've told the police all about it. One morning, Kate found the letters addressed to the lady living here before scattered all over the floor." He shook his head, and Aileen sensed he remembered something. "It's stupid. Your grandfather's postcard strangely ended up in the fire basket and the needlework under the table. Kate swore she'd left them inside the tin and the letters inside the bureau."

"That's very odd. Did she ring the police?"

"We blamed the ghost of William. We laughed so much about it." He paused. "I even made 'wooo' noises and tapped her on the shoulder to make her jump. She punched me in the arm."

Aileen was surprised to see his eyes fill.

"She reported it, but the police just gave her a crime number and didn't come here."

"She'll be fine," replied Aileen, tapping his hand reassuringly.

"We laughed about what she'd say to the police. Nothing missing, no forced entry, and a ghost as the prime suspect."

Aileen noticed his smile and eyes brightening as he talked about Kate. "Why don't I make some tea, and we'll ring the hospital in an hour or two."

Aileen walked into the hallway and retrieved a small package that had clattered through the letterbox. She examined the label. "Kate must have sent for something from the genealogical website."

"She seems to enjoy being a detective," said Jake, standing in the doorway.

"There's another handwritten letter too. Who writes letters these days?" she asked, holding it up to show Jake.

"What is it with this house and bloody letters?" he replied.

CHAPTER 30

"Kate, can you lift both arms for me?"

She had no idea why the young doctor was asking, but she obliged him. He gave her a thumbs up as if satisfied and then leant forwards and shone a piercingly bright light into each eye.

"Your pupils are fine. Is the pain relief sufficient for you?"

Kate nodded obediently. She was still struggling with the news she'd received from the doctors earlier. On the brighter side though, her skull fracture was linear, and the pain, with luck, would only last three or four weeks. The bruises around her shoulders would fade, and the cut at the side of her head was stitched. She couldn't remember that being done or being anywhere near a CT scanner. It was the additional diagnosis that had floored her.

A uniformed police officer walking into the six-bed hospital bay pushed her thoughts aside. The doctor stepped back and gestured towards the chair beside Kate's bed.

Sitting down, the policewoman cocked her head and gave Kate a sickly smile. "I wonder if I might ask you some questions about last night? That's if you think you're up to it?"

Kate nodded again. She felt she was doing a lot of nodding because the extra diagnosis had filled her head, and now, even forming words seemed complicated.

"I'm PC Eleanor Heath," she said, and Kate watched as the young, dark-haired constable took a notebook from her pocket. "So, you've sustained some serious injuries. Do you know how you came to fall and hit your head?"

Kate paused for a moment. *She's going to think I'm nuts, but here goes.* "It's all hazy, but two men were in the house."

"Two? Were you having a drink with them?"

"Was I?" Kate stared straight ahead.

"Can you describe them?"

"One was a sweet elderly gentleman."

"Older, you say. Roughly what age?"

Kate looked at the PC, who poised her pen above her notebook. "Well, that's the thing. Hard to tell. He wore one of those shirts, the type men used to wear years ago. It had a detachable collar."

The PC pursed her lips.

She has no idea what I'm talking about because she looks about eleven. "Sorry, before your time, I expect. He wore a brown tweed suit that was quite worn and looked too big for him." Kate could see the doubt in the young woman's eyes. "He smelt of smoke a bit and had a crumpled packet of Woodbines in the top pocket of his jacket." *How am I suddenly remembering all this?*

"Woodbine? And did he hurt you, Kate?"

"They're a cigarette brand and, no, not at all. He sat beside me and said I'd be all right. He talked to me for ages about his life and his regrets. He was very kind to me."

"But when..." She checked her notebook, "A Mr Jake Madden found you, he said you were alone."

"Jake found me?"

"That's right, and he called the ambulance. So, this older gentleman must have left by then."

"But the gentleman was—" The name was on the tip of her tongue, but she couldn't form the name for some reason.

"What about the other man, Kate? Can you remember anything about him?"

"Erm..."

"We found some fingerprints on the French doors in your dining room."

"You did? But that was—Yes, Howard. Yes, Howard came round, and we had some wine."

"Would that be Howard Vaughan? He lives in the building opposite you, I believe?"

"Yes, that's right... But he didn't... It's all a bit of a blur, I'm afraid."

PC Heath stood up. "That'll be all we need at the moment, Kate."

"But... but I can't remember when Howard left." Kate's eyes blurred, and she was aware of her heart pounding.

"Best you leave now," a nurse suggested to the policewoman. She checked the drip beside Kate's bed. "It's okay. The concussion will affect your memory, and you need to relax." She passed a tissue to Kate. "By the way, your partner Jake and friend Aileen called the ward asking after you."

"My what?"

"Jake, your partner. Isn't he the father of your—" She stopped mid-sentence after noticing everyone in the hospital bay staring over at them.

"What on earth am I going to do?"

The nurse pulled the curtains around the bed and sat beside Kate.

"I'm hav... having a baby," she cried. "But... But I thought it was the menopause."

"But, Kate, lots of women have babies in their forties these days."

A thought popped into Kate's head. *Yes, Dorothy did.*

She rested her head back on her pillow and closed her eyes, willing herself to sleep. If she napped, she wouldn't think or remember. Sleep came quickly, and her dreams were not full of Lionel's face but full of the kind old gentleman who'd chatted to her. She woke up with a start and still couldn't quite place him. *It'll come to me, I'm sure.*

"I'm having a baby," she mouthed. It helped to say it, even if she was the only one to hear. The doctor told her they'd not realised she was pregnant when they'd done the head scan, and Kate had voiced her concerns about the quantity of wine she'd been drinking lately. She'd laughed nervously and far too loudly as the doctor made a cheeky comment about her being a geriatric mother. However, he'd reassured her that the risks were low, and they would monitor her from here on to be on the safe side.

Thoughts of Lionel invaded her mind, so she rested her head back again. He'd have been shocked at the prospect of being a father again in his fifties. But she had an overwhelming sense of relief too. Not because he was dead; she'd never have wished that. But because she'd found out he was married before finding out she was pregnant. *I wonder whether he'd ever have come clean and told me.* She smiled, placed a hand over her abdomen, and wished her parents were still around to see their grandchild. *Your life has taken an unexpected turn now, girl!*

Seeing Jake and Aileen entering the ward, even though it wasn't visiting time, made her smile.

"You look much better than the last time I saw you," Jake said, pulling up two chairs. "We've bought you a few things from home. The hospital said we could bring them in and stay for fifteen minutes."

"How are you, dear?" asked Aileen as she sat and slid her hand gently over Kate's.

"I'm bruised around my neck and shoulders." *Maybe that's why I had to lift my arms earlier.* "And I'm a little concussed, and my ankle is twisted. I'm on painkillers and dehydrated," she said, looking up at the drip beside her bed. "And there are stitches in the side of my head, but apart from that, I'm fine!"

She could see the concern on both their faces, and she knew her words didn't portray how uncomfortable and confused she felt.

"But they did say I could go home in a month or so. They want to keep an eye on my skull fracture and my blood pressure."

"We can take care of you when you're discharged," Jake said with his face reddening a little.

She ignored what he said. "Thank you for the bag. It'll be nice to put on my PJs and have my toiletries. By the way, Jake, when did you become my partner?"

Aileen stifled a laugh, but his face reddened even more.

"Oh, sorry about that. We'd never have found out how you—"

"It's okay. I'm teasing you. Anyway, when I tell you my news, you'll be glad you're not my partner."

They both sat open-mouthed as she announced she was four months pregnant.

"I don't know what to say." Jake shuffled in his chair.

"I do! That's wonderful news. Congratulations," said Aileen, squeezing Kate's hand. "How do you feel about it?"

Kate shook her head. "Shocked. Very, very shocked. I thought I was menopausal. But I haven't felt well since I moved into number 81. A bit nauseous and so damn tired."

Jake nodded. "All makes sense now. It wasn't always the wine then."

Aileen glared at him. "I'll help you, Kate. That's if you'd like me to."

Kate smiled. "Yes, Aileen, I'd like that. I don't know anyone or have any fam—"

"Have the police spoken to you?" Jake asked.

"Erm, yes, but I'm not sure I was much help. Everything is such a blur."

She noticed Aileen shaking her head at Jake. "You need to rest and not worry about all that."

He mouthed "sorry" at Aileen as she retrieved a letter from her handbag and passed it to Kate. "We thought this might be important as it's handwritten."

Who on earth could that be from?

"A package arrived too from one of your genealogy sites, but I'm sure that'll keep," Aileen continued.

"Oh, I'd forgotten about that." Kate let the letter slip from her fingers.

"More research?" Jake asked.

"You must rest when you get home," said Aileen. "You've been so kind to me, but I'm sure there's nothing more to find out about my family."

Kate looked at Aileen and then at Jake. *There's something about their eyes, or is it their chins?*

"Look, the truth is the website had an offer on DNA tests, two for the price of one, so I placed an order. Thought it might be fun."

"Not much wrong with your memory, if you can remember ordering," said Jake.

"Yes, yes, it was just before... just before..." Kate sighed as she lost her train of thought. "Aileen, I never showed you the letter from William's friend Charles. I realised just before... Well, you must read it when you get back. I don't want you thinking he was all bad."

"Don't worry about it all now," said Aileen.

She looked towards Jake's arm and then back at Aileen. "Are you both returning to my house after you leave here?"

Jake nodded. "I'll check everything's locked and secure, so don't worry."

"Look, why don't you two spit in the test tubes? I've had enough testing and prodding today to last me a lifetime."

"I'm not sure I want to know more about my genes. I told you what an arsehole my father was," he said.

"You've turned out all right. You're quite nice at times," she replied, reaching out and touching his arm.

He looked up and smiled and covered her hand with his. "You're not too bad yourself."

They held each other's gaze, only looking away at hearing Aileen give a slight cough.

Kate dropped her hand back onto the bed, and he placed his hand just inches away. She fought the urge to touch him again. *Don't be daft. You're pregnant with someone else's baby! As if he'd be interested in you.*

"Is that the only tattoo you have, Jake?" Aileen asked, pointing to his arm.

He nodded.

"It'll be a laugh doing a DNA test," she added, winking at Kate.

Does she know what the letters spell on Jake's arm?

"We can see if you have any foreign blood, Jake," Kate said, winking back at Aileen.

"Some Italian might be nice. I tan very easily and am very smooth and sophisticated." He ran his fingers through his hair, and they all laughed.

"You're more likely to be Irish with a surname like Madden," Kate said, looking at Aileen.

"May the leprechauns dance over your bed and bring you sweet dreams," he announced.

They laughed again.

"I have bruises. Don't make me laugh anymore."

Jake looked at Kate, then at Aileen. "I have absolutely no idea how those words came out of my mouth."

A nurse at the other end of the ward checked her watch and raised her eyebrows at their laughter. They hurriedly said goodbye, and Kate waved one last time before they disappeared out of the ward.

After opening the letter, she read and reread the words, and her eyes welled. She clasped it to her chest as she finished. *I can't believe it.*

"No. No more tears," said a bubbly, young nurse as she approached the bed. "You'll be going home in a few weeks."

Kate held up the letter.

"Not bad news I hope," said the nurse, swinging the table over Kate's bed, ready to place down an evening meal.

"A few happy tears mixed in with some sadness."

"I'll let you off. Pregnancy hormones can play havoc," she said, placing a roast chicken dinner down.

As she ate, Kate placed the letter beside her plate to enjoy the best parts again.

> My name is Hannah Attwood. My late father gave me your address, but they told me you had moved when I called on the owners. I badgered them for your forwarding address. I hope you don't mind.

Kate ate and sipped water. The chicken was dry, and the vegetables overcooked for her liking. But she tried to wash down as much as she could.

Luckily, I had a long conversation with my
father two days before he died. We laughed
so much, and he told me something important. He told me about his love for you.

Kate looked up, struggling to picture Lionel's face. She'd almost swept those loving grey-blue eyes from her mind. But now, she longed to see them again.

He was a good and loving father, and his
news came as no great shock to me.

Since my early teenage years, I knew my
parents' marriage was... Well, let's say not
very happy. Dad travelled all over with his
work, and my 'Uncle Jim' moved in when he
was away.

Kate sighed. "Oh, Lionel, my love, why didn't you tell me the truth?"

The lady in the bed opposite looked up from her meal and held Kate's eyes. *Shit, I said that out loud.*

Her eyes welled again as she read on.

THE VILE MAN MOVED IN PERMANENTLY TWO DAYS
AFTER DAD'S FUNERAL. MY SO-CALLED MOTHER
CARTED MOST OF DAD'S BELONGINGS OFF TO THE
CHARITY SHOP OR THE COUNCIL TIP, BUT I SAL-
VAGED A FEW KEEPSAKES, WHICH I WILL TREASURE.

"Hey, what have I said about crying?" The young nurse stood with her hands on her hips. "Come on now, Kate. There's sticky toffee pudding and custard for afters."

Half crying and laughing, Kate pushed her half-eaten chicken meal away and reached for the pudding.

HE CONFESSED TO ME HE DIDN'T TELL YOU HE WAS
MARRIED. I NOW REGRET SCOLDING HIM SO MUCH
FOR THAT. NOT REALISING THAT WOULD SADLY
BE THE LAST TIME I WOULD EVER SPEAK TO HIM. I
THINK AS TIME PASSED, IT BECAME MORE AWKWARD
FOR HIM TO ADMIT IT.

"That's better. I can see you're more of a dessert kind of woman," said the nurse, passing by again and puffing out her cheeks.

"I'm not fat. I'm just eating for two!" Kate laughed.

Calling over her shoulder, the nurse replied, "Yes, and I've no such excuse. I just love food."

Kate laughed before enjoying the last spoonful of sticky toffee.

> I WOULD LOVE TO SPEAK TO YOU ABOUT MY DAD, AS HIS DEATH MUST HAVE ALSO BEEN A GREAT SHOCK FOR YOU TOO.

Kate held the letter to her chest again and closed her eyes. *I miss you so much, Lionel.*

"Shall we both pop back inside number 81 and do those DNA tests?" Jake asked as they walked back to the hospital car park.

"Oh, you're keen all of a sudden," Aileen said as she unlocked her car.

"What Kate wants, Kate gets!" he replied as she started the engine. "I'm so relieved to know she's going to be okay."

"You like her, don't you?" Aileen asked as they set off.

He shook his head and glanced out of his window. "I've been fighting it ever since I met her. I've only known her a few days, and I've just split from my ex."

"Oh, I see. Timing is not great."

"Kate makes me laugh. She moved to a town where she doesn't know a soul. She buys a house at auction that she didn't even come and see, then spends hours researching stuff about people who lived there a hundred years ago."

Aileen smiled. "And they're my relatives, not hers! I'm so grateful to her because I feel so much better now since finding out about Dorothy... even if her father William was a right—"

Jake stared straight ahead for a moment. "That Lionel must have been crazy to deceive her as he did... she's so lovely. And wow, she can 'alf talk after a drink of wine."

"Has the news of the baby changed everything?" Aileen glanced across at him.

"That's the crazy thing. I'm not sure it has. Finding out about your grandfather and your mother's life has made me think."

"Jake Madden thinks!" she replied and pulled a face at him. "Come on. If Kate can tease you, surely, I can too."

He grinned and paused before saying, "We thought William, your grandfather, was a terrible father, but that unopened letter painted another picture."

"Oh, I'll read it when we get back. We'll never know for sure why he left his daughters in England. Maybe the grief of losing Theresa consumed him?"

"And in his defence," said Jake, "He may have had every intention of his daughters going to Canada eventually."

She nodded. "Perhaps he just couldn't handle the responsibility? Times were different then. Men weren't so involved in raising their children."

"That's true. Times were hard, and there was a war on."

Aileen turned into Whitehall Street, thinking how to phrase her next question. *Tread carefully. Kate might be completely wrong.* "So, tell me about your father, Jake."

"Not much to tell. I never knew the bloke. He just cleared off. Mum cried for days when she saw this tattoo." He turned his arm slightly to show her. "I was a rebel as a teenager. Don't know how Mum coped with me."

"Is his name on your birth certificate?"

"Yes, but God knows why she put it down."

"Perhaps she thought he might come back someday?"

He looked across, doubt written all over his face.

"Not to worry. You're nothing like your father, I'm sure."

"Aren't I? I have commitment issues just like him. I didn't want marriage or children with my ex."

"She wasn't the right girl for you." As she parked, she asked, "Do you know your father's name?"

"Sean, Sean Madden," he replied.

She smiled but said no more.

As he got out, he glanced over at the flats opposite. Howard's curtains were drawn.

"Leave it to the police, Jake," Aileen said, seeing the irritation on his face.

"He needs sorting for creeping around Kate from day one for some reason. Always in his bloody window nosing. I'm surprised he's not there now watching what we're up to."

"It'll all come out in the wash. Kate's going to be okay. That's the main thing."

"No, there's more to it, and anyway, I think Howard made a pass at her."

"It still might have just been an accident. You don't even know he was there."

"He was there all right. I can feel it in my gut."

"I'm sure the police will get to the bottom of it, Jake."

A red car pulled up in the street, followed by a police car. A young policewoman who they'd seen earlier was with two other officers. Aileen didn't recognise the smartly dressed gentleman in the red car.

"Come away, Jake. Let's get inside," she said, tugging at his arm.

As they entered the house, he picked up the small package, and Aileen followed him to the kitchen. He tore it open and read the instructions out loud.

"We just have to spit into these tubes then?" she asked, examining one.

"Yes, and this clear liquid held in the lid is released once we push it into the tube."

They could barely spit for laughing so much.

"Kate would have loved to have seen this," he said, finally screwing the top onto his tube.

"Yes, she certainly would," she replied, wiping away her tears of laughter. "Amazing what's in your spit." She studied his face as he placed both tubes in the return envelope.

He must be at least twenty years younger than me. That's why Kate hasn't said anything. She's just not sure.

"Kate will laugh even more if I have foreign blood in me," he said.

"I think we've probably all got some of that. A bit of Viking blood." Aileen used her forefingers to make horns out of her head. "Well, we'll have to wait and see. I'll post this on my way home."

"That's great, and I'll call you tomorrow if I hear any more."

"Yes, ring in the morning and see how she is, Jake. I'm sure she'd appreciate that. Here, let me give you my number."

"And don't you forget to take that other airmail letter. It's in the dining room," he said.

William

Howard kicks away one of the square boxes littered on his floor and sinks into his armchair. His eyes are bloodshot, and his shirt is unbuttoned to the waist. The curtains are drawn, and an empty whiskey bottle lies under his chair. Lighting another cigarette, he adds to the dark grey fog in the dimly lit room. He glances at his front door, waiting for the knock we both know will surely come.

"You've made your bed. Now lie in it." The words slip from my lips. My father's words, perhaps?

But I feel I must try to lift Howard's mood. Who am I to preach to the poor chap? I let my family down just as badly. But I never drank that much or left a woman unconscious. That's unforgivable.

"You didn't leave Emillie unconscious, but you hit her."

"But she could wind any man up."

"More excuses, William."

If Howard looked at the framed photograph of his three daughters, it might give him a reason to turn back. But his only focus is finding more booze and taking tablets from a small brown bottle.

I shout at him, "Think of your daughters. No man ever found happiness in the bottom of a whiskey glass."

"You didn't think of your daughters."

Howard rests his head back and mumbles, "I bloody 'ate women." His chin lowers as he nods off, then jerks back up. His eyes widen as he says, "They lie to me, use me, and then wonder why I drink."

Now, whiskey has rarely passed my lips. I'm more of a brown ale type of man. Too much always made me a very sentimental and talkative old fool though.

"Ah, away to bed, William," Theresa would say as I draped my arms around her and nuzzled her neck. But she'd never begrudge me having a drink at the Gullet Inn. She was a good wife, the best.

I watch as Howard heads down a path of despair. I remember the path. I remember it well. It's airless and narrow and lets the rain in. The death of little Bridget, James, and then Theresa sent me down that path.

"There's always hope, William... without it, what's the point of living?"

"Yes, there's a flicker of hope, Howard."

He's looking for oblivion, and the tablets and whiskey should do it. He snatches the bottle beneath his chair, hoping to top up his glass. His eyes widen in disbelief as he sees it's empty, and it shatters as he throws it at the fireplace.

"Did that make you feel any better?" I ask.

Lifting himself out of the chair, he uses the walls for support as he heads for the kitchen. He kicks at the unread newspaper in the hallway as he passes. I can see the desperation and hunger in his eyes as he flings open every kitchen cupboard.

"I must have some bloody whiskey somewhere," he says.

He pauses at the kitchen table and picks up two official-looking letters.

"Yeah, yeah, I've broken my restraining order... again," he says, looking at the first.

I read the second letter, looking over his shoulder. It's from Hargrove Solicitors and says he has no claim to 81 Whitehall Street.

Well, that's no surprise.

He screws them up and throws them towards the sink. He lights another cigarette, returns to the living room, and ransacks his sideboard.

"Shit," he says, turning the photograph of his daughters face down.

"You've not lost them. Not like me. For God's sake, man, you still have a chance to make amends."

He falls back into his chair and unscrews the small bottle. After stubbing his cigarette into the overflowing ashtray, he tips the tablets onto his side table. He eyes the remaining drop of whiskey left in his glass.

"Yeah, that'll be enough." He takes four or five tablets in his hand and swigs back with the liquor.

"Just face up to your mistakes," I say. "I don't want to see more death. Not all it's cracked up to be, mate."

Four more tablets slip down his throat.

"Fight the darkness. Look for a flicker of hope. Find a brighter path." I'm unsure where my words come from, but they do little good.

There's anger in his eyes. "I should 'ave took my time. Worked on Kate," he says.

I'm surprised he can still speak.

"A damn good-looking woman like that, with a bob or two in the bank, she could 'ave been the answer to all my problems."

"Just like I was to you, William."

I hear the voice and turn. "I beg your pardon?"

As the words leave my lips, I see her. She's unfocused at first, and I'm afraid to move. Afraid the vivid colours of her will disappear.

She unties the ribbon from under her chin and removes my favourite bonnet, the pale pink one. We lock eyes the way we used to.

Her soft, lilting voice fills the room. *"Howard blames everyone else."*

Howard rubs his unshaven chin. "I'll say... say she slipped." He nods, almost resting his head on his chest each time. "Yeah, that's what I'll do."

"For Christ's sake, be quiet, Howard. I want to speak to Theresa."

She throws me a familiar look. She hates me cussing.

"Will God forgive him, do you think?" she asks. *"Is he sorry for what he's done to his daughters, wife, and Kate?"*

I'm surprised to hear her say the name Kate. "How do...?" But voices outside distract me.

"Howard, are you in there? It's Bill." The knocking turns to a hammering.

Howard gives no reply. He slumps forward, and his whiskey glass falls from his fingers.

"Come on now, Howard. The police are here too. They need to speak to you. Let's sort this out."

Two police officers thunder through the door, followed by a young woman dressed in uniform. I've never seen a woman in a police uniform before.

"She... she slip... slipped," he says under his breath. "Hid Betty's will... she shouldna done that." He exhales, and his oblivion arrives.

Theresa has left, and I'm in darkness again.

CHAPTER 31

A month later

"Aileen and I can stay with you for a few days if you'd like."

Kate nodded but didn't reply. "Have you heard how Howard is?" she asked as she climbed into Jake's van.

"Why would you care?"

She wound down the window for some air. "I feel sorry for him."

"Have you not got a bad bone anywhere in there?" He turned on the engine and headed out of the hospital car park.

"Oh, plenty. I had an affair with a married man for a start."

"Is that the best you can do?" He glanced across at her. "Howard could have killed you, Kate."

"But he didn't." She fought against her tears and tried to push away the anxiety brewing inside as they neared Whitehall Street. "I've got lots to look forward to. What's he got?"

"Well, he brought it all on himself. He fixated on the house for some reason, and he's been as creepy as hell around you. And are you forgetting he left you unconscious?"

"Drink does that. He needs help," she said as they turned into Whitehall Street.

Jake shook his head at her. "You're unbelievable. So, you still can't remember if he pushed you?"

"Let's not talk about it anymore."

Once inside number 81, Kate gripped the banister and climbed the stairs one by one.

"Don't lock the bathroom door. Just in case you faint," Jake called from the hallway.

She obeyed his instructions, and although she appreciated his concern, she needed a few minutes alone. A calmness descended on her as she entered the bathroom, and she longed to hold on to it and not be full of worry and what ifs.

Pushing her hair behind her ears, she stared into the bathroom mirror, her eyes misting. She was pale, and even though the zig-zagged stitches into her hairline had been removed, she couldn't help wondering how long her hair would take to grow back. *What a mess I look.* She was tempted to reach for her makeup bag but decided there wasn't much point.

Kate clasped the side of the washbasin to steady herself and looked down, exhaling. The moment she lifted her head, he was there. He stood behind her, wearing his brown tweed suit, collarless shirt, and nifty hat. With a broad smile, he raised his hat in greeting.

"William? William?" she mouthed.

Sunlight cascaded into the bathroom as she fought the urge to turn around. William bowed his head and placed his hand on it.

"Thank you. Yes, my head's a lot better," she said. "Was it Howard that night who pushed me over?"

Fishing in his pocket, William pulled out his Woodbine cigarettes and lit one before nodding.

She recognised the packet. She recalled the smell. *Yes, it was him. William was by my side that night.*

"Smoking is bad for you, William."

He gazed back at her with a wry smile and shrugged as if to say, "It's too damn late for me."

"Thank you for staying beside me and telling me all about Theresa. You loved her with all your heart. Was it all too much after she died?" She studied his pained expression. "I'm sure she'll forgive you, William. Just like I've forgiven Lionel."

He crossed his arms and rocked them as if nursing a baby.

"You know I'm pregnant?"

He smiled.

"I'm going to be okay, with Jake and Aileen helping me. Are you okay?"

He held up a small, faded black-and-white photograph.

She leant closer to the mirror, screwing her eyes up to see. "Your wedding picture?" *It's another one. There's no crease down the middle.*

William kissed the picture and held it to his heart.

"Have you seen Aileen?" Kate asked.

A solitary tear ran down his sunken face, and he pointed to Theresa's hair in the picture.

"Yes, Aileen's hair is beautiful too. Dark and wavy. Just like her grandmother's."

"Everything okay?" Jake's head appeared around the bathroom door. "I thought I heard you talking to someone."

"No, I'm fine. Everything's fine."

She turned back to the mirror but saw nothing.

"Thank you, William," she whispered after Jake left the room.

Did I just have a conversation with William?

Jake plumped the cushion on her armchair as she entered the dining room.

"Don't fuss," she snapped. "Jake, I'm sorry. You're right, and I do need to rest. Still feeling disorientated."

"You're bound to. Concussion, remember?" he said with a cheeky grin.

Yes, that's it. I'm concussed.

"The hospital sent you home with some painkillers. I'll put the kettle on so you can take some. Aileen will be here soon."

Kate nodded and sank into her chair. She closed her eyes in an attempt to control her breathing.

"Do you like it?" Jake asked as he placed a tray of teacups on the dining table.

She hadn't noticed the sideboard sitting alongside the bureau. It was polished, and all the brass handles were replaced and gleaming.

"Wow. Jake, it's beautiful."

"A mate of mine renovates furniture, and he said it was a pleasure to work on it. He came the day you went into the hospital and spent four days solid on it."

"You'll have to let me know how much I owe him. He's done an incredible job. Was it difficult to get up from the cellar?"

"No, not at all. Just the two of us, and it was lighter than I thought... almost as if we had another pair of hands."

Kate smiled. *Maybe you did have a helping hand.*

"I've put rat poison down. Rustling and scratching galore down there. My other mate checked the place for dampness and said it's all fine."

"I can't thank you enough." She looked out over the garden. Jake had laid the turf, and its lush green had transformed the garden. "It's wonderful. You've worked so hard while I've been away."

"Come the spring, we can plant up the flower beds," he said with satisfaction.

We? Did he say we?

"My baby will be nearly..." She paused as their eyes met.

"Yes, that's right. And there'll be plenty of room for a swing now," he said. "Not sure your new BMW will fit the bill much longer though."

She laughed. "Let's not get ahead of ourselves. Could I have a drink of water please?"

He nodded and hurried out of the room.

She picked up her laptop from the side table and switched it on.

"Hey, you're supposed to be resting," he said, passing her a glass of water.

"It won't do me any good sitting here just thinking."

"You're as stubborn as hell."

"It takes one to know one, Jake."

She sensed he was about to say something more but left mumbling about pottering in the garden until Aileen arrived.

Kate logged on to her usual genealogy site and clicked on DNA results. The site linked Jake's name to other people who had also taken a test. *Wow, that's fascinating.* It gave potential relations from first to sixth cousins. The name at the top of the list made her gasp: Aileen Thompson, half-sibling/first cousin.

"Oh my God, was I right?"

It said they shared 1,750 centimorgans. She googled the word and downloaded a chart.

Aileen's smiling face appeared around the dining room door. "How's the patient today?"

"Ah, come in, come in. I didn't hear the door. I'm fine. Glad to be home."

Jake stepped back inside.

"He's like a mother hen, clucking around me," Kate said.

"He's been worried about you."

Jake's face reddened.

"Well, we both have," Aileen added.

"I'll finish off a bit in the garden and get out of your hair," he said.

"No need. I'm sorry... sorry for snapping at you. I want to talk to you both anyway." She closed the laptop. *Where on earth do I start?*

They looked at each other before pulling out a dining chair and sitting.

"Jake, you've told me a little about your father," she began.

"That's right. He was a proper bast—"

"What was his name again?"

He pulled up his shirt sleeve to reveal his tattoo of Madden. "Sean Madden, and he buggered off before I was born."

Kate glanced at Aileen, who was holding her hand to her mouth.

"My mum said he was a fly-by-night," he continued.

"What does that mean exactly?" asked Aileen, staring at him.

"You know. He was a wheeler-dealer. Fingers in a lot of pies."

Kate couldn't help but smile at his explanation. "He was a petty criminal."

Aileen stood up from the table. "But... but—"

"Let me," said Kate. "Jake... in Aileen's adoption file, there was a letter from a Catholic priest. He thought Aileen's father was a Sean Madden."

Silence filled the room.

"Ha, there'd have been loads of men with that name, and besides, and no offence, Aileen, I'm quite a bit younger than you."

Aileen sat again. "None taken."

"You mentioned your mum had a nickname for him, Jake?"

"Yes, she called him Mad Madden."

Aileen stood again and began pacing. "That's the exact name mentioned in my adoption file."

Jake leant back in his chair with his hand behind his head. "Probably a big Irish family. Sean's a common name. Madden too." He glanced at Kate, but she gave no back up to his reasoning.

She stood and placed her laptop on the dining room table for them to see.

"You should rest, Ka—"

Aileen interrupted him. "You've got our DNA results, haven't you?"

Kate nodded.

"What am I? Italian?" He laughed, and Kate elbowed him.

"Just be serious for a minute."

"What are we looking at?" he asked, staring at the screen.

"This list shows your DNA matches. Your long-lost cousins. Cousins, you never knew you had."

Aileen bit her lip as the colour drained from her face. "I'm at the top!"

"What?" Jake moved closer to the screen and screwed up his eyes.

"You share what's called centimorgans. In your DNA, you share 1,750 centimorgans," said Kate.

Jake and Aileen stared at each other. "I don't know what to say," said Aileen.

"Me neither," he said, shrugging.

"Now, see this chart," said Kate, pointing. "First cousins share between 137 and 530 centim—"

"And how many centimorgan things do half-siblings share?" asked Aileen.

"Full siblings share between 2,209 and 3,384, and half-siblings 1,317 to 2,312." Kate ran her finger across the chart.

"We share 1,750," said Aileen, her eyes tearing as she looked at Jake.

Jake's eyes widened, staring at Aileen and then at Kate. "So, you're telling me Aileen is my half-sister?"

"Yes, that's exactly what I'm saying."

"You're saying we have the same father?" He didn't wait for an answer or react to the tears flowing down Aileen's face. He raised himself slowly from his chair and left the room.

Aileen's eyes followed him, and she reached for the tissue box. "So, this is... this is why you were keen for us to take the DNA tests?" she asked, dabbing her eyes. "I had my suspicions too, you know. I noticed Jake's tattoo the morning they took you to the hospital."

Kate nodded and covered Aileen's hand with her own. "I'm so, so sorry. I should have told you both what I suspected. It just all seemed too crazy to be true. What were the chances of me employing him to do my garden and you turning up when he was here?"

Aileen pushed back her chair. "Yes, it's unbelievable. I'd better talk to him."

"No, let me. After all, it's me that's—"

"It's a shock, Kate, but not a bad one. I felt there was more to come out about Sean Madden."

Kate headed to the kitchen and peeped around the door. Jake stood with his back to her, his head down and both hands gripping the kitchen worktop.

"I'm so sorry, Jake. I had no right to—"

He turned. "Thank you."

She reached out with both arms, and he fell into them. His closeness made her hold her breath... but it seemed so natural being close... so easy.

"It's a hell of a shock." He pecked her cheek and then lingered.

His smell washed over her with their arms entwined and his face so close. If she moved just an inch, her lips would meet his, and she wanted to. She desperately wanted to and for him to turn too. But he slowly pulled back, and she searched his eyes for a sign hinting that he'd felt something as well.

"Life certainly hasn't been dull, Kate, since meeting you and coming to this house."

"We can agree on that," she replied,

With his familiar teasing smile, he said, "Let's see. We found out about William, a man who died in 1915, and we thought he'd been rifling through the bureau."

She stifled a laugh.

"You spent hours researching a piece of needlework made by the dead man's sister-in-law. Oh yes, and we spent an afternoon visiting Hills Lane, where her Irish family lived in the early 1900s."

"Jake, the lane is such a pretty, oldy worldly place with cobbles and stunning Tudor buildings at each end."

"I'm not saying it has all been pointless, or I haven't enjoyed being here. Being here with you." He hooked hold of both her hands. "And you invite a stranger into your house, and she turns out to be my half-sister."

"Are you both okay? Can I come in?" Aileen asked, her head appearing around the kitchen door.

Jake beckoned her and, holding out both arms, he hugged them.

"Hey, don't squeeze," said Kate, stepping away. She placed her hand over her bump. "Mustn't squash the little one."

"This house is something special," said Aileen.

"Excuse me, the garden's pretty special too," he added.

They all turned to look out of the kitchen window to admire his handiwork.

"I'm sure it would impress Lizzie Doyle. God bless her soul," said Kate, linking her hand to Jake's and Aileen's. The sun emerged from behind a cloud, illuminating the red quarry tiles. "Thank you for being here. I think we three have lots more to talk about."

"You need to rest now," said Aileen. "You're looking a little flushed. Why not lie down for a while? Jake and I will go do a food shop. We could have a nice meal together this evening."

"That's a great idea. I'll cook," he said.

Kate and Aileen looked at each other, both with raised eyebrows.

"Really?"

CHAPTER 32

As Kate woke and looked at her phone, it surprised her that it was 5:30 and dark outside. She couldn't remember getting into bed. Aileen had been right; she did need to rest for her own sake and the baby's. She looked up at the ceiling with both hands on her abdomen, reliving her and Jake's hug. The urge to kiss him had almost overwhelmed her. *God, I'd have made such a fool of myself.*

It had been a friendly, caught-up-in-the-moment hug, and she tried to reason with herself. *For God's sake, I'm pregnant with someone else's baby, and I'm older. Too old for him?*

Before going downstairs, she looked out of her bedroom window at Howard's flat. The curtains were drawn, and the place was in darkness. She could remember more about the night she fell than she'd let on to Jake and wondered if Betty had known what Howard was up to. And it worried her how he might have coerced the poor old lady into changing her will.

As she went downstairs, she heard Jake and Aileen laughing in the kitchen. She was glad they were there, relieved she wasn't alone with her nagging concerns. *Is there another will? Will I lose the house?*

"How are you feeling now?" asked Aileen as Kate walked into the kitchen.

"Gosh, I've been asleep for ages," she replied, yawning. "I'm pleased you're both still here."

"I think this calls for a drink of some sort," said Jake, reaching down to the wine rack. He examined the label on every bottle. "I'm guessing Pinot Grigio is your favourite, Kate?"

"Don't tease. I know what I like, that's all."

She watched him as he searched the kitchen cupboards. He turned around, grinning and with three glasses splayed in his hands.

Ah, that smile. "Think you're forgetting something, Jake," she said, running her hand over her bump. "I'm already worried about how much wine I've drunk the last few months, not knowing I was pregnant."

His cheeks coloured. "Of course, I'm sorry. I'll put the kettle on instead." He fumbled as he reached for the kettle, and Aileen watched with an amused smile.

When Kate caught her eye, Aileen flicked her eyes towards Jake and then back at Kate. Then she nodded her head towards Kate and tilted it towards Jake.

Kate pursed her lips and shook her head but sensed a redness creeping up her neck. "No. No. It's fine. You and Aileen can both have a drink."

"You're sure?" he asked. "I could do with one, to be honest."

"Yes, it's fine. I'll waddle back to my armchair and put my feet up."

"I'll bring the tea to you," he called as Kate and Aileen headed for the dining room.

Jake had set the dining table with a cloth and cutlery.

"He's been busy," said Aileen. "It's fillet steak, chips, and salad for dinner."

"What?" asked Kate,

"You must rest and let us spoil you now you're home from the hospital."

Kate gazed out over the garden. "Not been a dull moment since I moved in here."

"We could both stay a few days if you'd like. If you don't want to be on your own."

"I'd be grateful if you did, and it'll be nice for you and Jake to spend some time together."

"Yes, it's a lot for us both to take in. It's a real mystery why Charles' letter was unopened and hidden in the bureau."

"Doubt we'll ever know. But I hope Lizzie forgave William."

Aileen smiled. "Me too. It's strange how I've been off work for almost six weeks, but I will ring them later... I feel ready to go back... ready to carry on."

"It's not long since you lost your mum, but I'm pleased you're feeling like that."

Aileen reached inside her bag. "I'd like Lizzie's sampler to stay here, Kate. Let's get Jake to put it up above the fireplace."

"That'd be smashing. She's back where she belongs, and it's time for us all to move on."

"On that subject... how do you feel about my half-brother caring about you?" Aileen asked, pulling a playful face.

Kate ignored the question. "So, do you think it's true? The DNA, the story about Sean Madden?"

"While you were asleep, Jake rang his aunty, his mum's younger sister."

"And?"

"She confirmed that Sean Madden was much older than his mum. Her parents were livid at the time. And in my adoption file, it said my father was much younger than Dorothy."

"Yes, it did," said Kate.

"Dorothy bagged herself a toyboy!" said Aileen.

They locked eyes, then burst out laughing. *Maybe I could too!*

"What's so funny?" asked Jake, coming into the room carrying a salad bowl. "It's almost ready now. The steaks are in the pan."

"Thank you, Jake, and we're looking forward to it."

"He can cook too, as well as being a dish himself!" Aileen added once he'd left the room.

Kate flung open her arms and looked downwards. "Aileen, look at me. I'm four months gone!"

"It's written all over his face," she whispered as he reappeared. "At least now you know why you've felt so off-colour."

"Yes, and so flaming tired."

"What have I missed?" he asked, placing bottles of ketchup and mayonnaise on the table.

An awkward silence followed, only breaking as Kate's mobile phone rang. She reached for it. "Yes, I'm home now and feeling a lot better." She paused. "Thank you."

Jake and Aileen exchanged puzzled looks.

"It's the police," she mouthed before continuing. "No, I'm sorry. I'm still struggling to remember what exactly happened."

She noticed Jake raise his eyebrows.

"Will he make a full recovery?" She nodded. "So, you'd advise me to do that? Okay, that's kind of you to let me know."

"Well? Are they going to charge Howard or what?" Jake asked as she hung up.

Kate looked away.

"Sorry, my mouth runs away with me sometimes."

Aileen shook her head at him. "Let's enjoy our evening. Is the steak ready, Jake?"

They sat silently, staring out the French doors until he returned carrying two plates, each piled with chips and a juicy-looking steak.

"Are you trying to feed me up?" Kate asked as she sat down at the table. "I know I'm eating for two, but—" She tensed as he sat beside her, his leg almost touching hers. "But, wow, this steak looks delicious."

Aileen agreed. "He has hidden talents!"

Kate was pleased no one mentioned Howard's name again as they ate. Instead, Aileen teased Jake that he should apply to appear on the Great British Bake Off.

"Listen. A lot has happened since moving here." Kate paused and helped herself to more salad. "I wanted to tell you about the letter you brought into the hospital. It was from a girl called Hannah Attwood. She's Lionel's daughter."

"That good-for-nothing Li—"

"Sssh," said Aileen, glaring at Jake.

"It was a lovely letter. I didn't know he had a daughter, but Hannah knew all about Lionel and me."

"But wasn't he cheating on her mother?"

"Always two sides to a story, Jake," said Aileen, kicking him under the table. "Things are often not what they seem. Will you write back?" she asked.

"Yes, I will. And after all, my baby will be a half-sister or half-brother to Hannah."

"I'm sure she'll be thrilled to hear your news. Somebody else will find a half-sibling," said Aileen, smiling.

"I hope so. It'll be a little part of Lionel for us both to hang on to. Her mother has moved some other chap into the house already."

"Blimey. She didn't let the grass—" Jake stopped mid-sentence.

"I loved him very much, and I think he would have told me everything in time."

Aileen reached her hand across the table to Kate's. "It'll be nice for you, Kate, to get to know Hannah."

"It seems like we're all finding family at the moment," said Jake.

A picture of William popped into Kate's head. She was tempted to tell them about her conversation with him earlier. "Pity William's not here to have a drink with us." Her thoughts tumbled out of her mouth.

"What?" said Jake. "He wasn't much better than our fly-by-night of a father."

This time, both women glared at him.

"I hope Dorothy forgave him for abandoning her and her sisters," said Aileen thoughtfully. "I hope she knows I'm fine and spending time in this house. We'll never know why William left his daughters."

"And do you forgive Sean Madden for abandoning us, Aileen?" he asked.

"I do, Jake. Yes, I do."

He stared out of the French doors.

"Penny for your thoughts, Jake," Kate said as she studied his face.

"It's been quite a day!" said Aileen, swigging back the last of her wine. "I'll see to the dishes."

As Kate turned to Jake, hoping they might be alone for a while, there was a knock at the door.

"Who on earth could that be?" *Hopefully, not the police.*

Kate followed Jake to the door. A petite woman, casually dressed, stood at the door, and three young girls waited at the end of the path.

"Are you Kate Walker?" she asked.

"Yes, that's right."

"I'm sorry to bother you. I'm Anne. Anne Vaughan."

Howard's wife? "Oh, hello. Is everything okay?" Kate asked. She could see a small removal van parked opposite.

"We're all fine," she replied, waving back at her daughters, who were either engaged on their phones or jumping on and off the kerb. "I wanted to thank you and return this key." Anne placed a key in Kate's hand. "Think Howard kept hold of this after the previous owner... Mrs Harris had died."

"That explains a lot," Jake said, returning to the dining room.

"I hear you haven't pressed charges against him," Anne said.

"Well, I wasn't sure... concussion, you see."

Anne looked at the side of Kate's head and raised her eyebrows. Kate instinctively put a hand on her bruised shoulder.

"Look, I've been there, done that, many times with Howard. He's admitted he tried to get Betty to change her will."

Kate bit her lip, unsure what to say.

"I used to lie to the police all the time for the children's sake. But you're just a good person."

"Everyone deserves a second chance," Kate said. "Everyone."

"Believe me, Howard's had plenty of those."

Anne looked back over the road again. "All his furniture, not that he has much, is going into storage. Hopefully, he will get the help he needs now that he's been admitted to the hospital."

"Admitted?"

"I thought the police would have told you. He's had a breakdown and been sectioned."

"I'm so sorry."

"Don't be. From what the police told me, this had nothing to do with you. It was all about this house." Anne stepped back to look up at number 81. "He's an alcoholic... has been for years. Why he imagined Mrs Harris would leave this lovely house to him is beyond me."

"And the restraining order?" Kate asked.

"Oh good, the police have told you then. Once he's discharged, and I don't think that'll be for quite some time, Howard can't go within twenty miles of you or this house."

"That's reassuring, Kate, isn't it?" said Jake, returning to her side.

Yes, it is.

"But to be honest with you, Kate, I'm considering moving away. My aunt has offered us a home with her. She has no children of her own, you see. A fresh start is what we need. Not just me, but for them too." She glanced over at her daughters. The eldest was now shrugging and beckoning her mother. "I'm coming. I'm coming."

"Yes, new beginnings are what we all need in our lives."

Kate looked up at Jake as he spoke and smiled. Jake's hand touched hers as they watched Anne turn and walk down the path.

CHAPTER 33

William

I'm in the house with Kate, Jake, and Aileen. It's such a lovely evening, and I'm enjoying their company. It's wonderful that Aileen will sleep in the house tonight, just like her mother did. As all my precious girls did.

I just saw Jake and Kate holding hands. They haven't known each other long, but this is the start of something. A picture of my family pops into my head, but it fades as I hear familiar voices in the hallway.

I move slowly towards the door, afraid of what I might see or that the noise might stop. The hall is full of dancing colours and lilting Irish voices reverberating in the hallway and up the stairs. I try to focus my eyes. Lizzie is standing in front of me. I notice her hair's clipped back tidily, just how it always used to be. Her voice cuts through the others.

"I see you're still smoking, William. It got the better of you in the end though."

Lizzie is right. She was always right.

"Think you've spent enough time in my old house."

"But I've been searching for..."

"Your family?"

"I... I don't know what—"

She breezes past me and enters the dining room. Jake is putting Lizzie's sampler on the wall.

"Well, that suits just fine. The Doyles will never be forgotten now. My old cake tin did its job well."

I look up at the sampler and wonder if Kate, Jake, and Aileen have noticed that it's brighter. It's no longer just the initial T that is vibrant.

"It's taken a long time, William, but everyone has forgiven you now... My old bureau and sideboard have polished up nicely... what secrets they kept." Lizzie looks out of the French doors and smiles. *"My wonderful garden looks just the same."*

"I helped Kate decide how she wanted it," I say.

"Thank you. You looked after her very well, William, when she fell. I picked your daughters up many times when they fell."

I bow my head as shame envelops me. "I let them down."

"But life moves on, William, and regret and guilt weigh people down. You're a great-great-great-grandfather now, by the way."

"Am I?"

She beckons me to follow her back to the hall. Now she's holding a small child, and I strain my eyes. It's my boy, my son.

John Rupert holds out his chubby fingers towards me. I reach out, and Lizzie passes him to me. I feel him. Feel his happiness and his innocence.

Lizzie stands to one side and gestures behind as if she is introducing me to someone.

"Hello, Da," chorus three young women.

I shake my head. It's Ada, Ethel, and my little Dorothy. And my, how they've grown!

I pass my son back to Lizzie and cup each of my daughter's faces in turn. They're beautiful women and still look so much like their mother.

"I see you've met my daughter," says Dorothy.

"Aileen's a wonderful woman, and she's been such a help to Kate. Have you seen her too?" I ask.

"Yes, I've been beside her for quite some time, especially since her adoptive parents passed."

I bow my head. "I'm so sorry I left you all."

To my surprise, they all step forwards and hug me. I wish Kate could see, but she's too busy chatting with Aileen and Jake.

"I'm so sorry I hid that airmail letter in Aunt Lizzie's bureau," says Ada. *"I've only just told Aunt Lizzie that. I thought it was from Emillie, you see. I was worried she might come back and live with us. She never did come back to England though."*

I cringe at the mention of Emillie. "It's okay. You weren't to know it was from my dear friend Charles. I'm the one who needs to apologise."

"Emillie was a wrong'un, William," says Lizzie. *"She stopped posting the money orders. I should have done more... Ada did warn me what she was like."*

I crumple to the floor, and pain runs across my chest. "I hit Emillie."

"Well, that brazen hussy probably deserved it." Lizzie stops and crosses herself.

"Come on now," says Ada, helping me up. *"We all need to say sorry sometimes."*

"I am sorry. I took the easy way out... avoided the situ—" I realise now Emillie had her own reasons for leaving Shrewsbury. I'm ashamed that I thought she cared about me.

"Well, water under the bridge now. We're all meeting back at Hills Lane for a Doyle family party. You'd be very welcome, William. Everyone from the lane will be there, including little Bridget," says Lizzie.

"Is she bett—"

"She's grand. Hope you've got a coin in your pocket for her."

I put my hand in my pocket and pull out a sixpence.

"Are we all set?" asks Ada. *"Lots more family for you to meet, Da. Uncle Shay, the Mahoneys, Peddler, and all your friends from the Gullet are waiting. Spect James and Patrick will be playing football or at the station watching trains."*

"Did he become a train driver?" I ask.

"He did indeed, Da."

"There'll be plenty of brown ale," adds Ethel, smiling. *"And Grandad John managed to get us a rabbit."*

"Yes, Ma's made us a stew, so we better not be late," says Lizzie.

Questions fill my mind, and the sea of people parts and voices hush. The Theresa I loved and still love with all my heart skips forward.

She removes her bonnet and shakes her dark wavy hair over her shoulders. I notice her eyes soften, and a familiar smile spreads across her face. She holds out her hand, and I take it. Warmth spreads across my chest and down my left arm, and I step forwards, and we embrace.

"I was the first to forgive you, William. The others got round to it eventually."

As I leave number 81, I can't resist looking back one last time, and I call out, "Enjoy the house, Kate. We've both found our family now."

Printed in Great Britain
by Amazon